Fiction

SOMETHING IN THE AIR

HELEN ROLFE

Boldwood

First published in Great Britain in 2025 by Boldwood Books Ltd.

Copyright © Helen Rolfe, 2025

Cover Design by Alexandra Allden

Cover Images: Shutterstock

A CIP catalogue record for this book is available from the British Library.

Paperback ISBN 978-1-83561-098-5

Large Print ISBN 978-1-83561-100-5

Hardback ISBN 978-1-83561-101-2

Ebook ISBN 978-1-83561-099-2

Kindle ISBN 978-1-83561-097-8

Audio CD ISBN 978-1-83561-106-7

MP3 CD ISBN 978-1-83561-105-0

Digital audio download ISBN 978-1-83561-103-6

This book is printed on certified sustainable paper. Boldwood Books is dedicated to putting sustainability at the heart of our business. For more information please visit https://www.boldwoodbooks.com/about-us/sustainability/

Boldwood Books Ltd, 23 Bowerdean Street, London, SW6 3TN

www.boldwoodbooks.com

For my readers, thank you for flying with me in this new series!

CAST OF CHARACTERS

The Whistlestop River Air Ambulance (The Skylarks)

Red team
Maya – pilot
Noah – critical care paramedic
Bess – critical care paramedic

Blue team
Vik – pilot
Kate – critical care paramedic
Brad – critical care paramedic

Other
Frank – engineer
Hudson – patient and family liaison nurse
Paige – patient and family liaison nurse
Nadia – operational support officer

The Whistlestop River Freewheelers

Rita
Dorothy
Alan
Mick

1

The Skylarks huddled together in the kitchen at the Whistlestop River Air Ambulance base. Beyond the window sat Hilda, their trusty helicopter, ready and waiting on the helipad for the next job. The evening crew had arrived to take over from those who had been on the day shift and as the crews overlapped, they gathered to celebrate patient and family liaison nurse Hudson's forty-sixth birthday.

Nadia lit the candles on the decadent chocolate drip cake.

'Did you seriously make this?' Hudson asked. 'It's... well, I'm speechless.'

Maya, pilot in the red team, laughed. 'First time for everything.'

'Yes, I made it.' Nadia was happy with the result too. She'd assembled four layers of rich chocolate sponge filled with chocolate cream as well as pieces of dark and white chocolate. A glossy chocolate ganache covered the sponge layers topped with white and dark chocolate curls.

'It looks and smells divine,' said Maya.

'I love baking.' Nadia was forever making things for the two crews – the red and the blue teams – and what was known as the wider team which encompassed anyone who was involved with the Whistlestop River Air Ambulance. 'It's no big deal.'

'No big deal?' Hudson's eyebrows rose at the sight of the impressive cake. She'd hidden it away so he had had no idea what was coming until he'd been ushered into the kitchen this afternoon.

'Just blow out the candles already!' Bess hollered. She, like everyone else, was probably desperate to try a slice.

Together the crews sang such a loud rendition of 'Happy Birthday' that Nadia almost had to cover her ears, especially when someone added in a high-pitched whistle at the end as Hudson blew out the candles.

'What did you wish for?' Nadia asked him.

'Now that would be telling.'

She removed the four and the six from the top of the cake and set them aside. 'I cheated a bit with those,' she said of the two numerals.

'Would've been a fire hazard with forty-six little candles. Much safer this way. And it looks—'

The big red phone at the airbase rang out announcing a job, putting a stop to the celebrations. The blue team leapt into action at the call from the HEMS – Helicopter Emergency Services – desk and because it was a local job at which pilot Vik knew there was no great place to land, the crew decided to take the rapid response vehicle parked out front instead.

Once the blue team, apart from Vik, who wasn't needed, had all set off, Nadia picked up the cake knife to do the honours – the blue team would get plenty when they were back; she'd made enough for everyone to have a couple of slices – and they all knew the score. Jobs could take anything from under an hour to hours on end and sometimes the crew might have back-to-back jobs meaning even more time away from base.

And nobody else wanted to wait for cake for that long.

Nadia was about to cut into the sponge layers when the front doorbell of the airbase building sounded. 'I'll go and get that,' she said, pausing. As the operational support officer, her job was to ensure the smooth running of The Skylarks' operations, so it was more than likely for her. She was expecting a delivery of office supplies.

She handed the knife to Bess to take over, and went through to the reception area. The main door was usually unlocked but not as day approached evening and Nadia prepared to go home. She wasn't subject to shifts like the two crews; she did a regular day, although more often than not she stayed back, doing unpaid overtime. It was more than a job to her; it was a joy to be a part of, and there was always so much to do. Plus, The Skylarks had always felt like family.

When Nadia walked through to reception, she expected someone to be hovering at the door but all she could see was a sizeable cardboard box left in front of it.

'Do you think that's for me?' Hudson had followed her from the kitchen. 'Could be a nice birthday gift.' He rubbed his palms together.

Nadia retrieved the bunch of keys from the desk drawer and picked through for the correct one. 'I hate to disappoint you, but I'm expecting a delivery of stationery – Post-its, notepads, a few manilla folders.'

'Best birthday gifts ever.'

She laughed. He'd already got some great gifts from the team; he was popular. Especially with her. He was kind, he was a family man, she liked him more than she should. This morning, she'd presented him with a box of chocolate brownies, but he wouldn't read too much into it because she'd done the same for plenty of other people she worked with. And so her feelings for him stayed buried and that was the best thing all round.

'Did your kids give you something special?'

Hudson's face lit up the way it always did when he talked about his two children. 'Carys did me a handprint – her grandad may have helped – and Beau gave me a new thermal cup for my coffee.'

'So cute – Carys, I mean, and that's a nice gift from Beau. He knows you like your coffee.'

'I certainly do. I'll have a coffee with one of those brownies later on, if I can fit it in after the cake, and the kids will help me out.'

She and Hudson had always got on, ever since he'd joined The Skylarks as one of their patient and family liaison officers over five years ago. They'd always been able to talk. In fact, it was that way with the whole team: The Skylarks, who took to the air to save lives; Hudson and Paige, who worked as patient and family liaison nurses; Frank the engineer; and the Whistlestop River Freewheelers who were volunteer riders, drivers, and call handlers, and were responsible for delivering bloods and essential supplies for the air ambulance as well as other medical establishments. And it was good to see Hudson happy today. Lately, she'd got the feeling there was something going on with him that he hadn't yet shared and whatever it was shrouded him with a fog of sadness and gave the impression that he had the weight of the world on his shoulders.

Nadia found the correct key and went to unlock the door. She was single, but Hudson wasn't, and lately the energy between them had contained a spark of something she wouldn't want to admit to. At least not to anyone but herself. She'd never be the one to destroy a relationship, especially when there were children involved. She'd been on the receiving end and would never be that person. But what made it tough was how Hudson seemed to act around her, as if he too wanted more, more than he could have and more than she could ever give.

When Nadia opened up the front door to the airbase headquarters, their conversation stalled completely.

They both stared down at the cardboard box.

'Did it...?' Hudson began.

'It did... it moved.'

'I don't think it's filled with Post-its.'

Hudson crouched down and pulled back the unsealed flaps as Nadia knelt down beside him, her blonde bobbed hair blowing across her face in the spring winds until she hooked it behind her ears.

Neither of them could immediately find the words to convey what they were looking at.

This morning, Nadia had woken from a dream and promptly decided it had been a nightmare. It had left her distressed, spent. Because in the dream, she'd been given the one thing she'd always wanted, but then it had been cruelly severed away from her when she'd woken up. It had felt so real, to have that gift, that one thing.

And now here it was again. Right in front of her.

But this was no dream. This was reality.

There was a baby in a cardboard box, swaddled in a blanket and abandoned, left here at the door to the airbase.

2

'What have you got over there?' Maya came into reception where Nadia and Hudson were still frozen in place at the front door.

When Maya stepped closer, the piece of cake she had in a serviette didn't make it any closer to her mouth. 'Is that...'

Hudson scooped the baby up into his arms. Nadia couldn't take her eyes off the little one, who looked remarkably content despite being left outside in a box.

'A baby,' breathed Nadia as she held out her arms to take the infant from Hudson.

Maya gently pulled the edge of the soft blanket so she could see the baby's face properly. 'Don't tell me this precious thing was in the box.'

'Left here, yes. She was abandoned.' At least she presumed it was a girl given the pink blanket and the same-coloured Babygro her little body was dressed in.

'How could anyone do that?' Maya said softly.

By this time, paramedic Bess had come through to see what was going on. 'My goodness, did someone leave this little one here?'

'In the cardboard box.' It pained Nadia to repeat it, it was so cruel an action.

Bess went over to look inside the box and pulled out a piece of paper. She unfolded it and showed it to the others. 'Her name is Lena.' The four letters were written clearly, carefully.

Nadia looked down at the little girl again. 'Hello, Lena.' Somehow it made it better that the baby had a name. 'How about I check you over quickly, make sure you're okay?'

Hudson headed over to the reception desk. 'I'll call for a road ambulance.'

Nadia's job with The Skylarks was predominantly an admin role but one which entailed a lot of medical knowledge and experience, both of which she'd gained working as a nurse prior to coming to Whistlestop River. She was more than qualified to assess Lena and ensure the infant was stable to transport and so she headed to the office where she laid the baby on the top of the table so she could check her over before the ambulance arrived. She wanted to be sure they weren't dealing with a baby with immediate health concerns and this became more than simply transporting an abandoned infant.

When Lena began to grizzle, Nadia lifted her into her arms again. 'You're doing just fine, aren't you, little one?' She held her warm body against her. The bright lights probably hadn't helped to settle Lena; the undressing had probably made her aware that something wasn't quite right. It might be spring but the weather in late May still allowed a chill to snake its way through the airbase in the late afternoon.

Hudson met her on her way back to reception. 'The wait for a road ambulance is too long. I've called the hospital and notified them of the situation, let them know we'll be on our way soon. Bess and Noah are still here and are happy to do overtime but the rapid response vehicle is out. So Vik will take Hilda.'

Vik headed for the internal door to the hangar. 'Flight conditions are good; Maya and I went through them at handover.' He looked at Lena. 'We don't want to take any chances with an infant this young. I'll start Hilda up, see you out there.'

Bess held out her arms. 'Let me take the baby to the aircraft.'

But Nadia didn't want to let Lena go. 'I'm coming with you.'

'There's no need.' Bess was used to getting out of the airbase pronto, and as they talked, she was already heading in the same direction as Vik had gone.

'There's room for me; weight-wise, we're set.' Nadia knew how it worked. The aircraft had strict rules every time it took to the skies and one of those rules was to do with calculating fuel and how much weight they were carrying on board. The patient this time wasn't an adult, not even a teen, but a baby that by her estimate couldn't weigh more than a few kilograms.

'I'll see you both out there.' Noah, the other critical care paramedic with the red team, put his helmet and jacket on ready for the mission, because he'd need to be on board should the crew get called to another job after they transported the baby. It didn't matter to him or Bess that they'd finished their shift; they went above and beyond the call of duty whenever it was required. He'd already retrieved the bloods and the drugs that weren't always kept on the aircraft, and he set off towards the helicopter.

Bess shrugged on her heavy-duty jacket, picked up her helmet and held out her arms again. 'Give her to me while you put the spare helmet and jacket on.'

Lena seemed happy enough to be passed between them.

Hudson appeared in the hangar next. 'How is she doing? It's a good job we answered that door when we did.'

'Ain't that the truth,' said Bess.

Nadia gave her summation to Hudson, who would most

likely write the report as she put her arm into the other sleeve of the jacket. 'Her nappy wasn't full but not dry either so she seems hydrated. There are no obvious marks on her torso or elsewhere; she's content. It seems as though she's been well looked after.' Her words felt clinical but looking at Lena, this felt like anything but.

The sound of the aircraft's blades whipping against the air on the helipad grew louder as if to remind them of their mission.

Hudson reached for the spare helmet. They all knew the score with flying in the air ambulance even if you weren't part of the crew that regularly took to the skies. It was safety first. He put it on Nadia's head, fastened the strap beneath her chin. She looked into his eyes, closer in proximity than they'd ever been before.

And then the moment was over as she took Lena from Bess and they headed out towards the aircraft.

Hudson walked alongside Bess and Nadia, shouting over the din of the helicopter. 'I'll take a look outside, all around the airbase and surrounding fields. Whoever left her might not have got far after they rang the bell.'

'Okay.' The downwash from Hilda took Nadia's words away and she held Lena, who had started to grizzle, closer to her chest as they climbed into the aircraft.

Noah slid the side door to the helicopter shut. He and Nadia were sitting in the back with the baby and would communicate with Bess and Maya in the front via the headsets on their helmets.

With Lena secure in her special seat and wearing a tiny pair of ear defenders to protect her sensitive ears, Noah gave the go-ahead that they were ready.

'Clear on the left,' came Bess's voice over the headset.

'All clear for take-off,' Vik confirmed.

Lena began to scream the second Hilda lifted into the air. Nadia longed to take her in her arms but she was in the safest place possible so instead, she reached over and placed a hand against Lena's chest, just softly, giving her the assurance that she wasn't alone any more; someone was here for her.

The journey wasn't a long one. Vik announced an expected arrival time of three minutes almost as soon as they were up in the skies and flying over the beautiful town of Whistlestop River, the town Nadia had made her home in for the last eight years. But she was too preoccupied watching Lena, shushing her even though the baby wouldn't be able to hear the soothing sounds, to look out of the window and appreciate the river below, winding, curving, glistening in the sunshine.

She wondered whether Hudson had found anyone or anything outside the airbase: perhaps a hint as to who had left the box there. But there hadn't been an update over the radio; she expected whoever was responsible had fled.

At first, Nadia had wondered who could ever do such a thing, but as Hilda soared through the skies en route to the hospital, her thoughts turned to concern for the person – a mother, most likely, in a highly emotional state, perhaps with physical or mental health issues. The baby couldn't be more than a week or two old but thankfully, she appeared remarkably unscathed.

As soon as they touched down on the hospital's helipad, Nadia told Bess and Noah that she'd take it from here. 'You will be available for another job should you get a call or you can all head back to base. You've already done a full shift.'

A nurse met them and ushered them inside the lift that took them down to the appropriate floor. They followed the winding labyrinth of the hospital until they came to paediatrics, all the while Lena nestled contentedly in Nadia's arms.

Nadia had known this baby less than an hour and already she felt attached, like she never wanted to let her go.

She knew Lena wasn't hers; she had no claim on her. But as she handed her to the nurse once they reached the paediatric department, the tug at her heart, that feeling she'd never forgotten, was right back, stabbing at her emotions and twisting them around and around every time she looked at the infant.

It was the same pain she'd felt when she lost her own baby, not once, but twice.

3

Hudson was due to pick up the kids from their grandparents but because of the drama unfolding with baby Lena, he wanted to get up to the hospital, find out what was going on.

He was lucky. His parents lived locally in Whistlestop River and they always stepped up to help him out, tonight being no exception. He wasn't sure where he would've been without them. They had known for a while what his ex-wife Lucinda was like – unreliable when it came to sticking to timescales, at least out of the office environment – and were never surprised when Hudson called them last minute to ask that they mind three-year-old Carys because Lucinda had had something come up at the last minute. Fifteen-year-old Beau was past the age of needing them to watch him but he often went to their house simply because he liked their company. In fact, Hudson was pretty sure Beau preferred being with them to him. He supposed he should be grateful. At least Beau let some family into his teenage world.

Hudson parked at the hospital. Inside, he followed the signs, walking the maze of the building, saying hello to a nurse here and there. Part of his job remit with The Skylarks was to build and enhance relationships with hospitals so he knew a lot of the staff from previous encounters. His role also involved supporting patients who had been treated by the air ambulance team so that they could make sense of their experience, and a big part of his job was supporting families after their loss of a loved one. It was the bit he was particularly good at, but also the bit that tried him the most. He'd been here at this hospital only a couple of weeks ago to meet with a family whose daughter, despite The Skylarks' best efforts, hadn't survived. The family had needed to fully comprehend what happened, at least the best they could, and they had important questions about the care that was provided to their daughter in the pre-hospital environment. It wasn't an easy job for Hudson on those days as relatives found themselves in the painful position of being unexpectedly bereaved, but Hudson hoped he brought them some comfort and made things that little bit easier to bear.

Unlike the crew who took to the skies, Hudson didn't work erratic shifts. Sometimes they happened, of course, like now, but usually he had more organised and social hours which fitted in with him and the kids. He'd been part time when he started with the Whistlestop River Air Ambulance and had been able to juggle work with being the parent who stayed at home the most, but when Lucinda moved out of the family home eight months ago, he'd had to return to full time given the change in his financial situation.

When he reached paediatrics, he spotted Nadia coming along the corridor. She looked drawn, tired, not her usual self at all.

'How's the baby?' *Please let it be good news.* If he believed it would make any difference, he'd cross his fingers on both hands.

Her face brightened. 'She's doing well. She's going to be

checked thoroughly by a doctor but preliminary checks by myself and the nurses haven't found anything of concern. We think she must have been fed before she was left outside the airbase.'

'No other signs of dehydration?' Even if the baby had been fed, time was getting on and hunger and thirst could creep up easily.

'No. She isn't lethargic; she had a bit of a cry earlier with plenty of tears.' She smiled; mostly, you didn't like to see a baby's tears, but it was a good sign that the baby was hydrated.

Nadia led the way back into the ward and over to one of the cubicles, coming in behind a guy in a white coat who strode with purpose right over to Lena. 'This must be the doctor to do the formal assessment.' Her gaze drifted back to Hudson. 'It's way past the end of your day. You didn't have to come all the way out here.'

'It's my job, remember: patient and family liaison. And The Skylarks don't clock off if they're needed.'

'You're right. Perhaps I'm the one who shouldn't really be here; it's just, well, she's so small—'

'It's good that you came. It's good that you care.' He watched her shift along near the window so she could observe the doctor doing the checks. 'I'll take you home when you're ready,' he told her.

'Thank you.'

Hudson stayed while the doctor examined Lena. Prior to his role with The Skylarks and before Carys was born, Hudson had been a full-time nurse, so he knew what the doctor was likely looking for. The doctor examined Lena's eyes for their appearance and movement – he'd be checking for cataracts. He placed a stethoscope against Lena's chest to check her heart. A lot of babies – adults too – found it cold and it jolted them but Lena seemed mesmerised by all the attention. The doctor was likely checking for heart murmurs. They were common, and meant the heart had an extra or unusual sound caused by disturbed blood flow as it negotiated its way around the tight bends inside a young child's heart. They usually turned out not to have a serious underlying cause – Beau had had one when he was born and both Hudson and Lucinda had held their breath until the doctor confirmed it was an innocent murmur which went away soon after. But hearing anything was out of the ordinary with your baby was a unique form of torture.

Lena underwent other physical examinations including the checking of her hips, screening tests she may have had as a newborn already but without any record, it was best to do them again. For the most part, she took the examinations well but it wasn't too long before she got tetchy and Hudson couldn't blame her. Her face turned pink; she gnawed at her clenched fists.

The doctor handed a grizzling Lena to Nadia because Nadia, just like a parent, found it hard to stay back. Hudson didn't feel it was his place to ask her, but he sometimes wondered why she'd never had a family of her own; she was a natural and she seemed to have a desperate longing. Or maybe he was reading too much into it. Maybe his knack of observing how people reacted and felt had gone into overdrive.

Alongside the doctor's assessment, a junior doctor had been taking notes and he carried on with those as the consultant addressed Nadia and Hudson. 'Given her size, weight and appearance, I'd say that this little one was born slightly early. She's approximately ten days old, maybe less. But she's healthy, she's strong. She's been well looked after.'

A nurse came into the cubicle. 'The police are on their way and social services have been notified.' She leaned in and rubbed the back of her finger against Lena's cheek. 'Now let's get this little one a bottle of formula. It's been a couple of hours since you found her.'

'The mother or whoever abandoned her outside the airbase must have fed her right before she was left.' Nadia cradled Lena in her arms. 'She's too little to go too long without food. She's done well to last.'

The nurse went off to make up the formula and Nadia sat in the chair next to the bed in the cubicle on the ward. Alongside them, ready for Lena, was a clear plastic cot-bed but Hudson suspected that even after a feed, Nadia would be in no rush to transfer the baby.

Hudson crouched down on his haunches. 'You doing okay?' He was used to this. He worked closely with patients and their families to explain interventions, their medical care, the holistic approach to their recovery. And Nadia right now felt like someone who needed that support. This case had hit her hard – it happened sometimes. He wanted to ask why she'd taken it so personally – was it just because Lena was so little? Had something happened to a baby she knew?

But it wasn't his job to pry. It was his job to support.

Nadia didn't shift her gaze from Lena as she lay there in her arms. 'I'm just glad we found her soon after the bell rang. Sometimes, we don't answer; sometimes, we're in the hangar and don't hear, or the crew could've been out on a job. I might have left, we—'

He did his best to keep Nadia calm. 'What might have happened isn't the focus now. Lena is healthy and safe, that's the main thing.'

As Lena became more fractious, Nadia stood and started to pace beside the window in the small space that belonged to this child for now. Medically, she almost had the all-clear, once she managed formula and had had a few nappy changes. Then all they'd need was social services to find a suitable placement for her and she'd be off. Although this was an unusual case, Hudson would keep in close contact with social services and the foster carer; he'd be ready to provide information about the appropriate support services if and when the mother or whoever had left Lena came forward.

The nurse came back with the formula and Nadia settled into the chair once again. But Lena didn't take to the bottle straight away. The teat went in and she turned her head away and screwed up her face some more. Nadia tried it again, and another time.

'Let me try a different type of bottle,' the nurse suggested.

But that one was no good either.

The nurse put a hand to Lena's head, the downy blonde hair curled beneath her fingers. 'I wonder whether this little one has been breastfed and isn't used to bottles.'

If that was the case, it meant that whoever had left her had really tried hard to care for her, as breastfeeding was rarely easy. Hudson wasn't sure whether that made things better or worse but it did make him hopeful that the mother would come forwards and get the help she needed.

The nurse, who Hudson had met a couple of times before, picked up on Nadia's distress. 'She'll eat eventually but if not, we'll try using a teaspoon just to keep her hydrated. Would you like me to try her with the bottle again?'

'I'm happy to keep doing it, if that's all right?'

'Of course.' The nurse excused herself to go over to another cubicle where she was needed. Hudson knew what it was like. It would be lovely as a nurse to focus on just a couple of patients at a time but it didn't work that way. Sometimes, you saw so many, it was hard to keep each case clear in your head, much to the frustration of the parents, as well as the nurses.

Nadia stood and held Lena against her body, swaying gently to calm her.

And then she sat down and tried the bottle again. But it still wasn't happening.

When the police arrived, she stood up, Lena cradled protectively in her arms once more.

There were two officers, one of them being Conrad, Maya's ex-husband. Hudson couldn't stand the guy. He was a total prick, full of self-importance, but as a detective who worked in the next town along from Whistlestop River, he was also known for being relentless when it came to getting to the bottom of a case. So, in that respect, it was good to have him on board.

Hudson and Nadia answered Conrad's questions the best they could. But there wasn't much to go on at all.

'And you answered the ring at the door to the airbase straight away?' Conrad's colleague asked.

'Yes, immediately,' said Nadia, although she clarified it with, 'Well, the time between hearing the ring and opening up the door after I'd found the keys delayed me by, say, five minutes.'

Conrad, lips downturned in thought, pushed them for more information. 'Think hard. Did you see any cars nearby that looked out of place? Had anyone unusual been hanging around the airbase today or recently? Any little detail you can remember might help us.'

But Nadia shook her head. 'I'm sorry. I can't remember anything else.'

'Me neither.' All Hudson could remember was seeing the baby and Nadia unable to take her eyes away from her. He wished now that he'd gone straight outside and had a look around. But hindsight was a wonderful thing. 'The cardboard box is back at the airbase if you need it, but there are no markings on it; it's plain.'

'Hmm... not helpful.'

Did Conrad mean the box wasn't helpful or they weren't? Hudson suspected both. This guy seemed to have a knack for making you feel guilty even if you weren't.

Conrad spoke over a crying child in the bay diagonal to theirs. 'Would you be open to doing a television appeal tomorrow?'

Nadia looked at Hudson, then at Conrad, whose focus settled on her. 'You want me to talk on camera?'

'Usually, it's the police who do the appeal,' Conrad explained, 'and I'll be there. But the baby was left at the airbase and you found her. It will make it more personal, in my opinion.'

'Anything I can do to help.'

'Do you need me to speak?' Hudson put in.

'Too many cooks...' Irritation laced Conrad's voice.

The man was an arse – Maya's frequent description of him – and for a detective, his people skills were seriously lacking. Unless they were all missing something members of the public got to see. But as long as he did the job, that's all anyone really wanted.

Everyone longed for a happy ever after in these sorts of cases. Hudson had been involved in a case with an abandoned newborn baby three years ago. The teenage mother had given birth and dumped the baby in a bin in the toilets at her school. The baby hadn't survived despite the air ambulance arriving at the scene quickly after the infant was found. They'd delivered pre-hospital emergency care but it was too late. Hudson had acted as patient and family liaison with the mother, a fifteen-year-old, and her parents, who'd had no idea their only daughter was even pregnant. He'd been the bridge for them to find support and counselling, but they'd never fully get over it. And the case had haunted him with Carys's arrival being around the same time. He hadn't been able to fathom how anyone could put a baby into a bin. The case had given him nightmares for weeks and he was only relieved that Lena hadn't met the same fate.

When Conrad and the other officer had their statement, Conrad told them he'd be in touch about the television appeal.

The nurse came back over with a bottle after the officers had left. 'Third time lucky?'

Nadia puffed out her cheeks. 'I'll give it a go. She seems to be calm enough again.' She sat down in the chair and, with Lena in position, took the bottle, guiding it to the baby's lips. 'Come on, Lena. You can do this.'

'Stubborn little miss,' the nurse sighed when Lena turned her head away, the milk from the teat squirting over her delicate features.

Nadia wiped the baby's face and just when they all thought it wasn't going to work and the nurse said she'd go and get a teaspoon and try an alternative method, Lena turned her head, the teat slipped inside her mouth and she rhythmically gulped down the milk until there was nothing left inside the bottle but air.

A collective sigh of relief had Nadia, the nurse and Hudson sharing smiles. And when Nadia handed over the empty bottle, she sat Lena on her lap, one hand supporting her chest and the weight of her head, the other rubbing her little back to elicit a burp.

And it was a big one that made them all laugh.

'If only it were so acceptable to burp that way after a good meal when you're an adult,' said Hudson when the nurse left them to it.

Nadia laughed. 'If only.'

Before they left the hospital, it was confirmed that Lena

would remain with the doctors and nurses until social services appointed an approved foster carer.

'I'll come up here again tomorrow to see her,' said Nadia as Hudson pulled out of the car park.

'That's a nice idea.' Even though he was driving, he sneaked a quick look to see she'd turned in her seat to face him.

'You don't think it's weird?'

'The Skylarks are forever crossing boundaries. And I think we do it well.' Nadia was in charge of keeping the team operating effectively, managing their schedules, ensuring they ran efficiently, but she cared; they all did. It was part of what made them all keep coming back to the job.

'She's all alone in the world,' said Nadia, her voice catching on her words.

'She's not alone; she's safe. And she's in good hands. And whoever left her, they either weren't thinking straight or they felt they had no choice.' He couldn't be sure of the circumstances but a parent rarely left their child on a whim. And one as well looked after as Lena? It hinted that whoever had abandoned her, whether it was the mother or someone else, they loved her very much.

'I was so relieved when she took the bottle. Do you think the nurse was right: that Lena was likely breastfed and wondered what on earth was going on? She must've known none of us were her mother; she was waiting to be in her arms.'

'Maybe, but she was pretty happy with you.'

'How long until she's placed with a social worker?'

She sounded worn out. He wanted to ask why this case had hit so hard, ask whether she needed to talk. This woman had a huge heart, a warmth, a way with people that he'd admired right from his very first day at the air ambulance base.

'It could be anywhere from a few hours to a few days, but

they'll do it as soon as they can. She doesn't have health concerns that require a stay in hospital; better to get her to a homely environment.'

He pulled in at the kerb outside her house.

'Thank you for bringing me home, Hudson. You'd better get back to your kids.'

'No worries at all, and my parents leapt in to look after Carys. Beau went because he enjoys their company.'

'Is Lucinda out of town? On your birthday?'

He'd mentioned his parents without even thinking. 'Couldn't be helped. Oh... and thank you for the brownies and the cake again – haven't had any of the latter yet but tomorrow is another day.'

'Let's hope they've left us some cake back at the base. And you're very welcome for the brownies.'

With a smile and yet another thank you, Nadia got out of the car.

As he drove to his parents' to collect the kids, Hudson thought about the woman he'd married and the woman he was getting to know as a friend. They couldn't be more different, both in looks and personality. Lucinda had a sharp brunette bob with eyes that missed nothing and her appearance was on a par with her work ethic, her utter drive and determination in her job as an actuary with an insurance company. Nadia on the other hand had soft blonde waves in her hair and a smile that was impossible to ignore. She was a people person, like he was, and she had a way of talking to you that made you feel as if you were important, as if you mattered.

And now he drew another comparison because the way Nadia had been with Lena today had him imagine what she would be like as a mother. She'd be the one to volunteer at nursery, to accompany them on school trips, to let them get messy with paints at home, take care of them when they were sick. Lucinda loved Beau and Carys, Hudson knew that, but she'd never wanted a family as much as Hudson had and had never done those things. They'd fallen pregnant by mistake with Beau and he knew that had Beau not come along, it was unlikely they ever would've stayed together. Lucinda cheated on him a few years into their marriage but when he found out, she insisted she didn't want to end their relationship, that nothing mattered more than keeping her family together. She told him then that they should keep trying for another baby, the second baby they'd never been blessed with despite their efforts. And so, with the lure of the bigger family he'd always longed for, he'd accepted that she made a terrible mistake and they'd tried to make their marriage work.

They were still trying to make it work when Lucinda found out she was pregnant with Carys. That was when Lucinda's biggest lie had come to the fore. Hudson's way of coping was to focus on their family; her way of coping was to throw herself into her work for as long as she could, working right up until the day before she gave birth. She took minimum maternity leave before she got back to what she loved best – her job and the part of her life that was solely hers. She had a harder edge when it came to family than he did. And that harder edge was what had come between them as a couple in the end. She'd had another affair, she wasn't very good at hiding them, and making their relationship work became impossible. They'd tried for the sake of the kids but it was obvious that staying together for Beau and Carys would likely make everyone unhappy.

He pulled up outside his parents' home. All he wanted now was for Beau and Carys to settle into this new life of theirs, seeing both parents separately, spending the majority of their time with their dad. Lucinda had cheated on him twice at least when they were married – twice that he'd found out about anyway – and now she had a new boyfriend. She'd introduced the guy to the kids even though the divorce had only been finalised last month and while Hudson didn't mind that she was moving on, he did mind when it affected the children. And from what he could make out, Beau wasn't overly keen on this new man at all. He wouldn't tell Hudson anything about him; he always asked his mother if *he* was going to be there when she came to pick him and his sister up.

Hudson went inside his parents' home to be greeted by the sound of laughter – his mum's and Carys's. He wanted to immerse himself in the sound; he wished he could hear more of it at home, especially with Beau.

All he wanted these days was for his kids to be happy, to feel safe and loved because his kids were his whole world. Nothing else mattered as much as they did.

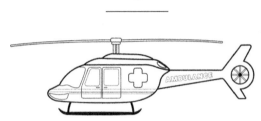

4

Nadia was nervous. In the reception area of the airbase, she watched the television camera operators outside hovering, ready for her. Various onlookers had begun to assemble and she wasn't sure whether she could do this. Conrad, lead detective on the case to find the missing mother of baby Lena, had asked her to speak and appeal to the mother to come forward.

'Are you sure someone on the force wouldn't be better at this than I would?' Nadia fussed with the frill collar of her floral blouse, an open collar that in some way felt as if it was getting tighter, as if it might hamper her efforts to speak.

Conrad faced her square on. 'In cases like these, women... mothers... often relate to other women. Based on my experience, I made the call to hold the appeal here at the airbase where the baby was found and to have you speak as you were the one who found her. It gives the case a personal, softer edge. It might make all the difference.'

'What if it wasn't the mother who left the baby here? It could've been the father, or a relative?'

'Highly unlikely.' His sense of superiority shone through. It was part of his personality, whether justified or not. 'And if it wasn't the mother who left the baby, the appeal won't go to waste. Someone somewhere must know something. I'll keep digging until we find out who this baby is.' He lifted his hand in acknowledgement to someone beyond the doors of the airbase before he looked back at Nadia. 'Ready?'

Of course she wasn't, but if she could help in any way, she would.

They both stepped outside and into the spring sunshine.

Conrad stood taller, his chest puffed up; he was getting camera-ready. In a suit because he was a detective rather than a police officer, he was full of self-importance just as Maya always said he was. But Nadia couldn't care less how much he thought of himself or how much he talked the talk. All she wanted was for him to be as good at his job as he claimed to be and when Hudson nodded over to her from nearby to encourage her, she took a deep breath, ready to do this.

The first attempt to film the short segment was hampered by the shrill ringing of the telephones, which sounded all around the base for The Skylarks.

Shortly after The Skylarks took to the skies in the helicopter behind the airbase building, the crew began their filming again. It took three takes but Nadia was at least used to being a spokesperson for the charity, which made public speaking a little easier. Not that there were that many people here; most would see it on their TV later or online, wherever the segment was shared.

Notification came a little over an hour after the segment was recorded with the time and the channel where it would first be broadcast. The Skylarks were still out on the job they'd been called to and in the office between tasks, Hudson put the television on and stood beside Nadia, ready to watch.

Nadia, one arm across her body, her opposite elbow resting on it with her fingers to her lips, was paranoid she'd not done well enough to convince the mother to come forwards. 'I hope I did okay.'

'I think you did better than okay.'

'Any second now...'

They waited for the segment to come on.

'You know I can't stand Conrad, but he made a good call having you talk. I wouldn't mind betting you come across just as kind on camera as you are in real life.'

Nadia wasn't a nail biter but if she was, she knew her nails would be destroyed by now. 'Let's hope it helps.'

Within thirty seconds, there she was, on screen with the police detective.

The segment began with them standing there, the sound of the helicopter fading away in the background – the crew must have recorded the take-off and cleverly edited the footage to make sure the air ambulance was a part of the finished television coverage. What Nadia and Conrad each said had been pre-decided and the importance of what she was doing had dampened down her nervousness.

Conrad's voice, usually a boom, and commanding presence changed tone when he spoke. And even though nobody was keen on Maya's ex-husband, Nadia had to hand it to him. Today he had done a good job.

'Yesterday, just after 4 p.m., a baby was left in a box at the doorway to this very building.' Conrad briefly put a hand out to indicate the glass doors behind them and the signage above which read *Whistlestop River Air Ambulance*. 'Myself and my fellow officers would like to praise the team here for their fast thinking and the transfer of baby Lena to the nearest hospital where she remains safe and well. Here with me today is operational support officer, Nadia Sutton, who found the baby yesterday.'

It felt odd watching herself on screen. She remembered Conrad handing over to her, the feel of all eyes upon her.

'We know the baby is called Lena because her name was written on a piece of paper tucked beside her in the box. I could see that Lena had been well looked after and, following a thorough examination by doctors at the hospital, I'm delighted to say that Lena is not injured and there are no immediate health concerns. However, we desperately would like to locate Lena's mother or whoever left Lena with us. If you are listening, please do come forward.'

Conrad took over. 'We have trained officers and medics ready to provide support. Please get in touch by calling the emergency services or going into a station or a hospital.'

As the segment concluded, Hudson switched the television off. 'You did great, you know. This will be shown online, hopefully often, and on the television again. We've done everything we can.'

'So why don't I feel any better?'

He came to her side, put his hands onto her shoulders. 'Because you care; never apologise for that. But remember she *is* safe, she *is* well.'

She wanted him to wrap her in his arms, to feel the security of his hold, but she knew she couldn't let herself want that. They were friends; that had to be as far as it went.

'I'm going to call the hospital, see what stage they're at finding a foster carer.'

'Can you let me know what they say? I'll be in my office; I've got some calls to make.'

'Sure.'

She left the main office where the team gathered for meetings and followed the corridor through the reception to the other side where her little office stood. She closed the door behind her. She needed some time to get herself together: the events of yesterday, a restless sleep, a television appeal, Hudson – her emotions were bubbling towards the surface in ways she couldn't quite get a hold of. She kept thinking of Lena, in a box of all things, the mother, whoever she was, what would happen from now.

When Nadia emerged, Hudson was on the phone in the main office. The Skylarks were heading back inside the building from the hangar. Brad, one of the critical care paramedics, took the cool box of bloods through to the room where they were stored until they were needed for the next mission. He'd be putting away the drugs too which were always kept in the building rather than the helicopter and signed out before each job. Business as usual around here when Nadia felt as if her world had been tilted, that she was having to face up to all that she'd lost, all over again, given the events of the past twenty-four hours.

When Brad came out of the room and met her in the corridor, she mustered as much enthusiasm as she could manage by announcing, 'There's birthday cake, remember. Nobody got to eat much last night.'

He looked weary.

'Tough job?'

'I'll say. I need some cake first, a cup of coffee, then I'll be ready to go through my notes with you; is that okay?'

'Fine with me,' she said, leading the way to the kitchen. She didn't ask for more details, not right now; he looked like he needed some time to de-stress.

Hudson joined them and, without her having to ask, gave her the update from the hospital. 'Lena is still thriving, drinking formula like there's no tomorrow. A foster carer with the appropriate approval level has been appointed and they'll be going to the hospital with the social worker midday tomorrow.'

'That's good. She'll be somewhere safe.'

'I'll make a call to the police, check whether they've heard anything.'

'Thanks, Hudson.'

'My pleasure. But right now, I'd better make sure I get a slice of my cake, preferably a very big one. I can't believe I've held off until now.'

Nadia distributed slices of cake, Hudson made the mugs of coffee and when Kate, the other paramedic on the blue team, appeared, she said she'd grab hers later. It was time to clean Hilda. The whole crew were responsible for cleaning the helicopter, nobody escaped the job, and Hilda was due her maintenance check tomorrow so would be taken away and another model left in her place.

Nadia took her cake to go and told Brad, 'I'll be in my office whenever you're ready.'

She wondered whether she would ever get a turn to decompress from everything that had happened recently, the pain it had brought up. If she closed her eyes, she could imagine, almost feel, Lena in her arms. Holding the baby had gone some way to comforting her from her own previous losses but at the same time, it had opened up wounds that had never really healed.

Nadia finished her piece of cake and confirmed the final head count for the crews and the staff for the main fundraising event of the year scheduled for next month. It was the annual dinner dance and would be held at a magnificent venue on the coast. The fundraising team, who worked remotely and didn't come into the airbase all that often, had done a stellar job of pulling this together. There would be a three-course meal, followed by a silent auction, and then dancing late into the night. Nadia had been shopping last week and treated herself to a brand-new dress – black, almost floor-length, sequins – and couldn't wait to get all dolled up for a night with her colleagues. With any luck, they'd raise a great deal of money for the town's air ambulance. Maya's dad Nigel had a lot of business contacts and these days was one of The Skylarks' biggest sponsors. He'd arranged the beautiful venue at a heavily discounted rate and already Nadia could feel it was going to be an event never to forget.

Brad came in soon after she'd called through the final head count.

'I'm sorry it was such a tough shift,' she said.

'One of the hardest. The cake helped a little, thanks.'

Armed with a pad of paper and his notes as well as a good memory, he recounted the events of the emergency they'd attended. He was thorough; he had to be. Nadia's job was to listen, to go through all the information and then she'd be able to pass the case to either Hudson or Paige for follow-up. It was easier to have her go through incidents first so that she could manage the workloads of their two patient and family liaison officers and allocate work accordingly.

Nadia got all the details down. Paige's workload was ample for the hours she worked so this one would go to Hudson. Hudson would be the point of contact for the family, who would likely have questions about the care their loved one had had pre-hospital and what the next steps were. He'd handle it well because Hudson always seemed to bring light and hope with him. It was one of his many qualities she admired.

She looked out into reception to see whether she could grab Hudson to listen in but he was on the phone and so she and

Brad continued. He detailed every step of the job from The Skylarks' arrival to everything they did for pre-hospital care. The job had been a call to a road traffic collision and a young adult male had gone through the windscreen and was found lying on the bonnet. He'd had extensive injuries, a blood transfusion was done at the scene, but it hadn't been enough. He'd died before they got him to the hospital.

'You look like you could use a drink more than I could,' Brad said once they'd finished and Nadia had put all the details onto the computer. 'Harrowing, that's one word to describe today.'

'Oh, Brad, some shifts are like that, I know, I get it.'

'Let's hope tomorrow is better.'

They emerged from the office and she went over to Hudson at the reception desk. 'It sounds like a terrible shift for the crew today.'

'Yeah, not the best from what I hear.'

'I have all the notes ready for you. I was going to grab you but you were on the phone.'

'I called the police – nothing yet,' he confirmed. 'Come on, let's talk through the notes now and I'll grab Brad if I think I need more clarification.'

Back in the office, they went through the details. All the facts were there and the team were good at talking with one another if they needed anything else.

He stood up to go and Nadia picked up her bag.

'I'm off home,' she said. 'Early night for me, I'm shattered.'

He stopped in the doorway and smiled. 'You've forgotten.'

'Forgotten?'

'No chance of an early night. It's Dorothy's birthday; she's having a bash at the pub.'

Nadia's heart sank. She loved Dorothy, one of the Whistlestop River Freewheelers, dearly and he was right; there was no chance of sneaking off home because Nadia would never want to let Dorothy or anyone else down. But her energy levels were seriously lacking. She usually stayed behind and worked extra hours but even that seemed too much right now.

'Come for a bit; it'll do you good. I'm not staying for too long, and I won't be drinking; I have to collect Beau from a friend's.'

'What time does it start?'

'You really have forgotten.' He smiled. 'Half an hour, so I'm going straight there.'

'I'd better go freshen up and do the same then.'

And although she was tired, at least she was doing something with the people she cared about – she called them her family these days and she meant it.

After all, she didn't have anyone else. At least, not any more.

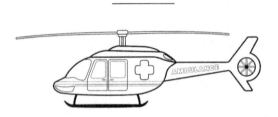

5

Hudson wouldn't have minded a few drinks tonight but the dad taxi took precedence, so he parked up outside the pub just as his phone began to ring.

He saw Lucinda's name on the display.

'Don't do this,' he muttered, tempted not to answer the call. She was supposed to pick Carys up from childcare and have her for the evening so at least he only had one of the kids to worry about when he had a social engagement.

It stopped ringing but started up again after barely a pause. And he couldn't ignore it. It might be an emergency – unlikely but possible.

'Hello.' He closed his eyes, waiting for the delivery of excuses.

And she didn't disappoint.

As he drove to the childcare centre, he called his parents on handsfree. They were used to this – didn't make him any less pissed off but at least he had a back-up.

Within thirty minutes, he'd collected Carys and dropped her at his parents.

'It's only for a couple of hours max,' he said.

'Don't worry about it; we love having her here.' His dad stood on the doorstep; Hudson's mum had already whisked her grand-daughter inside the house. 'I'm assuming you don't have time for a cup of tea.'

'Sorry, Dad, next time. It's Dorothy's birthday celebrations at the pub and I promised I'd go. Otherwise I would've cancelled when Lucinda let me down.'

'Tea next time.' He smiled. 'And no worries looking after Carys; it's what we're here for.' His hair was almost white now and he often joked that he fitted the role of grandparent perfectly these days. He'd had dark-grey hair for a long time and it was as though suddenly overnight, a white wash had come along and left its mark. It hadn't aged him though; his zest for life since retirement hadn't waned at all.

'Well, I really appreciate it. And I know it's short notice.'

'Grandparent duty is fine by us whenever you need it.'

'Thanks, Dad. She's got a change of clothes in the bag I've handed over; hopefully, you won't need them but just in case.' He started off back down the path.

'What was the reason this time?' His dad's voice followed after him.

Hudson turned back. 'She's cracked a tooth, has an emergency dentist appointment.'

His dad chuckled. 'At least she's original.'

Hudson had to laugh too. Whether it was an excuse or not he had no idea; all he knew was that Lucinda was good at making things up. She'd lied enough times over the years about little things – a meeting running over time when really she was going out for drinks, a gym session she didn't want to miss when really she was meeting up with a friend, a work trip that was four days when really it was only three but she'd felt she'd needed the extra day to herself before she came home. The lying had started early on in their marriage with a deception Hudson had found hard to forgive.

Hudson found out the truth years afterwards, a long time after they'd come to terms that for some reason, they couldn't conceive a second time. Lucinda had never wanted to go down the IVF route and he respected that; it was a lot to deal with and came with no guarantees. They had Beau and they adored their son and it would be the three of them as a family.

When Beau was twelve, Lucinda came down with a bout of food poisoning following a dinner out at a restaurant for their anniversary. They were back to arguing again and Hudson had wanted to make the effort to do something different. She was always at the office, he was working part time and running the house, but this night was an attempt to reconnect.

And reconnect they did. But not in the ways he hoped. The next morning, he'd gone to find her, to take her some water, some toast, see if she could keep something down before he went to work. But she was in the spare room, the little room that doubled as her study when she needed to do any work from home, and she was in the middle of a business call.

He sighed, set down the drink and the toast on her bedside table. At least she was feeling better.

He was about to eat the toast himself given it would be stone cold by the time she emerged from her work environment, when he saw a text flash up on her phone screen from the doctor. He picked up the phone – the text was a reminder for an appointment for today. He'd explained to her that food poisoning likely meant rest, plenty of fluids and didn't necessitate a visit to the doctor, but clearly she thought she knew best.

'What are you doing?' She appeared in the doorway and

when she saw her phone in his hand she came over and took possession of it.

'I was bringing you toast and some water.'

She spotted the plate and the glass. 'Oh, thanks.'

'You're feeling better?'

'Yes, much better.'

'Food poisoning usually lasts a bit longer; you're lucky.'

'Yes, I suppose I must be.'

Then why did she look so shifty and pale? 'What's the doctor appointment for if you're better?'

'You don't have to know everything.'

'So I'm not allowed to worry about my wife?'

She rolled her eyes. 'Just a women's check-up; it's been arranged for ages, nothing to do with the food poisoning.'

She was infuriating when she closed herself off like this, wouldn't talk to him. 'Toast is there,' he said, 'eat it or don't eat it. I'm not going to fight about it.'

He was going to be late for work if he didn't get going so he left her to it.

Ten minutes later, she came downstairs, clearly not expecting him to be hovering in the kitchen.

She clasped a hand against her chest. 'You made me jump. I thought you'd left.' She came closer, the plate cleared, her glass half-empty. And that was when she saw the stick on the kitchen table. And she didn't say a word, just set her plate and her glass down by the sink and looked out of the window, her back to him.

'Why didn't you tell me?' Hudson had gone to put something in the bin, realised the bag had a hole in it, and took the entire thing out to transfer the rubbish into a fresh bag. That was when the pregnancy test had fallen out. A positive pregnancy test.

'I would've told you.' She still didn't face him.

'Is that what the doctor's appointment is for today?' He felt his hopes, his spirits rise. 'This is... this is the best news ever.'

But when she turned around, the look on her face was chilling. 'No, Hudson. This is not good news.'

He was confused. 'But we tried for years. We both wanted this.' They'd assumed it was secondary infertility which happened to some couples. Lucinda hadn't wanted to undergo any invasive investigations; she'd wanted to let nature take its course. They'd clearly got lucky. Or at least that was the way he was looking at it.

He went over to her. 'I know it'll be a huge adjustment.' Perhaps she was panicking. 'We'll get used to it. Beau will have a little brother or a sister. He'll have siblings just like you did.' But when he tried to pull her to him, she shrugged him off.

'I need to get dressed, ready for the doctor.'

'I'll call in, take the morning off, come with you.'

'No, thanks, I'll go by myself.'

'Why are you pushing me away? What's wrong with you that you can't let me in?'

She stopped in the doorway, fists clenched at the sides of her silk dressing gown, and then she turned.

'I don't want this! I never wanted this!'

'But we both did. We were trying for ages...'

She growled. 'I was just telling you what you wanted to hear!'

It took a minute until realisation dawned. 'You pretended... You went along with it, you acted disappointed that it never happened.'

'It wasn't disappointment for me, Hudson; it was relief.'

She'd been deceiving him all this time, making him think she wanted to have another child when she had no intention of ever getting pregnant. 'How did you do it? Were you on the pill?'

'I've had the coil for years, but a lack of appointments meant I didn't get a new one.' She eyed the pregnancy test with disdain, lying there on the table, its vulgarity all she could see.

Looking back, Hudson knew that that day was the moment their fate had been sealed, the moment their marriage ended even though they welcomed Carys into the world and tried to be a family for as long as they could. Well, he'd tried anyway. Lucinda had returned to work, and to the long hours. She'd given up on their marriage way before he had. But eventually, Hudson had realised they really had reached the end of the road.

He hadn't been able to see the truth, he'd been tricked all this time, and for that, he felt a sense of shame, embarrassment that he'd been pulled along in her world, accepting what she said, assuming they even stood a chance.

Hudson locked his car in the car park at the pub and made his way in to join his teammates for Dorothy's celebrations.

Dorothy was already in situ and the only other person to arrive so far was Nadia.

'I thought I'd be really late,' he whispered to Nadia.

Dorothy gave him a big hug. 'You're the first two here so at least I have people to celebrate with.'

'There'll be plenty soon enough, I'm sure of it,' said Hudson.

'Seventy years young. Who would've thought I'd still be zipping around on a motorcycle!'

'Well, we're very glad you are.' Nadia smiled; she looked more chilled than when he'd seen her earlier and he wondered whether she was glad she'd come along. He was.

A couple of minutes later, when Hudson wondered whether Nadia hadn't been the only one to forget about this shindig before he reminded her, the pub doors opened behind them and a cheer went up when Dorothy's colleagues Alan, Mick and Rita came in along with pilot Vik.

Almost an hour into the party, Hudson whispered to Nadia, 'When do you think it's okay to sneak off?'

'I'm not sure. But what with the television segment today and not sleeping well last night, I'm hoping it's soon.'

He leaned back so he could look around the body of the crowd to where Dorothy was standing. 'She's well into the prosecco; she's enjoying herself.'

Kate from the blue team came over to chat to them, told Nadia all about the dress she'd bought herself for the upcoming dinner dance and asked Nadia all about hers. Hudson escaped the conversation by accepting the offer of a game of darts with Bess's other half, firefighter Gio, who was waiting for his brother Marco.

When he went back over to join Nadia, she asked him, 'What were you guys talking about?' Marco had arrived – he wasn't from Whistlestop River so must be visiting – and the three of them had huddled gossiping for a few minutes.

'Not about dresses.'

'Very funny.'

'The brothers wanted to know a bit more about Frank.'

Frank was the engineer at the airbase – a kind, gentle bear of a man who was dating the boys' mother, Marianne, so they had a vested interest.

'Imagine being up against the scrutiny of those two,' said Nadia. 'Mind you, I expect Marianne is prepared for it and it's nice that they care.'

'They're close. Kind of makes me wish I had a brother. Or a sister.' But Hudson had been his parents' miracle baby. After gynaecological issues left his mum and dad with about a 10 per cent chance of conceiving, they'd been overjoyed when Hudson came along.

Hudson had longed for a sibling growing up and talked about it a lot; it was the reason why his parents had finally sat him down and explained why the health issues his mum had made it near impossible. They told him they'd wanted a big family but for them, it simply wasn't meant to be. And he shared that vision of family; it was why he'd wanted Beau to have a brother or sister. Every day, he was thankful that Carys had come along.

The doctor's appointment Lucinda had booked for that day when she'd found out she was expecting for the second time had been to discuss her options – that delightful fact hadn't come out until midway through her pregnancy. It still made him shudder to think she might have had a termination but as she got her head around the idea of baby number two and she'd made the admission, she'd also said that she was glad she hadn't because she didn't think she would've forgiven herself.

He knew he probably wouldn't have forgiven her either.

Hudson nudged Nadia when Frank walked into the pub and went over to say hello to Gio and Marco. 'He's in for a grilling.'

Nadia watched the three men. 'He'll handle himself just fine.'

'I wonder if they have a strategy for quizzing their mother's poor boyfriend. We'll rescue Frank if we think he needs it.'

'Agreed.'

'Here's Marianne,' said Hudson.

'This is like a TV show for us.' Nadia giggled, the sound music to Hudson's ears.

Seeing Nadia like this, out of work, was an extra-special bonus. He'd been disappointed when she said she was heading home for an early night, and again when he thought he might have to cancel if his parents couldn't take Carys. Although he should've known they'd be fine with it; they very rarely said no and most of their commitments, their pastimes, took place in the daytime. It was very rare that at least one of them wouldn't be able to help out.

'Gio says his mum has settled in to Whistlestop River really well,' said Hudson. Marianne had moved down this way to sort out her issues with Gio and had never left.

'This town has a charm; it got a hold of me for sure.'

'Yeah, it's home.'

They watched Marianne head straight over to Frank and slip her hand into his.

'They're a lovely couple.' Nadia smiled. 'I'm really pleased he's found someone; he deserves to find love again.' They all knew Frank's history: that when his wife died, it had sent him to a pretty dark place.

'Family is everything,' he said, almost to himself before he turned to face her rather than watching everything else that was going on in the pub. 'I don't know much about yours. I've never really asked you.'

'Not much to tell.'

He wasn't sure that was true. And he wondered whether she was holding on to a sadness from the past, keeping things to herself rather than sharing them with anyone else. He knew that feeling well; it was why he'd kept his and Lucinda's difficulties quiet. That and the embarrassment that he'd been played for years, that she'd lied for so long and he hadn't had a clue. He'd half expected his own truth – the separation and then the divorce – to come out before now given Lucinda had had two flings during their marriage and was now seeing someone new. Perhaps she'd had the decency to conduct her extramarital affairs and her current relationship away from the town.

'I know you're from Switzerland,' he went on, his desire to know more about her ever present.

'How did you know that?'

'Pub quiz a year or so ago – there was question about lakes from what I remember and you nailed it, then you talked a bit about the place.'

'You have a good memory.'

'Must've been a nice place to live.'

'It was okay.'

When she didn't elaborate, he asked, 'Are you parents still around?'

'Not any more. They both passed away a long time ago.'

She really wasn't letting much go, was she? 'Do you have brothers? Sisters?' He felt like he was having a one-way conversation, or that he was another quiz master trying to get the right answers.

'No siblings, no,' she said. 'It's just me.'

He shook his head. 'In all the time we've worked together, I should know this stuff but I don't.'

'We know plenty about each other.' But her smile faded as she set down her empty glass, her hand cold and wet from the ice cubes that had caused condensation on the outside of the vessel.

'Do you ever wish it wasn't?'

'Wasn't what?'

'I'm sorry, I shouldn't have said that.' He was pushing it now and if he didn't stop, he might piss her off and that wasn't what he wanted at all.

'No, please. Go on...'

He hesitated. 'Do you ever wish it wasn't just you?'

After a beat, she admitted, 'It is what it is.'

'I'm sorry, I didn't mean—'

'No, don't apologise; it was a simple question.' She reached down for her bag.

He'd ruined the mood. He wanted to kick himself, hard.

'Are we escaping?' He watched her hook her bag onto her shoulder.

'I think it's okay to do it now.'

He downed the rest of his soft drink and followed her discreetly out of the pub. 'I feel bad leaving without saying goodbye but this is probably easier.'

'Dorothy is having a grand old time; she won't even notice we've left.'

Hands in the pockets of his jeans, Hudson hovered next to her on the pavement outside. A sweet, floral smell from the nearby magnolia flowers carried on the air around them and he wished they could spend more of the evening together.

She smiled at him. 'I'd better get going and have that early night.'

'I'd better get back to the kids.'

She looked up at the sky, the clouds shifting across it. 'It's such a beautiful evening. I love that it stays light so late.'

She was hovering. Did that mean she wanted company?

Was she waiting for him to ask?

Of course she wasn't. Because as far as she knew, he was married.

And even if he wanted to spend more time with her, he couldn't. His kids came first. This was a time to focus on them, to put his needs last at least for a while, until things settled down.

If they ever would.

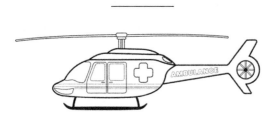

6

Hudson was doing dinner for the kids and, although it was a long way off, dreaming of the day when it wasn't such an ordeal.

He'd made Bolognese, a favourite and pretty much a staple in their house, but even that wasn't simple. Carys might only be three but she'd noticed the pieces of carrot he'd painstakingly chopped into tiny chunks to hide in the sauce and was refusing to eat it, and Beau, a fifteen-year-old who seemed to have weekly growth spurts, had already heaped another scoop of the meaty mixture onto the remains of his pasta, meaning there wouldn't be a big enough portion leftover to freeze for a family meal another day. It didn't matter too much but sometimes, a night off from full chef duty would be good.

'Slow down, it's not a race,' Hudson told Beau, who was shovelling the food in like there was no tomorrow.

'Ready, set, go!' Carys said, not once, not twice but several times, much to her brother's amusement. Maybe he was already thinking he might hoover up her leftovers himself, although that was brave; Hudson was pretty sure Carys had stuck her fingers into the food more than once.

Hudson picked up Carys's spoon for her. 'Come on, try to eat some more. Yummy, you love the tomato sauce.'

Her little face said otherwise.

'Come on, Carys.' He decided it was pointless pretending the carrots weren't there now she'd discovered them. 'You like carrots, bright orange, like the t-shirt you had on yesterday.' She loved to have sticks of carrot, cooked or raw, and dip them into red-pepper hummus. But, it seemed, that was vastly different to having them pop up unexpectedly in a meat and tomato sauce.

He picked up her bowl with an idea in mind. Anything was worth a shot. He went back to the pot he'd cooked the sauce in and ladled out another big spoonful into a different bowl. He patted it down so there was no orange to be seen and took it back over to her. She'd eaten some of the spaghetti from her other portion at least.

He set the bowl down. 'See, no more carrots, just Bolognese.'

'Dad, she's not stupid.'

Beau's comment earned him a dagger of a stare from his dad.

'Stupid!' Carys yelled.

'Cheers for that, Beau.'

Beau picked up the bowl of grated cheese from the centre of the table and shoved it Hudson's way. 'She likes cheese on top, remember.'

Ever since three months ago when Hudson found Beau drinking vodka at the house when he was not only underage but supposed to be watching his little sister, Beau's behaviour had at least simmered. Hudson had roared at him that day; he knew he'd scared his son into realising how dangerous it might have been not paying attention to Carys.

'Cheese?' Hudson asked his daughter, to which he got a toothy grin. And with a sprinkling of cheese, this time she accepted the spoonful of food. 'Cheers, Beau.' Hudson smiled at his son, who shrugged in that fifteen-year-old way that meant even if it was a moment of peace, he wasn't going acknowledge any sort of camaraderie with his father.

As Carys ate spoonful after spoonful, her little legs jiggling below the table, Hudson watched Beau, who, despite his moodiness and acting out since his mother left, was a good kid. And apart from that one time Hudson would rather not think about, he was really good with his sister. The other day, Beau had taken Carys after her bath and put her to bed so Hudson could clear the kitchen. He didn't usually but Hudson had been late home from work following a particularly involved patient case and so it put pressure on the evening routine. When Hudson went back upstairs, he'd heard Beau laughing, Carys giggling. She was too little to irritate him yet and Hudson had hovered on the stairs for a while just listening to the pair of them.

Beau was first to finish his dinner and with a touch to Carys's cheek which made her grin as he passed by, he took his bowl over to the sink.

'How's school?' Hudson asked before his son could escape.

'Dull.' But at least he was going.

'How are your friends?'

'Dad, don't be a loser.'

'Just taking an interest.'

Hudson was the one here at the house every single day and although he wouldn't change it for the world, he sometimes felt sorry for himself that he was still the enemy. Perhaps he was just the only one in the firing line. It was frustrating that Beau was nicer to Lucinda than him because she was the one who'd lied in their relationship, the one who had cheated. But of course the kids didn't know those things and they never would unless she chose to share those parts of herself. It wasn't for him to poison his children against their mother; he wanted them to have her in their lives. But it still felt unfair that he was treated like the baddie, because he'd been there for Beau a lot. Beau just didn't seem to see it. He'd been at every school assembly he'd been invited to, gone to every parents' evening, he'd done the pick-ups and drop-offs from school sports, it was him who'd looked after the kids when they were sick.

Lucinda had worked the long hours, which he didn't judge her for most of the time, but it was as though the work agenda always took precedence over anything going on at home. Even now, she was forever at day-long meetings, working with a new client, out of town on business. She kept in touch with technology when she couldn't be with the kids in person, but it wasn't the same. And Hudson was never quite sure how much she was telling the truth about where she was and how long she had to stay away, because lies had come so easily to her over the years. But that was for Lucinda's conscience, not his – he would protect the kids and it was up to her to prove that she was still the mum she claimed to be, that she loved them both and that of course she was always there for them. There should be a caveat to that which read, *When it suits me* but Hudson would never say that out loud; it would fuel her anger and the last thing any of them needed was more tension.

'I've got homework.' Beau moved towards the doorway but stopped next to Carys and poked out his tongue, making her giggle and do it in return – not really helpful at dinner time but Hudson didn't want to discourage the interaction because it brought out a happier side to his son, a side he didn't get to see much of these days.

Hudson wondered whether he really did have homework or if Beau was feeding him a line to get away. And the thought that he was learning that from his mother had him glad that the kids spent the majority of their time here, at this house.

He tried a subtle line of enquiry – no use questioning Beau's claim as it would be like throwing a grenade into the mix. 'What homework do you have?' His exams would be next year but this year was important too and Hudson wanted him to do well.

'Maths.'

Hudson wondered whether Beau had picked the one subject he knew his dad hated and wasn't likely to offer him help with. Lucinda was the maths whiz of their family. It came naturally to her.

But Beau was still hovering.

'Something on your mind?' Hudson carried on helping Carys, who didn't seem to have a problem with the taste of the carrot pieces now she couldn't see them under the sauce and the grated cheese.

'Did someone really leave a baby in a box?'

'How did you hear about that?' Hudson scooped up another spoonful of Carys's food and she obligingly opened her mouth.

'I saw that lady you work with on the telly. Was the baby dumped?'

'I wouldn't say dumped, but yes, a baby was left at the airbase.'

'Who would do that?'

'We've no idea but whoever it was likely chose the air ambulance base because they knew it was a safe place.'

'It's cruel, don't you think?'

Hudson tugged a baby wipe from the packet in the centre of the table and after a quick clean of Carys's face, much to her disgust, he gave her another fresh wipe to do her own hands. 'It is cruel if you think about the basic facts but there's usually more to it than what you see on the surface. Whoever did it would have had reasons neither you nor I can hope to understand, not right now.'

'Do you think you'll find the person?'

His son might be rude and snappy a lot of the time but inside that tough shell he displayed with Hudson was a heart of gold, a soft side, the son who had shed tears on his first day at school, the son who had done his best to stand up tall when he was tackled so roughly in a school game of rugby that he got a mild concussion. There was a time when Beau had been fascinated by his dad's job too – he might not be up in the air with The Skylarks but the fact that his dad worked for an air ambulance charity had, a few years ago, been something Beau boasted about to anyone who would listen. He'd loved to hear the helicopters going up in the air, had watched them from ground level until they disappeared out of sight.

Hudson missed that kid, he really did. And he hoped that one day, when things settled, perhaps he might get to see him again.

'I hope someone comes forward, I really do. For now, the baby is safe.' Hudson put a hand on his son's shoulder. 'Want some dessert before you go up?'

'Can I take it to my room?'

'Sure. Just don't get it on your books or your laptop.'

'I'm not Carys,' he said with a typical roll of the eyes.

Hudson dished up ice cream and distributed freshly washed and hulled strawberry pieces to each bowl and handed one to Beau.

'Dad... what if they never find the baby's mother? Or father?'

'Then she'll go into foster care indefinitely until a permanent family is found.'

Hudson wasn't sure but he thought he heard Beau mumble something as he walked off about it not being right, not being fair. Hudson liked to think that maybe his son was counting his blessings, that maybe this sort of thing reminded him of how lucky he was.

Hudson and Lucinda had made the decision to separate long before she moved out. They'd kept up a pretence in separate bedrooms while she found a flat to rent, and while they initiated divorce proceedings and the process began, with neither of them contesting anything along the way. They'd agreed that Hudson would keep custody of the kids while she had full visitation rights. She didn't use those rights as much as she could, but it was an arrangement they'd both been happy with and the one they saw as causing the least amount of upset and disruption for the kids. At least that was their prediction but it hadn't gone as smoothly as they'd hoped.

Carys had regressed with her toilet training and had frequent accidents, she'd been clingy, she'd been difficult to put down at night and almost impossible to leave at childcare or even with Hudson's parents. Slowly, she'd returned to her normal cute, content smiley self. She'd been the easy one compared to her older brother.

Beau was at an age where he had his own, sometimes very strong, opinions which were out of anyone else's control. He'd dealt with their initial announcement in his own way – at first he'd gone quiet and seemed calm but what followed was a storm unleashed in the form of rebellion at school. He'd skived off lessons twice, been in detention for talking back to a teacher and another time for failing to hand in homework for the third time in a row. For a while, he'd talked back to Hudson, shouted and sworn at him, in a way he never had before. He didn't do that so much any more, he was more likely to offer up the silent treatment, but Hudson wasn't sure which of those behaviours he preferred.

And Hudson had no idea whether he'd seen the worst from Beau yet or whether that might still be to come.

Throughout all of this, Hudson had kept his home life quiet from his life with The Skylarks. It had been his way of coping, at first to pretend it wasn't really happening and then just because he didn't want to be asked about it, he didn't want to admit what a total shitshow his life had become and how he hadn't been able to see what was going on. He always knew he'd tell people eventually but he wanted to get himself and the kids in a better place first. In the meantime, his parents had been by his side; they'd been his counsel, his outlet.

During the separation and the divorce proceedings, another relationship had been the last thing on Hudson's mind, especially when Lucinda had already met someone else who seemed a bit more of a permanent fixture given he'd met the kids. Whoever the man was, and Beau didn't give much away, the new relationship hadn't gone down well with Beau and Hudson wouldn't make things any more complicated for his son or his daughter. He vowed to leave his personal life until the kids' altered lives settled down and they felt safe, not like something else was about to blow their world apart.

That was all good in theory. But lately, he and Nadia had worked a lot closer together on some serious cases, especially since Paige had reduced her hours, and the more time they spent together, the stronger his feelings became. Seeing her with baby Lena at the hospital had ignited a burning desire to get to know her more.

But he sometimes got the impression she was hiding just as much, if not more, than he was.

7

It had been ten days since baby Lena was found at the door to the Whistlestop River Air Ambulance base and a week since she was placed with a foster carer right here in town. Nadia had, with permission from social services, arranged to go and visit the foster parent, Sybil, and see how Lena was doing.

Sybil answered the door with a toddler in her arms – a toddler who looked like they'd just woken up.

'Oh, I'm so sorry.' Nadia cringed. 'Is now all right? I thought lunch time would be best.' She was rambling like an idiot.

'Lunch time is fine.' Sybil smiled. 'Please come in, it's wonderful to meet you.' Without putting the toddler down, she held out a hand for Nadia to shake.

Nadia stepped inside the home, welcomed by the aroma of freshly toasted bread.

'I just wanted to see how she's doing.'

'Of course, of course. I saw you on the television; you did well speaking in front of the camera – not sure I'd be able to do it.'

'It wasn't so bad.' The toddler in Sybil's arms surreptitiously glanced Nadia's way before burying his face in his carer's shoulder again. 'Who's this little man?'

'This is Gus. He tends to be a bit quiet when he's just woken up. He'll find his voice soon enough though. Why don't you come on through,' she said to Nadia before leading the way from the compact hallway into a dining room with a couple of high-chairs and through to a small playroom with a wipe-clean sofa and toys neatly stacked in boxes around the edges. There was a large playmat on the hardwood floor, the sort made out of rubber in bright colours with pieces that came apart and slotted together like a jigsaw puzzle.

Lena was so content in the baby bouncer that Nadia almost didn't spot her in the corner. She wasn't yet old enough to be doing much at all but her eyes took in everything.

'Lena, someone is here to see you,' Sybil trilled.

Lena certainly knew her name or perhaps it was the playful, higher-pitched tone of her foster carer that made her look up at them.

Nadia crouched down beside Lena while Sybil nipped into the kitchen and came back with a little plastic plate lined with toast fingers. The toddler in her other arm reached out for one and sucked on it contentedly.

'She looks well.' Nadia watched Lena move her legs enough to make the bouncer go up and down slightly. She was nice and secure, cocooned in the soft insert, safe in the five-point safety harness that she couldn't possibly fall out of.

'She's taken to the formula well and goes back to sleep easily enough during the night after a bit of a pat. She's probably the easiest baby I've had in all my time as a foster carer. And given her start in the world...'

When Nadia reached out her hand, Lena's little fingers found hers. 'She has a strong grip.'

'I don't think she's suffered; she's a happy little thing.'

Nadia watched Gus shuffle from Sybil's lap but stay close to her side on the sofa. 'How long have you been doing this?'

'Close to four years.'

'Have you had many children here in that time?'

'You'd be surprised how many. Some stay a while; some stay no time at all. Gus here has been with me for two months.'

'It must be hard work.'

'Hard work but I love it.' Sybil smiled down at Lena. 'I'm glad whoever left this little one abandoned her at the airbase, somewhere there were medical staff present. Any news of her mother or whoever else might have been responsible?'

'We've heard nothing. But the television appeal will air regularly and the newspapers have coverage, as do social media channels. Hopefully, we'll get a lead somewhere along the line.' But if they didn't, what would happen to Lena long term? Nadia had swayed from thinking the mother didn't deserve this beautiful child if she could give her away to telling herself that the mother probably hadn't had much of a choice. There was every chance she had done something drastic because she wasn't in her right mind.

'May I offer you a cup of tea?' Sybil pushed Gus's plate upwards so it was level when he almost lost the remaining toast fingers by letting it tilt.

'I don't want to be any trouble.'

'It's no trouble at all, honestly.' She noticed Nadia watching Lena. 'She's doing well, don't worry about her; she's in safe hands now.'

'It could've easily gone very badly.' Nadia struggled as her imagination began to paint a very different scenario with Lena left in a park or at a bus stop or somewhere she may not have been given the care she needed straight away. Her train of thought kept asking *what if?* 'The front door to the airbase was locked the day we found her. We don't always hear someone when they come; sometimes, we're occupied out the back. It wasn't a given that anyone would check the doorway... If I'd clocked off early, The Skylarks may have headed out on a job and the baby would've been inside that box for hours.'

Sybil smiled kindly. 'It doesn't bear thinking about the what ifs.' She seemed well-practised with knowing the right thing to say and how to calm a person down; maybe it came with the job, with meeting people from all walks of life, some of whom would have struggles that might seem insurmountable.

Nadia gazed down at Lena; she couldn't take her eyes off her.

'You can hold her if you like.'

'Are you sure?'

'Of course, bring her into the kitchen and I'll make us that cup of tea.'

Gus took another look at Nadia before he darted over to one of the boxes by the wall in the playroom and began sifting through what looked to be farmyard animals.

'Careful where you tread,' Sybil warned as she walked away and sure enough, the animals came out one by one, some launching further than others. She must have eyes in the back of her head.

Nadia undid the strap of the bouncer and very carefully picked Lena up. 'Hello, you.' When she cradled her against her body, it felt familiar, that rush of endorphins that came with being so close to a baby. The action encompassed all of her emotions: the loss, the regret and what might have been, the hope. As she rubbed Lena's back, the little one able to see over her shoulder, it was difficult not to feel a bond when Lena's breath fell softly against her neck. Nadia almost didn't want to go into the kitchen; she could stay here forever, not doing anything other than holding the baby.

Gus had everything out on the floor and carefully, Nadia stepped over the toys and went to join Sybil.

Over a cup of tea consumed carefully and out of Lena's way, Sybil wanted to know more about the air ambulance and The Skylarks and Nadia was happy enough to talk about the job for which she had such a passion.

'I never realised you relied so much on fundraising.' Sybil had checked on Gus in the other room and hovered in the doorway between his play area and the kitchen. 'I probably had heard it before but maybe it hadn't registered until now, not until Lena came here and my ears kind of opened for anything involving The Skylarks.'

'Sometimes it works that way.' Nadia smiled. 'It's happened with patients we've rescued plenty of times. Everyone assumes the air ambulance is all part of England's healthcare, but it's only when you or someone close to you really needs the help that you piece it together and realise exactly what it takes for operations such as ours to keep going.'

'I already donated online. The day after I got Lena and I knew her story – well, as much of it as we can know right now. It's only a small amount but it's a regular monthly donation.'

'Then thank you from all of us,' said Nadia. 'We are extremely grateful. We have such wonderful support from companies, from members of the public like you. And not being totally government funded has its pluses. We make our own decisions; we do what we feel is best for the patients we will treat. None of us want that to change and our wonderful fundraising team work hard to keep us going.'

'When I was on the website, I read about the dinner dance coming up.'

'Our annual fundraiser.' Nadia adjusted Lena in her arms as she started to make a fuss. 'This year, the venue is on the coast; it's stunning. You're welcome to buy a ticket; there are a handful left.'

'I've got too much on this year, the logistics would be a nightmare, but maybe another year if I can plan well in advance.'

'We have a lot of events, not just that one; plenty are kid friendly. If you're a regular supporter, you'll be down to receive our newsletter so keep an eye out.'

Nadia stood up when Lena wouldn't settle. 'Do you think she might be hungry?'

When she turned, Sybil was one step ahead of her. She'd already plucked a made-up bottle of formula from the fridge. She put it into the bottle warmer. 'Would you like to do the honours?'

'I would.' She sat down again and sure enough, Lena quietened as soon as the bottle was within her tiny grasp and its contents began making their way into her tummy. She looked up as she drank the milk, her wide eyes transfixed on Nadia.

'It's good that you visited,' said Sybil. 'It's better to have lots of people looking out for a little one rather than just me.'

'Do all your foster children find families eventually?'

She tilted her head side to side as if saying it could go either way. 'Some are slowly reunited with their parents or a parent, but that will depend on whether they're suitable or capable of doing the job. Some children are placed with another family on a permanent basis. But we can't always do that in every case.'

'What happens when they're too old to be in foster care?'

'They'll be supported as they move to independent living but it's still so young to be going it alone.'

'I knew nothing at eighteen.' Nadia gazed at Lena, who was

still looking up at her, her little mouth perfecting a tiny 'o' shape as she drank.

'Me neither.' Sybil cut up an apple for Gus and called him through to the kitchen where he hopped up onto a chair at the table to eat his next snack.

Once Lena finished her bottle, Nadia burped her and then reluctantly moved to hand her back to Sybil. 'I'd better get going – back to work for me.'

'Well, thank you for stopping by.' She took Lena from her arms and Nadia bit back the feeling that she was losing something all over again.

This was crazy. Lena wasn't hers; she had nothing to do with her.

Sybil, with Lena in her arms now, walked through the hallway to the front door.

'Thank you for letting me visit.' Nadia didn't miss one more chance to hold her hand out to Lena, who wrapped her forefingers in her grasp. 'I like to hear how patients are doing and this little one might not be a patient as such but...'

'You have a good heart, Nadia.'

'Take good care of her.'

'I can promise you that.'

* * *

Nadia drove to the airbase but she didn't get out of the car straight away. Instead, she closed her eyes. She could still smell Lena's delicate fragrance as if it had clung to her clothes, her hair, everywhere to serve as a reminder. She couldn't get the thought of the baby's grasp around her fingers out of her mind, the way she'd made eye contact the whole time she guzzled her milk as though she and Nadia were each other's world.

Nadia only came out of her trance when Bess rapped on the window.

She tried to put a smile on her face but the minute she got out of the car, Bess asked, 'What's wrong?'

Nadia shivered when the sun went behind the cloud. 'Nothing's wrong as such, but I've just seen Lena. I mean, she's fine, but I can't stop thinking about what might have happened had we not found her.'

Bess was quick to put her arm around Nadia's shoulders. 'We're quiet at the minute; you can always talk to me if you need to.'

They got back into the car at Bess's suggestion.

'Less likely to be interrupted this way,' said Bess. 'So come on, what's the real reason seeing Lena is so tough?' Bess had an incurable need to know what was going on with everyone, to make sure she understood them.

Nadia gazed out of the window. 'I don't have kids... but I was pregnant... twice.' She steadied her voice. 'I always wanted to be a mum, you know. It was something I saw in my future but for some reason, my body has always had a different idea.'

'What happened?'

'I fell pregnant when I was in a relationship during nursing college. It wasn't planned, but I wasn't sorry. And just when I was getting my head around the idea, I lost the baby to an ectopic pregnancy. The second time, I was married, but again I lost the baby. That time it was even more dangerous; I was lucky to survive.'

'It must have been terrifying.'

'It was, both times. And devastating. I was told I could still get pregnant again but I never tried. Things with my husband ended and apart from a couple of casual flings, I never found the right person to settle down with, certainly nobody I'd ever want to start a family with.'

Bess had reached for her hand. 'I'm so sorry, Nadia.'

She squeezed her friend's hand right back. 'When we found Lena, all the time I've spent with her, the visit just now, it brings the heartbreak right back to me. I held her in my arms, she clung to my fingers, looked me right in the eye. But she isn't mine, she never was, no baby ever—'

Bess's arms wrapped around her, calming her, reassuring her that she was there. She didn't say that it was okay, she didn't offer any platitudes, she just stayed by her side.

Nadia wiped her eyes with a tissue and checked her mascara in the visor mirror. 'We'd better get inside.'

Bess didn't move.

'What's wrong?' She managed a smile. 'I'm fine, really. I promise you.'

And then Bess looked her usual solid self, with a smile, with the assertiveness they all knew her for.

As they walked towards the entrance doors of the airbase, however, Nadia wasn't convinced that everything was okay with Bess. Bess had listened to her and she wanted to do the same for her friend. 'Are you sure everything is all right with you?'

'I'm tired, that's all. Just been busy lately.'

'Ah, yes, didn't you have Gio's niece and nephew for a couple of days?'

'It was one night, one exhausting night. I mean they're great but they're little energy balls, especially for two novices like us.'

They didn't get to talk any more because a job came in and Bess leapt into action.

And Nadia felt the familiar comfort of her work, the team that felt like family, wrap around her.

It was the safety net she needed.

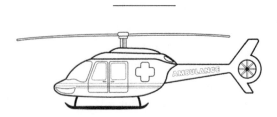

8

At the airbase the following day, Nadia finished her lunch in the kitchen. When she was done, she'd be spending a couple of hours liaising with the Whistlestop River Fire Service who were hosting tomorrow's major incident training day. When the various disciplines – the air ambulance, fire brigade, road ambulance, and other first responders – came together, it was more often than not in a high-stress, time-critical environment. These major training days improved communication and broke down barriers. They typically involved a series of workshops as well as simulations of situations the crews could find themselves in. They'd hosted this sort of training at the airbase before, but it was the turn of the fire service this time round. And while it wasn't to be held here, it was still part of Nadia's job to help organise the training days, put together the workshop content and liaise with the fire brigade on how to run the scenarios both crews would face. The red team would be in attendance on day one with the blue team having their turn the following day.

When Nadia went into the office, Bess was already in there.

'How are you feeling?' Bess kept her voice low in case anyone sneaked in on them.

Nadia sat down at one of the desks. 'I promise you, I'm fine.'

'I'm glad you told me. You shouldn't carry something like that on your own.'

Nadia got the impression Bess wanted to say something else but when she wasn't very forthcoming, she decided to leave it alone. 'You all set for tomorrow?' she asked instead.

Bess leaned back in her chair, her hands scooping her riot of curls up at the back of her head. 'I'm really looking forward to seeing what's in store for us.'

'Is Gio in the training session too?' Bess's boyfriend Gio had returned to work as a firefighter recently following an accident that had left his future career in doubt.

'Not tomorrow. He'll be on the opposite training day to me.'

'Doesn't his boss think he'll be able to concentrate with you around?'

'We're professionals, thank you very much.' Bess waited a beat before adding, 'We're moving in together.'

'That's wonderful! What happened to taking it slow?'

'I guess it feels like the right time.'

'His place or yours?'

'Mine. We thought about getting somewhere new that's both of ours, but it makes more sense to move into my house; it's plenty big enough now Marianne has found a flat of her own. He'll rent his place out for a while. Not as a safety net – at least I hope not,' she joked, 'but it's another income stream.'

Nadia opened the window to let in some fresh air. The cloud from yesterday had cleared and today they'd been blessed with the warmth of sunshine dazzling from up above.

She turned to find Bess watching her.

'What?' she asked. There was definitely something she wasn't sharing.

'Nothing.'

'Come on, out with it.'

'Just thinking about Gio and how quickly things happened – makes me wonder whether you've been out on any dates lately.'

'No, and no plans to.' And she was pretty sure that wasn't what Bess needed to say. It felt like she was grasping at anything else other than what was really on her mind.

'You know, there's a guy at the fire station, a colleague of Gio's I think might—'

'I'm too busy for a love life.'

'Rubbish. Nobody is too busy for love. Talking of love...' She picked up her phone, scrolled through to find a picture and turned the phone to face Nadia.

'Well, he or she is gorgeous.' She was looking at a puppy, a chocolate-coloured labrador retriever, its head tilted to one side, eyes wide in wonderment.

'He... and yes, he is.'

Hudson came into the office. 'So, you didn't back out?' he asked Bess when he saw the picture on her phone screen.

'What am I missing?' Nadia looked between them both.

Bess explained, 'A couple of months ago, Hudson let me know of someone selling puppies – gorgeous puppies – and Gio and I toyed with the idea of getting one. We committed but then changed our minds, then changed them back again.'

'You almost left him homeless,' Hudson teased.

'So dramatic,' said Bess.

Hudson handed a file to Nadia. 'Can you take a quick look through this for me? Check whether you think there's more to be done? I've coordinated a meeting with a brain-injury charity for Melanie, the little girl who came off her bike a few weeks ago.' Melanie had a brain injury as a result of her accident and it would take some adjusting for her and the rest of the family as she faced new challenges.

'Well done. The family will need some guidance.'

'I'll attend as well, but at least it's been set up, finally. There just aren't enough people working there unfortunately so it's been quite a wait to get this meeting.'

'At least the delay has given the family a bit of time to get their heads around what has happened and where they go from here.' She briefly perused the information. Hudson had done a good job as always, provided all the help that he could for the Scott family.

'They'll have a lot of questions.'

'I can't imagine what they're going through.'

It was the drawback, if you could call it that, of doing this job. Each of them felt every case keenly, and it was always worse when a child was involved. And babies? Well, that was a whole different game, especially for Nadia.

Bess was still peering at the photograph of the puppy and Hudson looked at the picture again. 'He's cute, but he'll be a lot of work. Hope you and Gio are ready.'

'Kind of.'

'What's his name?' Nadia asked.

'Zeus. Gio refused any suggestion of a cute name so I let him have his way. I'll choose the next, eh?' She laughed.

'Steady on – surely one puppy is plenty.'

'You tempted?' Hudson asked Nadia.

'Maybe… one day.' Perhaps it would stop her feeling so lonely. She didn't have much going on other than work, which she loved – it was the way she'd made it on purpose – but she had to admit the puppy was absolutely gorgeous.

'Gio and I have found some puppy classes,' Bess told them,

'and we've worked out a schedule for training him between us both.'

'Of course you have.' Nadia smiled. 'When did you guys ever do anything half-heartedly?' Both had strong personalities; neither of them would go into something with their eyes half closed.

'How will you manage with both of you working long hours?' Hudson leaned against the door jamb. 'I suppose there's doggy day care.'

'Yeah.' But Bess wasn't looking at either of them.

'Is that what you're doing?' Nadia asked.

Bess nodded and added an, 'Uh-huh.'

And Nadia went into panic mode. 'Don't tell me you're resigning. We can't lose you, Bess.'

'Don't be ridiculous, I wouldn't resign because I got a dog. And I love my job, as well as you guys.'

'Then what's wrong? There's something, I know there is.'

She looked at her feet: not a Bess thing to do at all. 'I wasn't going to say anything yet. It's so early...'

And now it made sense, the way Bess had looked shifty in the car when Nadia shared her own history and struggles.

Bess stammered over her speech, getting the facts out in the end. 'I'm going to have to take some time off... soon... I mean, it's why I'll be around for the puppy, but it's why we almost didn't get the puppy... it's...'

'You're talking in riddles.' Hudson laughed. 'You're taking leave to look after your puppy, is that what you're saying?'

Nadia knew that wasn't what she was saying at all. And she knew she shouldn't feel this way, not for a friend, but she had a sinking feeling. She should've known. Bess was renowned for having a big appetite and never held back but she'd not even eaten much of the lunch Nadia had brought in for the team a few days ago. She'd had a couple of doctor's appointments recently too, and now it all made sense.

Bess was pregnant.

'I'm not taking leave for the puppy, no.' Bess still looked as though this might be one of the most painful things she'd ever had to do. 'Gio and I, plus my mum and his, will manage Zeus between us, but in about seven and a half months, I'll be at home a lot more.' She couldn't meet Nadia's eye at first and when she did, Bess's eyes were filled with tears.

Hudson caught on. 'You're pregnant?'

'Shh... yes.' She let a smile escape. 'But I don't want everyone knowing just yet.'

'That's brilliant news,' said Hudson, giving her a hug. 'Congratulations.' He left them both in the office when his phone rang and he took the call.

Nadia hugged Bess. 'Congratulations. I'm really pleased for you. I mean it.'

But Bess's bottom lip wobbled and she looked at the floor. 'I was dreading telling you. I really was. I tried yesterday.'

'No, do not apologise. I'm so, so pleased for you and Gio.' And she was, despite the shock and her own personal history. 'Don't let what you know about me take anything away from that, do you hear me?'

'It happened so quick; we didn't expect it.'

'And that's wonderful.' Nadia took her friend's hands and gave them a squeeze. 'It's really amazing news. But Bess, how on earth are you going to cope with a baby and a puppy?'

Laughter took over from the tears which she swiped away. 'I've absolutely no idea. That's why we almost didn't get the puppy, but we decided we've got a while to settle him in before the baby comes. And we'd already fallen in love with him.'

She couldn't begrudge the happiness for her friend; that wasn't the sort of person she was at all.

'It's *very* early days.' Bess crossed her fingers on both hands. 'And I want to work until I really, really can't, so no going easy on me.'

'Done,' said Nadia. 'I guess this is why you're moving in together.'

'Yes. I swear Gio engineered this – he's been asking to live together ever since we started seeing each other.'

Nadia laughed. 'How does Gio feel about the prospect of being a dad?'

'He was shocked at first. I mean, happy, but a little stunned. We're both well into our forties, only got together recently really, and we never saw it happening for us. Hence the puppy.'

'You two are going to have your work cut out.'

Bess grinned. 'I'm having a geriatric pregnancy.'

'And you'll do it in style. I know you will.'

They hugged again right before the ring of the red phone in the office alerted The Skylarks to a job, for which Bess took down the details. Noah emerged from the kitchen with Maya, and Nadia met Hudson in the corridor as the crew made their way into the hangar and she came out of the office.

'How did you get on with contacting Mr Potter's extended family?' she asked him. Mr Potter was a patient the crew had attended to almost two weeks ago and they'd been trying to reach a member of his family ever since.

The familiar sound of Hilda being started up beyond the building signified the crew were almost ready to go.

'I got hold of a sister,' said Hudson. 'She's fifteen years his senior, though.'

Mr Potter was a seventy-one-year-old farmer who'd been trampled by one of his cows on his dairy farm. He was lucky to be alive after the 600 kg beast broke his ribs, punctured a lung and crushed one of his arms.

'I'll bet she was shocked, poor lady. Not the sort of phone call you want.'

'No, it never is.'

In the kitchen, Nadia grabbed a couple of mugs to make the coffee. 'She won't be able to take over while her brother recovers either.'

'Well, yes and no.'

'Are you telling me an eighty-six-year-old woman is going to come and run the farm for her brother?'

'Not exactly. But once she'd processed the shock and knew that he was on the road to recovery, she was all business. She told me she once helped to run the place. She knew all about the health and safety risk assessments, she clearly has a head for the business side and she's going to try to find someone from their network – her words – to take over while he gets better. I'm waiting for a call back from her with an update.'

'She sounds efficient, especially for her age.'

'She talked about moving in with him, followed that up by telling me he wouldn't like it when he found out.'

Nadia poured on the boiling water before handing Hudson a mug. 'Bess didn't think he was going to make it.'

'Shows how things can change in the blink of an eye.'

'They sure can.'

'You had no idea she was pregnant?'

For a minute, Nadia's thoughts were on the elderly sister, but she soon registered who he meant. 'No, no idea. It's great though, isn't it?'

'It is. A lot of work to have a puppy and bring a kid into the world at the same time, but she and Gio seem pretty solid.'

'How are your two?'

'Keeping me busy.'

Hudson usually wanted to talk about his kids but not today it seemed, not even with Bess's happy news. He went to the main office and Nadia went to hers via reception.

She started on some of her admin tasks. She needed to book in one of the rapid response vehicles for its service, go through a compliance report and place an order for a couple of items needed for the rear of the aircraft.

The distraction worked somewhat but when Bess got back to the airbase and Nadia found her in the locker room hit by a wave of nausea, it was hard to get her head straight and rid herself of the thread of envy that coursed through her, the unfairness that she'd almost had the same thing, twice, that it had been snatched away from her both times.

'You okay, Bess? Can I get you anything?'

Bess shook her head. 'I'm feeling a little bit sick, but I think a lot of it is tiredness, that's all.'

'Go upstairs, get your head down.'

'I can't, I haven't told Noah or Maya yet. They'll wonder what I'm doing.'

'I'll keep it quiet, say you're not feeling well; I won't mention anything else.'

She wasn't sure she'd be able to get the words out even if she tried.

'Thanks, Nadia.'

'Stop looking at me like that.'

'I can't help it.'

'I'm envious but not jealous – I'm happy for you. Remember that. Now get yourself upstairs before you get another call.'

Bess went up the stairs behind reception and Nadia updated Noah, told him Bess was resting but would be fine to go out when they were called to the next job, and she found Hudson in the office.

He put down the phone. 'That was Mr Potter's sister. She's found someone to stand in at the farm, to make sure the business doesn't go under, and she'll arrive in a couple of days.' He started to laugh. 'I'm sorry, it's not funny... It's just that she asked whether I could have a defibrillator on standby for her brother – for when he finds out that (a) she's coming to live with him, and (b) that someone else will be running his business for a while. And she wasn't even joking.'

Nadia began to laugh along with him. 'It sounds as though they've quite the relationship.'

'Siblings, eh.'

She had nothing to say to that. And he didn't seem to notice her silence.

'I'm glad I've got two kids; they'll have each other in the future if something like this happens.'

'They sure will.'

And she walked away without meeting his eye again since the mention of siblings because she'd lied to him. And it really didn't feel good.

9

The last week had flown by in a blur of work and parenting. Beau had gone off on a school trip for a few days and come back in better spirits and Hudson, with less tension in the house and a somewhat easier routine with the daughter who was young enough to view him as a faultless human being, found himself feeling more relaxed as a result.

Kate, critical care paramedic with the blue team, came into the office as Hudson was finishing a follow-up on Bruce Carey, the patient they'd airlifted to hospital almost a month ago and who had finally been able to go home. Bruce had suffered a stroke and was paralysed down one side of his body, making his job working in a factory no longer an option. The family faced a period of renovations in their home to allow for his disability, financial strain and adjustment, and all of it was hard to navigate, but that's what Hudson was there for – to give them access to the resources they'd need on their journey. It was one of the reasons this job was so rewarding.

'Four hours to go.' Kate tried to jolly Hudson up. His focus meant he didn't really take in much else until he was done, but now he was, he turned around from the computer monitor.

'Looking forward to it.' And he was, especially since he knew Nadia was going to be at tonight's dinner dance, their main annual fundraiser for the air ambulance charity. 'Are you excited, by any chance? You're as fidgety as Carys when *Peppa Pig* comes on the television.'

'I'm *very* excited! Four hours until I get to lose these unflattering trousers and clumpy shoes and put on high heels and a dress.'

Brad, the other critical care paramedic in the same crew as Kate, came in. 'I'm just as excited as she is, apart from the wearing of a dress and high heels, that is.'

'Hey, whatever you're into,' Kate teased before she flitted off in the direction of the kitchen.

Spirits were high with tonight to look forward to. Hudson was even staying over at the venue along with plenty of the rest of the team. It was half term at the moment and he'd hoped Lucinda would offer to take the kids away for the week, but two days was all she could get off work, she'd said. She'd taken Carys and Beau to visit her parents in Cardiff where they'd stay until tomorrow and the kids always loved it up there. He wondered whether Beau particularly enjoyed it because it was getting away from the norm, the familiarity and locality of his hometown. Perhaps he felt like he could finally be himself in another place without any pressure placed on him, because he always seemed happy when he came home.

In February, Beau had gone to visit Lucinda's parents on his own – his grandad had taken him to see the rugby, and his gran, by the sounds of it, had fussed over him with all his favourite foods. Hudson wouldn't mind betting they hadn't made him do a jot of homework either. Lucinda had two brothers and all three of them had excelled academically, they'd all found top jobs and earned a hefty salary each, and sometimes, Hudson wondered whether Lucinda's parents ever regretted pushing their kids too much. Or maybe the years had softened them and they had different priorities now their three had flown the nest. Lucky for Hudson, Lucinda's parents had always approved of him – they'd seen him as a good match for their daughter and he knew that was partly down to his different drive when it came to work. It wasn't that Hudson hadn't done well, but it had soon become apparent how much of a family man he was, and her parents had warmed to him instantly. At least he liked to think so and that was the feeling he still got. He missed them since Lucinda left and although he called them on the phone to say hello, he didn't visit; it wouldn't feel right. He wasn't sure how much Lucinda had told them about their relationship break-down but whatever it was had left them open to being friendly with him and that made it easier all round.

When Beau came home in February extolling the virtues of Cardiff and the open spaces at his grandparents' place, Hudson had asked whether one day, he wanted to relocate there.

'To be near Granny and Grandad?' Beau had asked.

'No, but for the place. You seem to like it a lot.'

Beau shrugged. 'It's different. I have time to myself. But I like it here too.' He'd exchanged a look with his dad, a look that said he didn't want Hudson to think he wanted to get away from him even though Hudson was pretty sure he'd thrown those words at his dad more than once in a fit of rage if things weren't going his way.

Nestled in a valley in Dorset, Whistlestop River wasn't some-where Hudson wanted to leave any time soon either. The town was a good size but hadn't lost its personality, people were friendly, the scenery amazing with the river meandering its way along and surrounded by miles upon miles of rolling country-side. The Whistlestop River Air Ambulance base was a major part of what Hudson loved too and he couldn't imagine working anywhere else.

At shift changeover time, the airbase became busier with the red crew taking over from the blue, who'd only just returned from a job they'd thought might be a hoax at first.

'I really thought it was prank.' Kate put her helmet back on the shelf in the hangar when the crew came in from the helicopter.

'What happened?' Hudson asked.

Apparently, they'd arrived on scene at a derelict farmhouse next to a pond and couldn't see a victim anywhere nor anyone waving to them to signify their help was desperately needed. The crew had been told a five-year-old boy had fallen into the pond and hit his head.

While The Skylarks didn't get many hoax calls, they did happen occasionally like the one they'd had last summer.

'We saw the pond, but no sign of anyone next to it or nearby,' said Kate. 'Vik hovered overhead and he managed to spot a second, smaller pond in the distance. He flew us closer and we found the patient. We took the little boy to the hospital and from what I can tell, he should make a full recovery.'

'That's good news,' said Hudson.

'I'll say.' Noah had just come on shift with the red team and was picking up his helmet because the crew already had a job.

All of them felt strongly about the crime of hoax calls but Noah had more reason than any of them. His late sister Cassie had required an air ambulance when she'd had an accident that cost her her life, but the air ambulance had been dispatched elsewhere already, to a prank call by someone who thought it was all a joke.

Hudson finished his day before the crew returned and Nadia held the door open for him at the front of the building.

'Escaping early to get ready?' he asked.

'Something like that. Kate has already gone; she couldn't get out of here fast enough.' She locked the door behind them seeing as the crew was out and only Frank, their engineer, was in the back finishing up a report before he too got ready for tonight's event.

He watched Nadia put the keys into her bag and look at the closed door to the airbase. 'You're thinking about Lena.'

'Am I that obvious?'

'Yes.'

'I'm being silly. I know nobody is going to leave a baby here again – although they could.'

'Unlikely though. Come on, let's think about how Lena is safe and well and let's have a good time tonight.'

'Still no word on the mother or a guardian?' She rummaged for her car keys in her bag.

'Not yet. Hopefully, we'll hear something soon. In the meantime, let's enjoy ourselves and raise a ton of money.'

'I like the way you think. I'd better get going, get organised before Dorothy turns up to give me a lift and sees that I am in no way ready.'

'I take it she'll be bringing you both in her car rather than on the back of her motorcycle.'

Nadia laughed. 'I didn't think to check but let's hope so. I'll see you tonight.'

'Look forward to it.'

Why was it that when you started having feelings for

someone beyond the usual boundaries, it turned you into a rambling wreck? He sounded overly enthusiastic, over-excited like a kid rather than a grown man.

But still, he'd meant it. He was looking forward to tonight. And if he was lucky, maybe Nadia would even save a dance for him.

* * *

Hudson wasn't used to feeling this free. Without his kids at the house, he'd taken his time to shower, packed his things, collected his hired tuxedo from where it was hanging on the hook behind the door, and relaxed as anything he'd packed up the car and picked up Brad en route.

After the satnav took them the wrong way at first – to a dead end in the depths of Dorset – they doubled back and, with a bit of navigating from Brad, approached the venue down a narrow, windy but incredibly pretty road surrounded by rolling countryside.

And now they were here, the hassle of the drive was well worth it because the venue was jaw-dropping. They'd seen it in the photographs, of course, but those pictures hadn't done the eighteenth-century house with panoramic views of the Jurassic Coast justice.

'Check this place out!' Brad, sunglasses on, rolled down the passenger side window as they pulled in out front of what looked more like a castle than a country house.

'It sure is something.'

'I wouldn't mind a whole week here.' Brad whistled as he got out of the car.

'Me too but I think I'd need a pay rise for that.' The rooms they'd booked had been heavily discounted, but still not cheap.

'I've got a couple of extra mouths to feed, remember, although feels more like feeding a whole football team on some days with Beau.'

'You wouldn't have it any other way.'

Hudson pressed his remote and the car boot obediently opened up so they could lift out their tuxedos encased in the special carriers and their overnight bags. They couldn't stand gawping at the house the whole time, even though Hudson wouldn't mind doing a lap of the building to see it from all angles, appreciate the salty tang of the sea beyond as the waves crashed in the distance. It seemed such a shame not to but hopefully, they'd have time for that later.

Tonight's ticketed dinner dance would bring together crew, staff, friends and family of The Skylarks and anyone else who worked for the air ambulance, their supporters, ambassadors, nurses and doctors and anyone from the general public who wanted to attend and support the charity. They'd picked a good evening for it too. The sun was shining; the clouds and the rain that had been forecast had been scared away.

The interior of the country house was as elegant as expected. In the foyer, tables ran along one wall housing items for the silent auction and, eager to get involved straight away, Hudson bid on the wellness hamper as well as the cooking class in London. There were some great items to go for as well as those – a flight in Hilda, a gardening hamper, a holiday for two in Jersey, a brand-new smartphone, a bottle of champagne, a golf lesson. Local and county businesses had been generous in their donations this year, which was a good sign.

Hudson and Brad checked in to their respective rooms and regrouped downstairs before heading into the main reception room where everyone else was mingling. Most were standing; some had taken seats on the fine upholstery. A fireplace on one wall would host a wonderful winter fire when the time came and beyond the doors leading to the rear lawn stood a big marquee which would be where the main dinner dance would be held. Even from here, Hudson could see the company responsible for the décor had done a brilliant job; it looked fantastic. White linen hung suspended from the marquee's roof, the elegantly decorated tables were ready for the guests, and there was a stage lit up at the very end where speakers would take their turn to talk about the charity and the whole purpose of coming here this evening.

Hudson adjusted his collar again. 'Not used to wearing a tux,' he told Brad as they moved over to stand beside the enormous Georgian windows looking out to the side of the house with uninterrupted views of the sea. He was also keeping an eye out for Nadia, but there was no sign of her yet. He only hoped the fact he kept looking around wasn't obvious to anyone else.

'I last wore a suit to my mate's wedding two years ago; apart from that, I don't think I've had any occasion to get rid of my Skylarks uniform or my usual attire of jeans – shorts if it's warm enough.'

Waitresses floated around the room, some with silver trays lined with flutes of prosecco, others with bottles of beer or soft drinks.

Kate arrived in a knock-out red dress on the arm of her father, William, one of the Whistlestop River Air Ambulance's ambassadors. Hudson had had plenty of dealings with Kate's father, a man who only had to smile to tell you he came with the best sense of humour.

'William, good to see you.'

'Good to be here. And this place is impressive; I've already told Kate I might have to come back sometime for a mini break, a little holiday.'

Kate dismissed the notion. 'He doesn't know the meaning of the word holiday; he works too hard.'

A chef who owned his own restaurant, William had held more than a few fundraisers himself, and Kate was probably right because as far as Hudson could tell, the man rarely ever took time off.

Hudson caught up with William for a while – he always asked after the kids as well as talking shop. He'd managed to arrange for a couple of items at the silent auction later – dinner for two at his restaurant, a night for two at a nearby hotel he'd got through a friend of his.

Vik, pilot with the blue team, found Hudson at the bar set up in one corner. The trays of prosecco were plentiful but beers seemed to have done a bunk.

'Beer?' Hudson checked.

'Please. I arrived late so I need to de-stress. I got lost... twice...'

'Dead end?'

'Yup.' Vik took his beer from the barman and clinked his bottle against Hudson's.

Rita, one of the air ambulance's Freewheelers, appeared from behind a group chatting. 'You both should've followed the postcode for the campsite. Brings you right here.'

'I'm not even going to ask,' Hudson said discreetly to Vik while Rita plucked a bottle of beer from the barman's outstretched arm; she'd obviously been up here already.

The atmosphere was lively, crowded; there were so many people Hudson knew and some he didn't.

By the time he looked up again, the next guest to come into the room took his breath away.

He watched Nadia as she kissed a lady on the cheek, gave someone else a hug, chatted to another person. His collar felt uncomfortable again; he tried to stay engaged in conversation with Rita.

Nadia was stunning. Her blonde hair was curled more tightly in ringlets rather than her usual waves. Instead of the usual business attire, she wore a v-neckline, sleeveless, black and gold, sequinned dress that flared flatteringly from her hips and showed her slender legs.

He couldn't take his eyes off her. But he should or it would be obvious to her and everyone else how he felt.

And he was, in the eyes of everyone else, still married.

She spotted him watching her. Hudson tried to gather himself, act as though she was just another member of the team or one of their supporters. But he wasn't sure he was doing a very good job. His racing pulse certainly said otherwise.

Vik and Rita had already moved away to talk to an older couple on their right, both long-term supporters of the air ambulance keen to catch up with some of the crew. The Skylarks were all happy to talk about their job, what it involved, make a bit out of their heroic efforts in this kind of setting when they knew it would help raise the air ambulance's profile.

And now Nadia was at his side. He leaned in and kissed her on the cheek, a cheek that took on a delicate pink tinge at his scrutiny. She didn't normally react that way; she was used to public appearances, people watching her, addressing a crowd. Out of the office, this felt completely different and perhaps it felt that way for her too.

'You look beautiful.' Hudson was sure his knees might buckle at any second, especially as the alluring aroma of a fruity, perhaps lavender-like perfume ignited his senses.

Hudson had vowed not to get involved with another woman until his kids were older and making their own way in the world. He'd thought it wouldn't be worth the hassle, the fallout, the stress it might cause the kids, particularly Beau. But the more time went on, the more he realised he couldn't control the way he felt. Nadia was fast becoming so much more than a colleague, a friend.

But would he ruin everything if he told her how he felt?

10

Nadia hadn't been nervous at all when she'd arrived at the venue. The first thing she'd done in her beautiful room in the country house was fling open the window to hear the sea in the distance and let the sunshine filter in, and then she'd taken a long, luxurious shower and got dressed for the dinner dance.

She'd been to enough of these fundraising events to know how it worked. Everyone gathered in the same place, people you saw regularly in their smarter attire, those you rarely saw welcoming you with open arms, introductions to people she'd never met and would do her best to remember so as not to cause offence.

After coming downstairs, she placed a couple of bids on items in the silent auction, which would close when they were all called into the marquee for dinner. She never wanted to win at these things but she always placed bids to try to get the price up and thus raise more money for their charity. The circulating drinks would help the process, as would the two ambassadors behind the table of items who were explaining to newcomers how this all worked as well as sharing the details of all the prizes. They were good at it, the sales pitch side, and she left them to it and went into the reception room where crowds were gathered.

What she hadn't quite expected as soon as she entered was to see Hudson at the opposite end, as though the crowds had parted just for them. In a tux, he looked more handsome than ever before and although she was eager to talk to him, her nerves made her stall her journey across the room so she could calm herself first. She talked to anyone who caught her eye, hugged supporters she'd known for years. Dorothy, stunning in the most spectacular turquoise dress, caught her and introduced her to a couple of friends she'd brought along. One of them was hoping to win the flight in the helicopter. 'Who am I safest with?' the woman asked Nadia. 'Maya? Or Vik?'

Nadia smiled. 'You'll be safe with either of them. I'll keep my fingers crossed for you, shall I?'

Talk turned to helicopters when the woman told her she'd been up in one years ago, over the Great Barrier Reef in Australia, and all the while, Nadia could feel Hudson's eyes on her.

'It'll be a different view,' Nadia assured her, 'but seeing Whistlestop River from up above is spectacular.'

The woman clapped her hands together. 'Come on, Dorothy, come with me; I'm going to keep an eye on those bids and see if I can go a bit higher.'

And then she was there, in front of Hudson and when he told her she looked beautiful, she blushed. That kind of reaction wasn't going to keep her feelings hidden, was it? But hidden was what they needed to be because he was married. Off limits.

With so many people in the country house, the temperature had risen and she was glad of a sleeveless dress. They worked together, had been this close plenty of times, if only she could remember that and try to act at least semi-human. And he would never cheat, she knew that much about him, so she should do her best to keep things purely professional.

'It's a sellout,' he said.

'We had a few tickets left yesterday morning but the last few went. This could be our best fundraiser yet.'

'What's the fizz like?' He eyed the glass she'd barely started.

'I'm taking it slow. Just the one. I find it best at these things not to have too many drinks until it's almost over.'

'Because then everyone else is so drunk, they won't remember if you make a serious faux pas?'

'Exactly.' She took a step back from him and looked around. 'Where's Lucinda? Is she here tonight?' A few days ago, she'd asked whether his wife was coming to this but thinking about it now, he hadn't ever answered her question.

'She's not, no.'

'I thought you said your kids were away at her parents'.'

'She's gone with them.'

Lucinda had been at the fundraiser a couple of years ago and from memory, she'd won a weekend at a yoga retreat in the Cotswolds after placing a winning – and very generous – bid in the silent auction. It was odd for her not to be here now. Everyone else had brought their partners along. It was a novelty getting this dressed up, to have a chance to be glamorous. Nadia certainly appreciated it.

He closed the gap between them again and she was about to take a step back, nervous at the close proximity, when he dropped a bombshell.

'Lucinda and I are divorced,' he said.

If Nadia had heard the news from anyone else, she would've doubted its credibility but hearing it from Hudson himself made it real. 'You're divorced? Since when?'

'It was finalised a month or so ago, but we separated in the latter part of last year. It had been a long time coming.'

'You never said a thing.' Her heart beat faster. He was single. Just like she was.

'Easier not to, I suppose. And I feel pretty dumb for not seeing what she was really like – or for ignoring it and assuming things would get better.'

'I'm so sorry, Hudson.'

'She moved out a while ago and I got used to being on my own but I needed to establish some stability for the kids, keep a bit of myself private until we all got our heads straight. That's another reason I never said anything at work.'

'It must be really hard for all of you.'

'We should've accepted it was over years ago. We're both happier this way but it's still been tough on the kids.'

Their conversation was halted by another one of their supporters who wanted to thank them for finding such a delightful venue. The woman kept them chatting for a while, talking about the stunning location, the elegant marquee, the silent auction.

'I've placed a good bid on every single item!' she said before she spotted a friend and flitted over to them instead.

'It's people like that who keep us going,' Hudson remarked.

'She was certainly enthusiastic – if she wins everything she's bid on, she'll be broke.'

Hudson's laughter was a tonic given what they'd been talking about, but Nadia couldn't ignore his admission about his marriage and act as though it had been run-of-the-mill conversation. 'So, given what we were just talking about, you're okay?'

'I'm okay.' He leaned so close to her that her heart began to thump harder, her hands felt clammy all of a sudden as though this was a date, not a work function. 'I know people say that it was a joint decision even if it wasn't, but this really was. The reason it didn't happen sooner was the kids; neither of us want them to suffer – we stayed together first for Beau and then for the two of them. We were over a long time ago.'

If she moved any closer, their lips would touch, and the thought sent her spiralling.

She wanted to reach for his hand and if her feelings didn't run deeper than a friendship, she might well have done. Was he telling her all of this now because he felt something more towards her?

He stepped back, smiled at someone who said hello on their way to the bar. 'Carys was unsettled at first but she's so young, the transition has been a bit easier. Beau... well, Beau is a teenage boy; I won't lie, it's been harder with him. He's been in a bit of trouble at school and I still worry what's coming my way with him.'

'You're a good dad, Hudson.' Nadia remembered on more than one occasion Hudson having phone calls with his wife that sounded full of tension, asking her what time she'd get away, requesting that she really make an effort. Nadia had tried not to eavesdrop but in a work environment, it was sometimes unavoidable. 'Do the kids see much of Lucinda?'

'Not as much as she promises half the time. She's forever coming up with excuses, but I've learned that I can't make her change; I'd exhaust myself trying. So I'm there to pick up the pieces, to leap in at the last minute.'

It was time to circulate again as more supporters demanded their attention and it was, after all, the whole point of tonight.

'We can talk later if you need to,' Nadia said quietly before they joined the throng.

'I'd like that.'

Was this dangerous water she was treading? He was still a

father, and a good one, and his kids were quite rightly his priority. She didn't want to interfere with that.

She talked with some of the town's locals who'd made the trip out here this evening. Originally, the fundraising committee had thought about having a marquee at the airbase, but they'd decided it wouldn't have the glamorous side to it that might attract a lot of supporters. Yes, it was easier to get to, but people wanted to be wowed by the whole night. And this country house with views of the Jurassic Coast certainly did that.

'The venue is just gorgeous,' one of their supporters gushed. 'And it was only an hour by minibus.' That was another thing the fundraising committee had organised – transport to and from the event because they knew that would lure even more people.

Nadia circulated, although all she wanted to do was have a heart-to-heart with Hudson because now she knew that he and Lucinda weren't together, she realised she probably hadn't been imagining it – that there might be something more than friendship between them. It wasn't just one-sided.

The announcement was made for guests to make their way into the marquee. Nadia checked the seating plan and weaved through the tables towards the centre where she found her place card. She scooped her dress beneath her and sat down. A balloon and streamer centrepiece with their table number stood tall and proud, the silver cutlery gleamed, the murmur of voices told her how much everyone was enjoying this.

'Where's the wonderful Bess this evening?' one of their oldest supporters, ninety-three-year-old Maud, asked. She seemed delighted to find she was sitting next to Nadia.

'You know The Skylarks – we can't stop what we do for a party.'

'A very good party.' Maud picked up a glass filled with a clear drink, a mint leaf and plenty of ice cubes.

'It is, but the red team drew the short straw this year and are the ones to stay behind. Bess will get to come along next time.'

Bess, still suffering from morning sickness at any time of the day, had claimed that it worked out better this way – she wouldn't have to make excuses for being tired or not wanting any alcohol. Next year, she intended to fully make up for it, she said.

Nadia had never had much sickness with either of her pregnancies. Maybe she hadn't got far enough along. She'd been tired with both though, before nature decided it wasn't her time and put an end to her dreams before she could feel any of the other changes in her body. She never got to experience a growing bump, the flutters and kicks of a tiny human, the nesting before the baby came, the labour and the utter joy of holding her child in her arms.

She bit back her sadness and smiled at a waiter who appeared and set down the glass of water she'd requested.

Maud lifted her glass of fizz towards Nadia's glass of water at her table setting. 'To the red team. May they fly safely tonight.' And when Nadia lifted hers to meet the vessel, Maud said, 'You need something better than water, dear.'

'All in good time. I need to be on my best behaviour for a while.'

Maud, full of mischief, leaned in and said, 'Then promise me you'll drink up and let loose.'

Hearing a ninety-three-year-old tell her to *let loose* made her smile as the other guests on their circular table took their seats.

The meal was delightful – fresh fish and vegetables as the main, a wonderful chocolate souffle for dessert and a cheese selection that almost rendered it impossible to move by the time they'd finished.

The silent auction followed the meal – good job as it gave them all a chance to remain in their seats and recover from the over-indulgence. Maud won the flight in Hilda and she was beside herself, so much so that Nadia was on standby to deal with an elderly person collapsing on her watch. But it seemed Maud was made of sterner stuff than that. And she wasted no time going to talk to Vik to see whether it would be him or Maya taking her up in the air.

Staff raced in to sort the tables in the marquee and shunt a few of them over to the edges to make a decent-sized dance floor. Nadia disappeared to the bathroom to freshen up before the whole team would be huddled together for a group photograph, and bumped into Kate, who was coming out the other way.

'Did that guy find you?' Kate asked.

'Guy? What guy?'

'There was someone looking for you... He didn't look like he was here for the actual event; he was wearing jeans.'

'Was it one of the minibus drivers?'

Kate's lips twisted. 'Hmm... don't think so. Very good looking, though. If he's one of the drivers then it's a shame I'm staying over.'

Nadia just laughed. 'Well, if I find him, do you want me to send him up to your room?'

'Don't tempt me. See you for the photo shoot,' she called over her shoulder as she headed back to the party.

Nadia freshened up, pressing a bit more face powder onto her cheeks, putting on more of her red lipstick. Her hair was behaving for once and she ran her fingers through the sides to separate the strands a bit.

She looked at herself in the mirror, her mind on Hudson

once again. He'd told her about the divorce and as far as she knew, he hadn't told anyone else. The thought had her hopeful that his feelings were growing for her as much as hers were for him. But would it be too messy and complicated to start something? Those kids would and should always come first. He had history, baggage, but then again, she certainly came with her fair share.

She returned to the marquee and joined the others for the photograph they'd frame and put up at the airbase. And when they were given their freedom again, she immediately found herself swept away in Frank's arms when he requested a dance.

'Were you ever going to take no for an answer?' Nadia laughed.

'No chance. Marianne is helping clear some of the tables so I'm on my own and need someone.' It was a sedate number, but it wasn't long before that was replaced for an energetic twist track that involved way too much moving after a heavy meal – not that it seemed to deter anyone else.

When others in the team joined the dance floor, including Hudson, Nadia wasn't quite so relaxed. She was self-conscious, worried about what she looked like, discombobulated by his presence.

After the partying was interrupted by the MC announcing the estimated amount raised that evening and a rapturous applause rang out along with whoops and cheers, hugs ensued between the team, supporters, anyone. The atmosphere was electric and whoever predicted this would be a wonderful fundraiser had been right.

She grabbed a glass of water from the table at the side and took it out of the back entrance of the marquee. She needed the fresh air. The sun had set while they'd all been enjoying their evening and the breeze gave her a welcome little shiver.

She hadn't been outside all that long before Hudson came and stood beside her.

'You escaped,' he said.

'I needed to. It's hot in there and frantic.'

'It's been a good one. Only one problem...'

'We have to better it next year?'

'Exactly.'

Their view was of the coast beyond. The lights of a boat in the distance and the moon up above reflected into the water and showed a beauty that existed no matter whether it was day or night.

'What I told you earlier...' Hudson began.

'Don't worry.' She turned to him. 'It won't go any further.'

'It's not that.' Hands in his pockets, he looked at the ground. She wondered whether he couldn't wait to loosen his bowtie or whether he wanted to keep the tux on the way she wanted to stay in her dress: to make this evening last for longer.

It was when he looked right at her, she knew he was going to say something about the way he felt.

He reached for her hand. 'I've been wanting to say something to you for a while. Not only about the divorce, but about... well, us.' He was nervous and it made Nadia feel calmer to know she wasn't the only one.

'Us?'

'I think you might have feelings for me that extend beyond a friendship,' he said.

'I do. But... I don't ever want to get in the way of anything.'

'You won't.'

'The kids.'

'They will always be my priority.' He groaned. 'Maybe you're right. Maybe I'm crazy to even think about having a life of my own right now.'

'You're not crazy.'

He reached out and moved the few strands of her hair away from her lips when the wind blew it there.

She looked up at him, at his handsome face, the olive skin, the five o'clock shadow, the endearing smile she could melt into. 'You really have feelings for me?'

'Most definitely.' He grinned. 'Do you think you might like to go on a date with me? Maybe even more than one?'

She smiled. 'I'd like that. But no rush, not if it's not right for you and your family.'

He let out the breath, looked at their hands, entwined, stepped even closer. He kissed her very gently on the forehead. 'That's all I need to know for now.'

She could've stayed in the moment forever. 'We should get back inside before we're missed.'

'Dance with me?' he asked as they made their way back to the marquee and rather than lively music, the track changed to the sort of music that drew couples in closer together. Some of those couples were in love – others were friends.

And Nadia and Hudson? They were somewhere in between.

Hudson led her onto the dance floor. He lifted one of her hands in his, he set his other against her waist and their bodies almost touching, Nadia tried to ignore the giddy feeling she had running through her, the feeling that made it near impossible to move.

Neither of them said a word; they just danced.

But as they drew closer to Kate, who was dancing with her dad, Kate caught Nadia's eye. 'He's over there, that guy I told you about.'

'What guy?' Hudson asked.

Nadia was about to say she had no idea when she locked eyes with the man who'd come in the back entrance of the marquee. Highlighted by the moonlight, it was hard to know if she was imagining it, it seemed so unreal.

Hudson followed the direction of her gaze. 'What's wrong?'

'Archie…'

And then it was as if her feet moved all by themselves.

She'd come out of Hudson's embrace, walked over to the man, stopped in front of him.

It had been almost twenty years since they'd laid eyes on one another, over two decades since they'd mourned the loss of their baby. Standing in front of her now was the same Archie she remembered with the blond hair that had faded, the piercing blue eyes she'd looked into plenty of times, the same habit of biting his cheek nervously when confronted by something he wasn't sure of.

Her heart thumped; her whole body tensed. 'What are you doing here?'

When Archie didn't say a word, Hudson interjected and introduced himself, perhaps to save Nadia from whatever he thought this was. 'I'm Hudson, good to meet you. You missed the silent auction, I'm afraid.'

'I'm not here for the auction.' His eyes never left Nadia, not until a little boy came to his side.

And when Nadia looked at the child, she felt winded. The resemblance was there all right and to see it was confronting.

'Can we go somewhere and talk?' Archie asked. 'It's important. I wouldn't have come otherwise.'

Nadia felt Hudson's arm go around her waist. But she pulled away and turned to face him.

'I'm sorry, Hudson, I need to deal with this.'

And she watched Hudson slowly nod, disappointment written all over his face as he turned and walked away from her, back into the crowds.

11

With Carys in the lounge playing with her toys, Hudson nipped to the back of the house to the utility room to sort the laundry into lights and darks. The big fundraiser and his night alone in a hotel felt like a distant memory already, even though he'd only left the beautiful country house and his crew mates six hours ago. How quickly he'd come crashing back to reality. He'd collected Carys and Beau from Lucinda's on his way through, given Lucinda lived in the same direction as Brad, who was catching a lift with him, and the moment Beau got in the car, Hudson got the impression his son would have preferred to spend a lot longer in Cardiff than he'd been able to.

This morning at breakfast, he'd expected to see Nadia. Everyone else was there and met at the agreed time of 8.30 a.m., but there was no trace of her and when he mentioned her to Kate, Kate told him that Nadia had gone back to Whistlestop River last night on the minibus with some other people from the town. She'd given up her room just like that, so whatever this guy Archie wanted with her, it had to have been important. And Hudson had a sinking feeling that there was a history between the pair and whatever he had dreamed might happen with Nadia one day would be just that: a dream. And did he really want to start anything with her now he knew there was another man on the scene? It was a complication he really didn't need, a fight he wasn't sure he had the time or energy for, no matter how strong his feelings were.

At least he'd had a good time up until that point. Hudson and the others had made the most of their temporary location and after breakfast, had walked along the coastal path admiring the views, inhaling the fresh sea air before they accepted it was time to set off for home. And he'd done his absolute best to push Nadia out of his mind – not that it had worked.

Beau appeared in the utility room. 'When's dinner?'

'Fifteen minutes or thereabouts. Chicken curry.' Hudson pushed a pile of whites into the washing machine.

'Cool.'

Hudson supposed that was high praise or at least acknowledgement. But conversation was over because Beau had already put headphones back on and Hudson saw the flash of his green hoodie as he turned out of the kitchen to go upstairs.

Beau might not be chatty but at least Hudson hadn't had to ask him to turn his music down since he'd come home. He'd blasted it out on more than one occasion in the past and Hudson swore it was his way of holding up the middle finger to his dad when he was irritated by him. Hudson had ignored it a few times but not when he had Carys to settle much earlier than her older brother. In the end, Hudson had bought Beau a pair of the enormous headphones that seemed so on-trend these days for Christmas and his son had taken to wearing them a lot. Hudson swore they weren't even connected half the time when he schlepped around the house. They were just a handy way of not having to talk to anyone.

Hudson quickly checked on Carys – she was still playing with a toy bus and all the little people that went inside. He went back to the laundry, put on the white wash.

He thought about that man again. Archie. Where had he popped up from all of a sudden and what did he want with Nadia? Whatever it was, they'd left the marquee, gone outside and he hadn't seen her since.

Nadia had never shared much about herself. Nobody really sat down and did that, did they? Things came out along the way – a phone call from a spouse or a mother-in-law, a mention of a sibling's birthday, talk of a bad relationship with an ex. But Nadia had never said much at all. She'd confirmed that she had once lived in Switzerland but even that was something he wasn't sure she'd ever meant to let slip. It was like she'd kept her entire life pre-Whistlestop River quiet, like she'd cut her ties with it and started over. He put it down to her being good at her job, super professional. But now, he wasn't so sure.

It had taken a lot for Hudson to admit his marriage break-down to someone aside from his parents. He hadn't intended to do it last night with Nadia, and definitely not at a party, but the way he'd felt when he'd seen her show up, the emotions zipping through him when he saw her in that dress, the way he'd felt every time they stood close to one another, he hadn't wanted to wait another minute. It had felt as though if he didn't tell her then, someone might possibly whisk her away out of his orbit.

Was that what this guy Archie was doing?

Asking himself the question had him realise how little he really knew of this woman he was getting closer to and had wanted to get to know more until last night. Now he wasn't so sure what he wanted.

He definitely didn't want complicated.

The washing machine churned its new load over and over.

He waded through the clean, dry clothes on the benchtop in the utility room and separated them into piles ready to put away and then moved on to sorting out the dinner. He'd made the curry last week so it was easy enough and he juggled playing with Carys and getting it ready.

He settled Carys in her highchair as Beau appeared. 'While I dish up, could you take your clothes upstairs?'

Beau looked up from beneath a thick fringe and groaned. 'I'm so hungry.' But he went to do what he'd been asked. He came back through with a pile of clothes in his arms. It was progress, a ceasefire of sorts when he didn't refuse to do something he was asked.

Hudson dished up and had all three dinners at the table by the time Beau came back and ruffled his little sister's hair, earning him an enormous grin. The little girl loved her older brother and vice versa. Hudson supposed by the time Carys got to the hard teenage years, Beau would be grown up and hopefully, he'd still look out for her.

When dinner was eventually over, it was onto the next thing: bathtime for Carys. Sometimes, he was tempted to skip it but given she'd smeared chicken curry in her hair, it was easier to put her in the tub and give her a hair wash than try to comb the mixture out somehow.

Once Carys was in bed after cuddles and a couple of stories, Hudson left her light down low. He'd switch it off properly later and swap it for the nightlight on the upstairs landing once the skies outside grew dark and no longer let a sliver of light slip through the door, which was left open a tiny crack.

He stopped outside Beau's door and knocked, gently the first time, with a bit more of a thump the second before he got a 'What?' in response.

'*Come in* would be better than *what*?' He had to speak louder than usual given Beau had the headphones on. 'I came in to see whether you had any cups or glasses up here.' If they were short on crockery, Beau's bedroom was the first place to look and sure enough, Beau plucked a mug from beside his bed, a bowl from the edge of his desk which had goodness knows what caked to it and a glass from his windowsill.

The doorbell sounded before Hudson even reached the top of the stairs and Carys appeared in her doorway.

He set down all the crockery, went over to his daughter and picked her up. 'Bedtime now, darling.'

The doorbell went again.

Carys rubbed her eyes, clutched her toy bunny against her neck. She'd been in a bed for over a year and the novelty of being able to hop out when she felt like it still wasn't lost on her. She needed a good thirty minutes of quiet to settle or any sound would grab her interest.

Like it had now.

The doorbell went a third time. And so he ignored the crockery on the windowsill near the top of the stairs and went down to find who was ruining his chance of a relaxing evening.

He found Lucinda letting herself in.

'I did ring the bell,' she said, looking up at him as he descended the stairs.

Carys let out an excited squeal and pushed against his chest as soon as they reached the hallway. He set her down and let her go.

Lucinda scooped up her daughter and hugged her tight. Looking at Hudson, she told him, 'Before you start lecturing me, Beau called me. He wanted help with his maths homework; that's why I'm here.'

'Letting yourself in.'

'Actually, I was trying not to disturb the bedtime *routine*.' She emphasised the word *routine* as if it was in quote marks. She'd have made the gesture had Carys not been in her arms.

Lucinda had never understood his insistence at routine for the kids, although she'd welcomed the calm and the quiet when she was trying to work and Carys went down like clockwork. She'd welcomed it when Beau was that age too.

'You couldn't have done this in the last twenty-four hours?' he asked. 'He's been with you in Cardiff.'

'We were visiting my parents; homework didn't come into it. Beau obviously got back into it today and realised he needs some help.'

'I thought you had work to do; that's why you couldn't stay in Cardiff longer. But you've time to be here now.'

'Oh, for goodness' sake, Hudson. I didn't come here to fight.' She pulled Carys's fingers from her hair. 'I could leave it for you if you want to help him.'

He felt a little bit blindsided that he hadn't even realised Beau was struggling, let alone that he'd contacted his mother with a plea for help. It made sense; she was the one you went to for maths homework, but still.

'You're here now.' He wished things were less tense, more civil, but it was hard when she showed up like this.

'You're always complaining that I let you down so don't moan when I show up.'

This so wasn't the same thing as cancelling last minute or forgetting a commitment. She dropped the ball often enough that he'd become a professional at picking it up again. And if she'd been better at timekeeping with her kids, she might have foreseen this, spoken with Beau about his schoolwork when they were away, avoided this evening's visit.

Beau appeared at the top of the stairs.

'Bring down the crockery, would you... I left it on the windows—'

Beau already had it in his hands.

'You couldn't have timed it any worse, you two,' Hudson grumbled, watching Carys already beginning to transition from nicely calm and tired towards agitated and most likely difficult to settle a second time.

Lucinda fought Beau's corner while their son took his crockery to the kitchen. 'You know what homework is like: sometimes you think you're on top of it, then you panic and need help. We've all been there.'

He wondered how much of his mood was due to her presence and how much of it was due to the way things had finished with Nadia last night and the fact his head was still preoccupied with the latter.

'I'll get my books.' Beau stomped past from the direction of the kitchen and back up the stairs to avoid the confrontation and Hudson would've yelled after him to tread lightly if he didn't think it would make the atmosphere ten times worse.

Lucinda still had hold of Carys, who had tucked her little head beneath her mum's chin.

'Here, I'll take her,' he said, his voice devoid of much friendliness.

'A slightly later than usual bedtime isn't going to ruin her, Hudson.'

Beau came back down and headed for the dining room.

Lucinda's dark hair concealed her face as she rubbed noses with Carys. 'Your brother needs me now; time for you to go to bed, little one.'

'This is confusing for her, you know that.' Hudson prised Carys's arms from around her mother's neck.

'It might be irritating but it's not confusing. I'm their mother.' She winced as Carys's hand caught in her hair again as Hudson took their daughter.

'And you don't live here. Not any more. We need some boundaries. I need the keys back for a start.'

'Fine. But we are both their parents, I won't be told that I can't ever stop by.'

He didn't have the energy to argue about this now.

'Mind if I make myself a cup of tea before we get started?' Her voice followed him up the stairs.

'Knock yourself out.'

He heard her harrumph as he put distance between them.

Hudson had expected his daughter to make a fuss at being taken away from her mother again, but perhaps she wasn't as attached to Lucinda as she had once been. Surprisingly, the thought made him sad rather than feel as though he had the upper hand.

Hudson settled Carys back into bed. He read her another story, but she wasn't too bad considering the interruption. Her little eyelids grew heavy as she succumbed to sleep quickly.

Back downstairs, he was more than ready to wind down. He'd slept okay last night at the hotel but not as well as he'd hoped given the drama with Nadia, and now, after getting the kids sorted, doing the washing and the dinner, and now a late-evening visitor, he was knackered. But he couldn't switch off, not with Lucinda in the dining room.

He didn't want a beer after the partying last night so he made a cup of tea and stood in the kitchen to drink it, leaning against the counter, gazing out of the window at the side of the house and the ivy that needed cutting back when he had a chance.

By the time Lucinda came into the kitchen an hour or so later, Hudson had calmed down a bit. He'd used his laptop, done some banking, paid a few bills and managed to reply to a handful of emails.

'Beau upstairs?' he asked.

'Upstairs and happier now we've been through some of his work. Maths is much harder than it ever was in our day... They do it all differently now.'

When he said nothing, she apologised again. 'I'm sorry for turning up at bedtime.' She rinsed her mug out at the sink and when she realised the dishwasher had only just finished its cycle, she left it beside the sink. Funny the routines you got into as husband and wife. He'd been the one to stack the dishwasher and put it on – she'd been working late so many times, it didn't make sense for her to do it. Usually, she'd empty it when she came home, inevitably very late, and put anything he'd left beside the sink into the racks. But now it was all down to him. That and everything else around the house that had once been theirs but was now his only.

'He might need some more help but it'll have to wait until next week now,' she said.

'I thought you were having Beau stay this Saturday night; weren't you going to take him to the movies?'

'I have to go away with work again. I've told him, he says it's fine.'

'What he says is one thing, what he really thinks and feels is another.'

'I have a career, Hudson. I won't apologise for that.'

'Didn't ask you to.'

'Beau says he understands and I think he's mature enough to make up his own mind.'

'He should always come before your job.'

She jutted out her chin. 'You weren't complaining about my

job when you got to be a stay-at-home dad and then only returned part time. It suited you then.'

'It suited *us*, not just me. And what about this new guy you're seeing? Beau doesn't sound too keen.'

'Beau isn't dating him, is he? And he's only been there once or twice when Beau was; they literally crossed paths very briefly.'

'You should still consider how he feels.'

'Stop lecturing me, would you.' She rested her arms on the back of the chair and less snippily told him, 'Like I said before, I don't want a fight.'

'Neither do I.' Although sometimes, he did. Sometimes, he felt like having a big old shouting match to get out all his grievances for the lying over the years, the cheating, the way she still seemed to be putting herself first. But she'd come here to help Beau, she could've been cosied up with her new man, so perhaps he should start cutting her some slack and move on from everything she'd done to him during their marriage.

It might well be the only way to stay sane.

'Did Carys settle okay?' she asked him.

'She did; I expect she's asleep already.'

'She still sleeps on her tummy after all this time.'

'The same way Beau did.' It had terrified them first with Beau and then with Carys. All the safety messages told you to put a baby to sleep on its back and they'd always followed the advice. But Beau and Carys both had other ideas as soon as they'd been able to move of their own accord.

It made him happy now to think of Lucinda watching their daughter sleep. Her love was still there, no matter how many times she let the children down by not turning up when she was supposed to or by putting off arrangements. He needed to remember the good things about her as well as her qualities that were beyond frustrating.

'I'd better get going,' she said. She left the kitchen and headed into the hallway where she bent down and picked up her bag. She came back, took out a bunch of keys, detached the house key from the loop and passed it to him. 'Here... you should have this back.'

He nodded his thanks and she left.

After he locked up, he went to check on Carys before switching off her light and replacing it with the nightlight on the landing.

He hovered outside Beau's bedroom on his way past.

His hand rose to knock, but he let it drop and instead headed back down the stairs. He'd let his son be for now, let him carry on with his work or whatever he was doing.

He picked up his phone from the kitchen table, started a new message with Nadia's name in the address field. But after a few botched attempts, he gave up.

If she wanted to talk, she'd get in touch.

And if she didn't, he'd just have to deal with it and go back to what they were. Friends. Colleagues.

Nothing more.

12

Nadia sat on the edge of her bed. The sun had only just come up; it was early. She had a day off today, prearranged, thinking she'd be relaxing in a beautiful hotel with her colleagues, congratulating themselves on the amount they'd managed to raise for the air ambulance charity last night. But instead she was stewing, she was worried, she was all over the place.

Her sister Monica, the sister she'd never told anyone about, was here in England.

And so was Archie.

And more confusingly, Monica was here looking for her, after all this time.

None of it made sense right now.

And to have this all blow up in her face here, in Dorset, in her safe place where nobody knew hardly anything about her background, made it so much worse.

She padded across the bedroom carpet, navigated her way past her overnight bag with things untidily scattered around it from last night as she'd tried to find her washbag and tooth-brush when she arrived home.

She'd considered staying at the country house after Archie and his son left, once they'd talked, but she'd made the snap decision to leave when she saw the minibus pull up outside nice and early for pickup. She saw it as her escape, a way to run away from the drama and the inevitable questions from everyone else about who the mystery man was, never mind what Hudson had to be thinking after Archie showed up. She'd run across the gravel parking area to the minibus, taking the driver by surprise given he was here more than an hour before the party would come to its close. He confirmed there was a spare seat for the journey back to Whistlestop River and so Nadia had run back into the beautiful venue, gone upstairs, got her things together and run back outside under the cover of darkness to hide on the minibus, away from prying eyes. The driver had been happy for her to stay onboard; perhaps he'd picked up on her distress and felt sorry for her. Others on the minibus had been in fine spirits when they finally left over an hour later but Nadia gave the odd smile and then settled with her head against the window, watching the streetlamps flash on by, passing cars, the blackness of the unknown outside. They could've been anywhere; the only scenery she recognised was as the bus slowed and pulled into Whistlestop River and began the rounds of dropping people at their doors.

She ran her fingers through her hair as she went into her bathroom. It had been tightly ringleted last night but those ringlets had loosened overnight, and given up by now. She switched the water on in the shower. It always took a couple of minutes to come through hot rather than tepid and she held her hand beneath the jets until it obliged. It was almost robotic the way she climbed in and stood letting the water soak through her hair, down her face, over her skin.

As she lathered up her shampoo, she thought about Hudson:

the way they'd got closer last night, how every touch from him sent a zing right through her. She remembered the admission that he had split up with his wife, the hope she'd felt that this might be the start of something between them. And then she remembered the look on his face when she told him she had to talk to Archie. It was obvious there was a history there with this man who'd shown up at the fundraiser but she hadn't had any choice but to deal with it straight away. And it was all too much to explain to Hudson at a party where she'd been taken by surprise. Hudson didn't even know she'd been pregnant before, twice, never mind that this stranger to him had been the father of her first baby nor that he was now married to her sister, the sister she'd never confessed to having. Nadia had walked away from Monica, the only close family she had, two decades ago and hadn't looked back.

The memory of talking to Archie bashed at the corners of her conscience as she lathered up her shower gel.

When Nadia had asked Hudson for some time with Archie last night, she'd needed it but she hadn't wanted it. What she'd wanted was to tell Archie to go away, to leave her to her own life, but when she looked into the eyes of the little boy with the same pale complexion and warm brown eyes as her sister Monica, she'd barely been able to speak. There was no doubt about it, the little boy was her nephew, and she'd never even known he existed. Prior to Archie showing up, she'd told herself over the years that perhaps her sister and Archie's relationship had fizzled out, but with this little boy standing right in front of her now, the wedding band on Archie's ring finger, it seemed they were in it for keeps.

'Daddy, I'm bored,' the child beside Archie had moaned as they stood outside the marquee.

Archie set down the rucksack from his back and pulled out

an iPad. 'I don't usually let him have much time on this but it'll give us a chance to talk,' he explained to Nadia as if he had to answer to her in some way. Perhaps he did, but not for that.

'I'm working. Showing up here is—'

'I know it's sudden, but please.' He spoke in a lower voice so his son wouldn't hear. 'I really didn't have any other choice but to do this.'

'There's always a choice.' Her heart thumped double time. 'Why are you here? And how did you know who I worked for, where I'd be tonight?'

'Excuse me...' A woman behind Nadia bumped into her and apologised. 'The ground is a little uneven.'

Nadia acted as though this was a completely ordinary encounter and hadn't almost knocked her off her feet with shock. 'Careful, it's worse out here; you don't want to fall in your heels and twist your ankle.'

'At least I know there are plenty of medics,' the woman chortled before she and her friend headed across the grass and around the house, presumably to the car park.

'I really need to talk to you,' Archie prompted as Nadia's smile slowly faded away again.

Nadia briefly looked behind her into the marquee, expecting to see Hudson hovering somewhere. But he wasn't. All she could make out was a sea of people enjoying themselves, coming together on what was supposed to be an evening of celebration.

'Please, Nadia. Do you really think I'd show up if this wasn't important?'

He had a hint of a Swiss accent but, like her and Monica, he was raised by British parents who had lived in an area with expats, he'd attended an international school much like the girls, and so you'd never really be able to pick where he was from.

'Where's Monica? Is she with you?'

His gaze flitted to his son, who was preoccupied with the iPad already even though they were standing around.

'Can we talk properly?' he urged. 'There's a bench, over there at the edge of the lawn.'

Nadia said nothing, but her feet took her in the direction he'd indicated across the grass just about visible in the moonlight and with the lights streaming from inside the marquee.

'This is Giles, by the way,' Archie said as they made their way over. 'Say hello, Giles.'

The little boy obliged but only gave her a cursory glance because he was far more interested in technology than in some random woman he'd just met. Nadia got the impression Giles had no idea that they were related.

With Giles at one end of the bench, Archie slid closer to Nadia. It felt odd to sit in such close proximity after all this time.

Her shock gave way to fury. 'Why are you even here?'

He checked Giles was engrossed and turned his body slightly, leaned a little more in Nadia's direction. 'Monica is missing.'

'What do you mean she's missing?'

'She came here to the UK; she came to Dorset – to find you.'

'But you just said she's missing.'

'I know she's in England but I've no idea exactly where.' He added some context – he'd noticed her passport missing, found an email from Eurostar, put two and two together and come up with five, it seemed.

'I haven't seen or heard from her.'

'But she'll be looking for you, Nadia. And she'll be doing it pretty blindly. She wouldn't have much to go on – you broke off all contact and made it impossible, so she came here without direction, with no firm plans of a place to go.'

'So this is my fault?'

'I didn't say that. Please, lower your voice.' He checked Giles was still engrossed and he was. 'Giles knows his mum is here; so far, I've told him we're having a bit of a holiday before we see her.'

'You still haven't said how you knew where I was.'

'I saw you on the television: the appeal. I went to the airbase, was told you were at a fundraiser. It wasn't hard to work out from there; the posters are all over town.'

She looked over at Giles again. 'Does he know who I am?'

'He thinks you're an old friend.' His brow furrowed. 'You were once upon a time. You were more than that.'

'Well, things got ruined, didn't they?'

He didn't respond but instead said quietly, 'I can't lie to my son forever, but I was hoping we'd find her before I had to. I was hoping we'd find her before—'

'Don't you have an app or something on your phone to track her? That's what I'd do.' She couldn't listen to any more. 'I have to get back to this event; this is work, this is important.'

'So is this. Monica is pregnant again.'

'Congratulations,' she said flatly.

'Nadia, it wasn't only that I saw you on the television that prompted me to come to see you; it was the fact that a baby had been abandoned at the airbase.'

Her pulse quickened and it felt like all the oxygen around them had suddenly dropped. It was a moment before she managed to ask him, 'How pregnant?'

'Thirty-five weeks when she came here, she'd be thirty-eight weeks almost by now.'

Nadia's emotions whirled up inside of her, she felt nauseous, she wanted to run away and yet she knew she couldn't. The timing... it could fit, couldn't it?

'Can I get you something – a glass of water?' Archie asked.

She looked at him. She felt like he'd asked her the most stupid question in the world.

Lena might well be Monica's baby, that was what he was saying, and nothing, certainly not a glass of water, was going to do anything to help her get her head around that.

'Monica should've been back in Switzerland by now. It was a risk travelling so close to her due date. She's not in a good place, mentally. It's not a rational thing to do, come over to look for someone when you've no idea where they are, not really, leaving her child behind, her husband, her life.' He was rambling and his voice shook. 'I don't know what to do, where she is, whether this baby you found...'

'So you think that Monica came to England, had a baby, somehow discovered where I worked and left it for me, is that it?' She began to laugh at the ridiculousness of it all. 'Is that supposed to make up for what she did? I lost a baby with you, things with us ended, she swooped in and took you for herself and now she has a sudden attack of conscience? Wants to give me a baby to make up for it?'

'Nadia—'

'No!' The sound of merriment floated out of the marquee and taunted her as the evening cooled and the air made her shiver as her fury at the unjustness of the past turned to tears threatening to spill.

'Is it really that far-fetched that she's had the baby and left it because she's not in her right mind?' Archie asked.

'Yes!'

'You didn't hear the way she's been talking about you lately: the longing to make contact, the regret, not to mention the guilt. She was always sorry for what she did. So was I. But you didn't want to hear it.'

'Damn right I didn't.'

'She was going on and on about not having you around when Giles was born, how she wished you could have been, how she didn't want our second baby to miss out on family. I've not seen her this bad in years. When I got to England, I phoned round all the hospitals to find out whether she'd ended up at any of them and that might be why she hadn't got in touch but I found nothing to help me. I then began to wonder whether, if her head is in a really bad place, she may not have given her real name at a hospital. And then today, Giles put the television on and the appeal was showing and I saw you.' He smiled. 'I saw you and felt like these twenty years faded away.'

'They haven't faded, Archie; I've made a new life.'

'Without me, without your sister.'

'I had to. We were together, you and I, before we lost the baby. I thought we could make a go of things and even though we split up, despite the fact we'd decided we worked better as friends, it didn't make it easier when my sister took you for herself.'

He let the moment settle before he asked, 'Have they any clues as to who left the baby?'

'In the few hours since you saw the television appeal again today?' She sounded patronising but this was all so much to cope with. 'No, Archie, they haven't.'

Lena couldn't be her sister's baby, could she?

No, it was ridiculous.

She pushed away the very real feeling of what it had been like to hold Lena, to feel the weight of her in her arms, the softness of her hair against her cheek, the way the baby had looked up at her as she took the bottle.

Had it been her own past that had made her feel an attachment? Or was Lena a part of their family?

The appeal had given her away. She hadn't given it a moment's thought. She'd never been on social media with her maiden name, so her sister, if she'd ever been looking, wouldn't have found it easy to trace her. Her romance with Jock Sutton had happened so quickly and not under the gaze of her sister that Monica wouldn't have known much about him, let alone how to find him. Nadia had met Jock in Switzerland shortly after her mother died from a sudden stroke. He was there for a conference and extended holiday and a few weeks later she packed her bags to return to England with him. To start over. She wondered sometimes whether having a different surname, no longer being Nadia Fischer, had pushed her into thinking marriage was a good idea, a way to disappear into thin air and leave all the hurt behind.

Her urge to get away from Archie and Monica, even though she wasn't even here, felt as strong now as it had been back then when she left Switzerland. 'Archie, I'm sorry you had a wasted journey coming here this evening, but I haven't heard anything from Monica. I suggest you call the police if you think the baby is yours. I can't help you.'

Monica had taken so much from her over time, including Archie, and with issues between the sisters that felt insurmountable, the clean break was the only thing that had kept Nadia sane. Nadia had left Switzerland twenty years ago with Jock, ten years her senior, and come to Dorset where he lived and worked as a surgeon. She'd found a job as a nurse at the same hospital but things hadn't been good for very long. The marriage had been short-lived, a mistake in the first place which ended with an unplanned pregnancy that almost took her life. They'd called it quits and it was soon after their separation that Nadia found a different family, with The Skylarks.

She began to walk away. The only thing to stop her was Giles running over and tugging at her hand. 'Am I allowed to run around the big tent?'

The skin-on-skin contact was something she felt hard to ignore.

But she couldn't get attached. She wouldn't.

'I want to stretch my legs,' he said. 'Dad is always telling me to do that.'

She felt the defences she'd put up melt away. 'I'm afraid it's not safe to run around, not for you or anyone else who might come outside, especially in the dark.'

'How do you know my daddy?'

Talk about a segue.

Archie had walked over too and all three of them stood beneath the moonlight, halfway between the bench and the party that carried on around them. 'It's a long story, Giles,' he said.

Nadia felt sorry for this little boy, this interesting, energetic nephew. And she felt another remarkable sense of loss when he looked up at her with innocent eyes.

She wasn't sure what made her do it. If Giles hadn't stopped her, she'd have been back in the marquee by now.

She bobbed down to the little boy's level. 'Your mummy is actually my sister.'

His eyes widened. And then his face fell. 'But I've never seen you. Is that because you live here? It's a long way on the train.'

'Yes, it is a long way.' It was all she had for now.

'Giles, how about we get going, leave this lady... Nadia in peace.' Whether Archie appreciated her divulging her identity or not, she couldn't tell.

'I haven't stretched my legs,' Giles pointed out. 'You said when we got out of the car that I could.'

'We'll go to the beach tomorrow.'

Nadia had been so busy feeling the past twenty years catching up on her that she hadn't spotted the exhaustion on Archie's face until now.

'Can I practise my forward rolls?' Giles wasn't asking his dad this time; he was asking Nadia. 'Is that allowed here?'

'I'm sure that would be fine, just away from the entrance to the marquee.'

'Okay.' He almost took off but paused. 'Will there be doggy do-dos?'

Archie interrupted. 'This seems a pretty high-class establishment and I haven't seen any dogs around.'

Giles started practising. One roll after another, on he went.

'I don't know where he gets his energy,' said Archie. 'The last few days I've been dragging him around so much, we've been in the car a lot, he's done well not to moan more than he has.'

'How old is he?'

'He's four.'

Nadia couldn't watch the child any more, even though her gaze was drawn to him: to his little smile, the way his eyes had shone with enthusiasm at the thought of being allowed to be out here at night and roll across a lawn that wasn't his.

'Archie, I really have to go. I hope you find Monica, I really do.'

His calm demeanour took leave. 'Nadia, this isn't just Monica taking a holiday; this is Monica travelling to another country, coming here and not letting me know exactly where she is, Monica not checking in every day with her husband and her son who she adores. This is Monica putting herself and our baby at risk. Monica who might well have left our baby at your airbase. I mean, it's possible, isn't it?'

She couldn't deny it. It sounded ridiculous, and yet...

But then she thought about Monica. Needy and

demanding Monica with the desire to be the centre of attention; it had always been her way. And Nadia had never been able to forget it either – Monica struggled at school, Monica got away with rudeness and wild behaviour, Monica did what she wanted and she was rarely pulled into line. All her actions, her decisions, they took centre stage and nobody else really got a look in, least of all Nadia. Monica's selfishness had taken time from Nadia and their mother; it had cost her Archie. Her best friend.

'Monica is a grown woman,' she told Archie firmly. She couldn't let this destroy everything she'd built up here: her stability, her sense of belonging, something that was hers and hers alone. 'This seems like another drama surrounding my sister, so what's new?' She sounded so harsh, so unlike herself. She felt like a teenager all over again, but for so many years, she hadn't had to deal with Monica and she wished she didn't have to now either. 'Call the police, Archie. Let them deal with it.'

'You don't even care?' He hurled the question at her when she turned her back on him.

She stopped in her tracks and spun round to face him. 'How can you even throw that at me? I always cared, I cared for years, and it didn't get me much in return.'

Desperation laced a voice that shook. 'She's not in a good place, emotionally.'

'She never was!' Luckily, Giles was still giggling so didn't respond to the raising of her voice. He'd moved on from forward rolls to doing what looked like an attempt at the long jump even though he had no sandpit.

'This is bad, Nadia. I wouldn't have shown up otherwise. Don't you think we both know that you want nothing to do with us? It almost broke Monica when you left. Your parents were both gone and you left without looking back.'

'Broke *her*? Over the years, she almost broke *me*, Archie. And so did you.'

'I know things happened between us all, things we might like to go back and change if we had the power to do that. But believe me, I wouldn't be here if this was a silly drama. She's changed, a lot. She's not that same person. And I really am worried about her. About my baby.'

She shivered, rubbed the tops of her arms and rejected his offer of his jacket. She didn't want anything from him, not any more.

'Did you know she came to England to look for you once before?' he asked.

'I don't believe you.'

'She did. She had no idea where to start but she knew Jock was from Dorset. She took off not so long after you left. She didn't want to be with me; she knew she'd hurt you by getting together with me. She came to find you; she wanted to make amends. She was over here for eight weeks, scoured the county by the sounds of it – the details of where she'd been didn't come out for a long time. When she came back to Switzerland, she wouldn't even talk to me. She pushed me away at first; she wouldn't let me or anyone else help. I thought...' His voice caught. 'I thought she might do something really stupid. I thought she was going to take her own life.'

'You're saying that to shock me.' Was his expression forced or was he telling the truth?

'I promise you I'm not.'

She stood there, the evening warm enough that she shouldn't be shivering and yet she was.

'Can we at least exchange numbers, in case either of us gets news? Give me that, please, Nadia.'

She reluctantly put his number into her phone and he gave his in return.

'You know, she might not even be here in Dorset. She could be anywhere; she could've gone to London – she always talked about the big smoke and the theatres and the excitement. Maybe you should try there if you don't have any luck with the police. Perhaps she's travelled home by now; you could check with a neighbour.' And before she walked away, she added, 'Wherever she is, I hope you find her and that she and the baby are safe.'

Somehow, her legs had carried her back into the marquee, back to the music, the laughter, the fun, the celebrations and coming together. And never had she felt quite so alone as she bypassed everyone to slip out and through the front door of the country house.

In the shower, after she recalled the events and conversation from last night, Nadia still couldn't believe any of it. The water still running, she leaned her forehead against the cool tiles. Monica. Archie. Lena. It was all too much.

She wanted to hear from Archie to know her sister was safe and yet at the same time, she never wanted to hear from him ever again.

She wanted all of this to go away.

But it wasn't going to, was it?

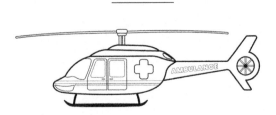

13

'The dinner dance feels like a distant memory.' Kate leaned against the sink in the kitchen after she passed Nadia a mug of tea.

The fundraiser less than forty-eight hours ago might feel like a distant memory to some of the team, but not to Nadia, who wished it was only the dancing with Hudson that she had to focus on in the aftermath.

'What made you rush off and give up that gorgeous room, not to mention the breakfast fit for kings and queens?' said Kate. 'Is everything okay?'

'Everything is fine. I remembered an important appointment the morning after, that's all.' It sounded plausible, didn't it? 'And I wasn't feeling all that great either – probably too much food and a mixture of drinks that I'm not used to, so I decided I'd hitch a lift with the bus, no harm done.' And now she was going too far, doubling up the excuses which sounded fake even to her own ears.

Nadia began to lead the way out of the kitchen. 'Tell me more about the breakfast; was it as good as the dinner?' She wasn't really interested but it was a semi-normal conversation she could cope with rather than the turmoil going on inside of her head.

'It was – pastries, fully cooked breakfast, pancakes... so much to choose from.'

'I can't believe you had room after the feast the night before.'

'Nadia, let me tell you how the human body works...'

But Nadia laughed, shook her head.

'It'll be us on duty next year,' said Kate as they reached the main office and she sat at the end desk. She wiggled the computer mouse to bring the screen alive. 'Had to make the most of it.'

Nadia picked up the paperwork she needed and didn't let her smile fade until she was out of Kate's vicinity. And moments later, she tried to put it right back in place when she bumped into Hudson. She hadn't seen him since the dinner dance and he was bound to have questions she wasn't sure she was ready to answer yet.

'I've got a meeting with the Turner family,' he told her without preamble. Maybe he didn't know what to say either. 'They've agreed to share their story to promote The Skylarks and the work we do here.'

'That's wonderful, well done.'

He wasn't looking at her – since when had he been one to avoid eye contact?

'Hudson, about last night.'

'You don't owe me any explanation.'

'I feel like I do, and I want to explain.'

When Frank appeared in the corridor, Hudson followed after Nadia as she went into her own office. He closed the door behind them.

'I lied to you,' she said.

'About being single?'

'What? No! I'm very much single, not seeing anyone at all.'

'Who was the guy?'

She hesitated. She may as well come out with it. If she didn't, she'd only be delaying the inevitable. 'Archie was once my boyfriend. He's now my sister's husband.'

'You have a sister?'

'I have a sister. Yes. I never told anyone that, for reasons that might take me a while to explain.'

He leaned against the wall. 'Wow, it seems…'

'Ludicrous? Weird?'

He smiled across at her. 'Not words I'd necessarily use, but why have you never mentioned your sister? I asked you in the pub outright whether you had any siblings and you said no.'

'I felt terrible lying to you.'

'So why did you?'

'There's so much about my life that I've pushed away and not told anyone about because I prefer not to think about it.'

He said nothing.

'I'm sorry.'

'No need to apologise. You know you ran away from the hotel and missed out on an exceedingly good breakfast, don't you?'

Did the attempt at normality mean they were okay?

He took a seat in the chair opposite her desk as she sat down on the other side.

'I'm not proud of myself for lying to you,' she said.

'I'm assuming there must be a deep reason why you didn't admit to a sister.'

His sympathy almost undid her. 'There's a lot of history, my family was… is… complicated.'

'I just wish you'd felt able to confide in me or someone else. I assume nobody else knows either?'

She nodded.

'So why is your sister's husband here? Is he local?'

'No, he lives in Switzerland, where I grew up.' She steepled her fingers, elbows on the table, and rested her head against her fingertips. 'He thinks that Monica, my sister, might have come looking for me.'

They were interrupted by a knock at the door – Brad looking for Hudson. 'The Turner family are here with the photographer.'

'Thanks, I'll be right there,' Hudson told him.

Hudson was good at his job and had set up this publicity opportunity with the family. Their story had a happy ending and they'd agreed to share it. There'd be a lot of emphasis on the role played by The Skylarks, which would help promote what the team did here and hopefully go some way to raising more funds as a result.

He stood up. 'We should talk more later. I can tell you've got a lot going on, but I'm a good listener. Ask the Turners.'

She returned his smile. He was being so kind to her.

'I'd better go, get the photographs taken beside the helicopter.'

'You can have my office for the interview if you like,' she said.

'I appreciate that. Thank you. The photographer will probably take half an hour, then I'll do the interview afterwards. How does that sound?'

'I'll be out of here in ten minutes then use the room for as long as you need.' She was talking to him like nothing unusual had happened in the last couple of days since her life had flipped, been thrown into disarray.

After Hudson left, Nadia re-read the text Archie had sent

that morning for the umpteenth time. He'd gone to the police as she'd advised; they'd taken him seriously and had followed up several lines of enquiry: they'd checked the hospitals in the country just as he had but nobody of Monica's description had been in; they'd checked with passport control that she was still in the country and hadn't yet left so that was reassuring, Archie said, although he was no closer to finding her. They'd also begun to look at Monica's online presence, see what they could find there, but so far, there was no news.

Archie's text had been lengthy; it explained how the police had asked him whether he thought Monica was in danger. He'd had to admit that all he really knew was that she would never harm her baby, that she wanted to find her sister after all these years, and he truly believed Monica was still here in Dorset. He'd offered to do a blood test, to see if baby Lena was his, but he was advised that at this stage, that wasn't necessary until they'd looked into this further.

They think I'm a nutjob, he'd written at the end of his text.

Nadia had almost wanted to reach out to her former friend, comfort him, tell him that everything would be okay, that his missing wife would be found and his baby would be safe. But she felt numb. So instead, she wrote a swift reply thanking him for the update and telling him that it was up to the police now.

She swilled the dregs of her tea and turned in her chair so she was facing the wall with all the framed photographs of the crew and their fundraising efforts. There was a beautifully framed picture of last year's big fundraiser: the gala held at a town venue when they'd raised thousands, the blue team in attendance this time. That picture would soon be replaced by one from this year, taken at the start of the night before the tables had been cleared and the dancing commenced. Another photo was of the sponsored run everyone here had gone in for, taken at the finish line, all of them gathered hot and sweaty given the hills in the area – their efforts were represented in a special gigantic fake cheque they were holding to show how much they'd raised. Another picture featured Nadia, Maya, Bess and Kate when they'd done Tough Mudder, a gruelling obstacle course and mud run – their faces said it all. Streaked with mud, they were jubilant, they'd had fun, her and her teammates – her family.

Monica had been family once. But she'd always taken; she'd never given. Was she about to take more from Nadia by coming here and forcing her to tell her truth she'd kept hidden for years? Nadia had never wanted that. She never wanted people to know that she could turn her back on her own flesh and blood; it seemed so cruel, so hard. Hudson already thought badly of her, she could tell. It was only because he was a decent person that he was giving her the time of day. She doubted whether he'd want any more than a professional relationship, a friendship at best, after this.

Nadia turned her focus to the volunteer applications in her inbox. They'd take her mind off things.

The Whistlestop River Air Ambulance could never drop the ball when it came to raising crucial funds. The dinner dance had raised thousands, it had defied expectations, but there was always more to be done and like many air ambulances, members of the public who volunteered were additional heroes to their team. She perused four separate applications, two from retirees, two from school leavers trying to get something on their CV that might give them a leg up when it came to looking for work. There were plenty of roles to fill – they could help at fundraising events, provide admin support at the airbase, drive fundraising materials to events, engage in public speaking. She followed up each application and requested the further details she needed as well as setting up suitable times to talk with the applicant. It was a part of the job she really enjoyed: getting more people involved. She'd wondered, when she left nursing, whether she'd crave that nurse-to-patient contact, the continual rotation of different people in her orbit. But she hadn't had a chance to miss it because, whilst the crews were relatively static here, the amount of other people involved was more than she'd ever realised.

There was a knock at her door as Nadia finished setting up a time with the last applicant. Kate came inside. 'Visitor for you in reception.'

'I'll be right there.'

Kate lingered a moment. 'It's the guy from the party.'

And her heart sank. Trying to avoid the past was pretty difficult when it insisted on showing up at your door.

14

Nadia went through to the reception to face Archie once again. Why had he come here? Did he have news about Monica and the baby?

Worrying about her sister was something she'd done her best to bury after having done it for so many years when they were growing up. But now, she couldn't help herself from wondering all over again where she was, how she was, whether she was okay.

Archie was sitting on one of the seats at the far end of reception and she went straight over. As soon as Giles saw her, he ran towards her with so much joy, she wanted to burst into tears and hug him tightly.

'I want to see a helicopter, Auntie Nadia,' Giles blurted out.

'Is that so?' How could she maintain a frown when this wonderful little boy seemed so enamoured by her presence? Perhaps she was simply a novelty.

'Can I go see one now?'

'I'm not sure whether that's possible today.' And how was she going to face a barrage of questions from everyone she worked with when he was calling her auntie?

In a completely different tone, she addressed Archie. 'What can I do for you?' She might be worried but she still wanted to keep the extent of her concern hidden; she wanted to keep that part of herself away from those who'd hurt her.

Taken aback by her formality, he addressed Giles. 'Why don't you look out of the big glass doors, see whether you can spot the helicopter if it goes up?'

'That's a good idea.' Nadia wanted to get this over with.

As soon as it was just them over this side, Archie asked, 'Has she come here? Tried to get in touch? I'm running out of options, the police have nothing so far, I don't know what to do.'

Being angry about the past and annoyed that it had found her in her safe place was easy to do when she was hiding behind terse text messages. It was much harder to do now they were less than a metre apart. Watching him, she could see the toll all of this was having on the man who had once been her friend. His usually handsome features held a sadness, a fear, and Nadia couldn't help it; her heart went out to him.

'No, I haven't heard anything,' she said. 'I assure you I will text or call if that changes.'

'Right.'

'Does Giles still not know?'

'No. But now he knows who you are, it's distracted him from thinking more deeply about where his mum might be. He thinks that we're here to spend time with you too. He's really excited about that, Nadia.'

What was he doing to her? Trying to make her holding them at arm's length impossible?

Disappointed, Giles came back over. 'I can't see the helicopter. Is it out the back?'

'It is,' she told him. 'It's on the helipad.'

'Have you been in it?'

'I rarely get to go out with The Skylarks; my job is here at the base.' Her smile faltered when she looked Archie's way again.

Vik had come into reception and Giles was onto it straight away and ran over to ask whether he was the pilot.

'Giles...' Archie's voice warned. 'I'm sorry,' he called over to Vik.

'No worries.' And then to Nadia, Vik said, 'Does this little guy belong to you? Because if he does, I'm happy to take him out to look around the helicopter if you need a minute.'

Her team knew nothing of who this man was, knew nothing about her history and yet they were intuitive.

'Would you mind?' she said. She would rather tell Archie to leave her alone when Giles wasn't here. He didn't deserve to pay the price for his mother's or his father's past mistakes. And she didn't have it in her to be so cruel.

Once Giles happily followed Vik to see the air ambulance for himself, Nadia turned back to Archie. 'I haven't heard a thing about Monica or from Monica. You don't need to come here. In fact, I'd really rather you didn't.'

'Like I said, I don't know what else to do. I'm sorry if that makes things awkward.'

'Are you? Because you're still here.' Arms folded, she stood her ground, although she wasn't sure she was even convincing herself.

'I'm here because I really think she'll turn up looking for you.'

'If she even knows this is where I work. Which, unless she's seen the television appeal, she won't. And the chances are slim of that, I'd say.'

'Are you kidding? I saw it online three times after I saw it on television. She could easily have seen it. She's been here a while, longer than me. And I still think about the baby, whether she's mine.'

Nadia realised that what came through in his voice the most was desperation, a need for answers. It was the way some of the patients' families she'd come across in her career sounded: the need to know what was going on, good or bad.

'I told you her head was in a bad place,' he went on. 'She had depression on and off over the years; it was why we put off starting a family: she wasn't sure whether she could handle it. And then she had postnatal depression after Giles. She wasn't sure she could go through it all again with a second pregnancy. Now I'm wondering whether she'd been right to worry about that and something really did snap.'

So the depression had found her sister again, more than once. It was almost too much to think about. But her caring nature meant she couldn't help but feel sympathetic because watching Archie reminded her very much of the members of families who'd given up hope, the families who knew bad news was on its way, it was just a matter of time.

Nadia uncrossed her arms and took a seat next to him. 'Even for Monica, leaving a baby seems way too far-fetched. I really don't think—'

'But it's not impossible. Don't you see?' Head in his hands, he was falling apart. 'When you first left Switzerland, she thought you might come back, but as time went on and reality hit that you weren't, that was when it really got to her. I don't think she ever fully moved on from what happened. She's softened over the years, Nadia; she's changed. You don't know her any more. You made sure of that.'

She got up. 'I can't do this. I'm at work; you'll have to go.' And she started to walk away.

He stayed where he was but his voice, firmer than before, followed her. 'She's your sister. Your family. How can you turn your back when she might be out there, her head all over the place, so messed up that she left her baby?'

'You don't know that,' she muttered, stopping by the reception desk before the corridor which passed through to the rear of the airbase and the hangar.

She leaned her back against the wall, closed her eyes. And she felt the tears well. The same tears she'd had when they were younger, at the frustration of her sister's messy life impacting everyone else.

She hated that she still cared. She'd been telling herself for years that she didn't and yet she knew that was the lie she'd repeated in her head in order to move forwards with her life.

She wiped the tears that formed unbidden and began to topple. But she wasn't quick enough to do it before Archie came over to her.

He came to her side, rested his back against the wall too and she was reminded of the way his body had felt against hers as young adults, students, the times they'd had fun, other times they'd been intimate. They hadn't been seeing each other as boyfriend and girlfriend for very long before she got pregnant and it was so much to cope with at a young age. When she lost the baby, they lost their way with each other, but she'd thought they'd always stay the best of friends. Except they hadn't. Everything had changed when Monica had stomped on in and taken that away from her older sister.

'Giles talked about you two falling out,' said Archie.

'What does he know?'

'Not much – we've kept it that way. All he really knows is that you had an argument a long time ago. I didn't think he'd be able to process the ins and outs; even I struggle to do that sometimes. But he says he understands.'

'How so?' She thought of the little boy who looked so much like Monica, it hurt.

'A month ago, he had a falling out with a friend at playgroup. All very high-drama stuff over a *Star Wars* toy but he didn't speak to the friend for a whole three days.'

She'd forgotten Archie and his ability to lift a situation even when it was dire. He'd always done that, but she'd left behind the memory as well as the person.

Neither of them spoke for almost a minute.

'Do you think you'll find her?' Nadia asked eventually. 'Do you think she'll just show up or come home perhaps?'

'She loves her son; she loves her baby. She loves me.' He croaked the last part as though this might hurt Nadia the most. 'I'm hoping we get news soon. I thought the police would laugh me out of the station but when I said she was pregnant and that the baby left here could be hers, they were a bit more serious. I told them about her history of mental illness – that's what it was, Nadia; it wasn't just her being your annoying little sister – she faced some real demons.'

'I know.'

He grunted. 'I apologise. I shouldn't be lecturing you.'

'You're not.' She stood up straight from the wall. 'We should check on Giles.' She led the way through the hangar and out near the helipad where Vik was showing Giles the cockpit.

'Dad, this is awesome!' her nephew cried out. 'I want to fly one day!'

'We'll see about that. Come on, time we left these guys to it.'

Giles predictably complained but good-naturedly. Whoever her sister was these days, Monica had raised a wonderful little boy. And Nadia had missed all of it. Without children of her own, the fact hit her with an unexpected wave of pain.

Giles needed the toilet before they left so back inside the airbase, Nadia pointed him in the right direction.

Outside the bathroom, Archie faced her. 'I can't leave England until I've found her.'

'I wouldn't expect you to.'

'She's really changed. I wish you could see it for yourself. We are your family.'

And yet she still resisted. 'Archie, *this* is my family.' Her arms gesticulated to their surroundings. 'My family is The Skylarks, the team here.'

Archie looked at her as though the bottom of his world might well have fallen out. He'd come here expecting his wife to have made contact. And now it seemed he didn't know which way to turn.

Giles emerged from the bathroom at the same time as Vik came along the corridor from the office. 'Thank you, Vik!' he called out.

'You're welcome, buddy.' He high-fived the little boy and Nadia swallowed down another wave of emotion. He was just like her sister had been at his age – bubbly, full of confidence, willing to talk to anyone no matter who they were. She'd been a beautiful kid until her teenage years when something in her seemed to have changed. Nadia had never seen it coming and she felt responsible for that in some way, like she should have.

The phones blared out their alert to another job and from where they were standing, they could see into the office where Kate was answering the call. Nadia explained to Giles what was happening when he slipped his little hand into hers. The sense of emergency must be frightening if he wasn't used to it and the feel of his skin on hers broke down a few more of her defences.

Vik was all business and went outside to start up the helicopter. Kate was scribbling down details of the job. Brad passed them in the doorway to get the drugs and the bloods. Nadia explained it all to Giles in a low voice so as not to interrupt operations going on around them.

'Collision between a car and a pedestrian,' Kate informed Nadia quietly enough that Giles wouldn't hear much.

Giles's hand still in hers, Nadia followed Kate into the hangar. 'How bad is it?' she asked. Giles was mesmerised looking around, too enthralled with the helicopter starting up to listen to them.

Kate pulled on her jacket. 'Female, age unknown, possible head trauma and injuries to the pelvis.' She picked up her helmet. 'There are signs she's recently had a baby – her abdomen, bleeding.'

Nadia's breath caught. 'Do you think...'

'No idea,' said Kate, who knew Nadia was hinting about baby Lena but didn't have time to pause and discuss it.

The whir of the blades on the helicopter beyond the hangar took Nadia's breath away. She locked eyes with Archie, and realised she was clasping Giles's hand too firmly as he began to squirm.

Nadia made a split-second decision. 'I'm coming with you, Kate.'

Kate stopped in her tracks. 'You're what?'

'Wait for me.' She dropped Giles's hand, grabbed the spare jacket, pulled it on and did the same with the helmet. When Frank came in with his toolbox, having been working on one of the rapid response vehicles, she told him to hold the fort.

He gave her a salute. He knew the deal.

Nadia didn't want Giles to panic so as she did up her helmet, she told Archie, 'This might take hours. Go to your accommodation; I'll call you.' And then she was following Kate.

On board Hilda, she simply said, 'If it's the birth mother, I want to be there,' as if that explained everything. And with no time to waste, Vik confirmed that weight limits and fuel were good to go and they lifted into the skies above Whistlestop River.

'ETA nine minutes,' said Brad from his position in the cockpit as the technical crew member.

An update came in from the HEMS desk. Nadia could hear it; they all could over their headsets.

'Victim. Female. In cardiac arrest. CPR being performed at the scene by an off-duty nurse.'

Nadia had to remind herself to breathe.

Please, please, please let the woman be all right.

Please, please, please don't let it be Monica.

If it was, this might be the only chance Nadia got to make peace with her sister.

She felt sick. With every whir of the blades that took them closer to the road traffic collision, she felt worse, as if the blades were physically cutting through her.

Flashing lights guided Vik to their landing site on a cricket pavilion near where the accident had happened. And as they were cleared to disembark, HEMS wanted an update of The Skylarks' ETA to the victim's side. This meant they were desperately needed, which indicated that the patient must be worsening and might not survive without their specialist care.

'Nadia!' Kate shrieked as she and Brad loaded up with all the gear.

Nadia had frozen. Her legs wouldn't budge.

'Nadia!' But Kate didn't wait. She couldn't; her job was to get to the victim, not to look after the woman who'd come along with them and couldn't move.

Nadia sat in the back of the helicopter listening to the updates from the HEMS desk come through one after the other from the road ambulance paramedics and then from her own team as they reached the victim and did everything they could at the scene.

Vik's job was to wait by the helicopter. He climbed in the back and wrapped a blanket around Nadia's shoulders. He asked no questions; she offered no explanation.

When a bystander came over to the helicopter, Vik apologised to Nadia before jumping out to talk with them. This happened a lot; people took an interest.

It felt like she'd been sitting there forever and then another update came, this time from Kate, letting everyone on the channel know what the status at the scene was.

'The patient re-arrested. There was almost forty minutes of prolonged CPR but the patient was pronounced dead at 15.43.'

Nadia leapt out of the helicopter. The blanket dropped from her shoulders. She ran towards the blue lights, she saw the crowd of first responders, the scene calmer than it would've been when they first arrived. She saw her crew; Brad came towards her.

'We tried our best,' he said.

Nadia's feet took her the rest of the way, flashbacks of Monica when they were little girls playing schools in the back garden, zipping up and down the pavements on their bikes, making cupcakes and splattering the mixture everywhere except where it was meant to go.

And as she saw the victim on the ground, blonde hair just like hers splayed out in disarray, she sank to her knees.

15

The interview with the Turners went well. The family were all in when it came to promoting the air ambulance, especially young Max, who couldn't wait to meet Bess and Noah, the critical care paramedics who attended the scene on the day of the eight-year-old's accident earlier this year. Max had been riding his skateboard in the street and had taken a tumble into the road. He'd been hit by a car. The air ambulance had been deployed and Max, with significant head injuries, was stabilised at the scene and transferred to a children's major trauma hospital.

The Turners' story, now he'd done the interview, would be written up after Hudson liaised with the communications assistant who worked remotely, and it would then go out as a media release which would hopefully lead to coverage in local if not national newspapers and publications.

Max's parents' emotions had really come through in the interview as they recalled the day they thought they'd lost their youngest son: how they felt as he fought to survive in intensive care for a period of time following the accident, and their absolute elation when he first opened his eyes and smiled.

Emotions went wild again when Bess and Noah showed up
in Nadia's office especially to see young Max. Neither of them
were on shift but they'd come in because Max really wanted to
meet the two people who'd rescued him from the road.

'They're true heroes,' his mother Jenny told Hudson as she
watched her son talking and laughing with the two paramedics.

'They're superheroes!' Max declared with a few sound effects
to boot.

'Without The Skylarks, we might not have him today.'
Jenny's voice caught. 'Thank you to every single one of you.'

Her husband reiterated their gratitude, the couple hugged
each other tight, and young Max made them all laugh with an
eye roll and his claim, 'They do this a lot.'

Hudson said goodbye to the Turners and assured Max he
could come back another day to see the helicopter. He'd
missed out on seeing it, perhaps getting a turn to sit in the
cockpit, because right now, it was out with the crew to rescue
someone else who needed a superhero at their side just like
he had.

Hudson found Frank in the hangar. 'Where's Nadia got to? I
wanted to tell her she can have her office back.'

'She went with the crew. Hopped on the helicopter, asked me
to man the fort.'

Nadia was a trained nurse but she rarely got involved in the
practical medical side any more. 'Why did she go out on the
job?'

'Beats me.' Frank patted his shoulder. 'Coffee? I'm making it.'

'Just had one, thanks, so not for me.'

They made their way along the corridor and before Frank
disappeared into the kitchen, Hudson saw two figures coming
into the building via the front entrance. And he wasn't quite sure
what to make of what he was seeing.

Conrad, detective in the adjacent town to Whistlestop River, and Beau at his side.

'I'll leave you to it,' said Frank, recognising Beau, and of course Conrad who, when he was married to Maya and as they went through a divorce, Frank had always kept an eye on. He might only be the engineer here but much like Nadia, he cared about every member of the team as if they were family.

'I think we need to talk,' said Conrad as Hudson joined them in reception.

'What's going on?' he asked Beau. 'Why aren't you at school?'

Beau had stayed over at his mum's last night and she knew the deal: no falling for claims Beau wasn't well, which he'd tried before and usually, she couldn't be bothered to argue.

'I had a headache first thing,' said Beau. 'I was going to go in but...'

Conrad prompted him to keep talking. Usually, the police detective was filled with so much self-importance, he didn't do politeness or patience and definitely didn't do any type of hand-holding for a teenager as far as Hudson knew.

Hudson led them over to the seating area. What was going on? Beau hadn't been well, hadn't gone to school, and somehow, he was with Conrad?

Beau looked up from beneath a fringe that was far too long – the kid wouldn't have it that he needed a haircut and was probably growing it out of spite from the time Hudson had heavily suggested it might need a trim.

'I need to tell you about the hoax,' said Beau.

'What are you talking about?'

'The one last summer. For the air ambulance. The fake emergency call.'

He had a bad feeling in the pit of his stomach because he remembered it, even after all this time. Last summer, The

Skylarks had been deployed to an emergency and landed in a field when they spotted what they thought was a person dressed in a hi-vis jacket. Except it wasn't; it was a scarecrow. The crew had scoured the fields to find a patient in need, in case it was a coincidence and there was a real emergency. The only saving grace had been that someone had subsequently called the emergency services to admit that the call was a hoax. Otherwise, The Skylarks might have been looking for a victim or victims for a very long time.

'I was involved,' said Beau.

'You made the prank call?' Hudson couldn't believe what he was hearing.

Conrad interrupted. 'There were a few lads involved; Beau says he didn't make the call himself but he refuses to give us any other names.'

'I'm not a grass!' Beau told them.

Hudson didn't get a chance to ask why he would tell a police officer, and why now, because Conrad took charge. 'Beau here was talking on the phone to someone; I overheard.'

'Were you boasting about it, Beau?' Hudson asked.

'No, I wouldn't do that.'

'Then what were you saying?'

'There's this girl... at school. She was going to go on a date with a guy and he's bad news. He was one of the boys involved with the hoax. I told her; I wanted to warn her.'

Conrad interrupted yet again. 'I wouldn't usually deal with cases like this but took this one on board seeing as it's Beau and because it's the air ambulance. Vested interest, you know.'

Vested interest? That was a joke. And did he think he and Hudson were buddies? Was that why he was saying he took the case? Hudson wasn't sure everything added up here; his head was all over the place.

Perhaps Conrad was just being Conrad – possessive, a giant pain in the arse. He didn't have any vested interest really – the only link he had was Maya, who was only polite to him because she was a nice person. Conrad had made himself such a nuisance around here before Maya put a stop to his interference once and for all that sometimes, he felt like a bit of the furniture, except not a nice piece, but rather one you wouldn't even give away to a thrift shop. Hudson would've thought the guy would be sheepish around the crew but no, here he was, bold as brass. Arrogant, that's what he was, and he probably thought – and he'd be right – that he had something over one of them now.

Hudson turned his attention to Beau. 'Whatever made you do it? You know how dangerous that is, that you could take time and resources from someone who really needs help. And this is my place of work...'

Beau hung his head. 'I'm sorry, Dad.'

'Are you?' Hudson didn't raise his voice much, certainly not here, but he could feel his temper rising. 'Your little joke could've cost lives. You're damn lucky The Skylarks weren't needed on another call.'

'I knew it was wrong—'

'Then why do it?' he roared, causing Beau to look up through his fringe in shock.

Tears tracked down Beau's cheeks. Hudson hadn't seen those for years; the anger always got in the way, and he was fifteen. He resisted showing emotions in front of anyone, especially his parents. He hadn't even cried when his mother moved out; his sadness was masked by fury, which he took out on Hudson in the days following Lucinda's departure.

'I didn't make the call, Dad, at least not the first one, but I was with a gang when they did it. We waited in the fields near the scarecrow, saw the helicopter land, then ran away. I hung back and made the second call.'

'Second call?'

'Your son called the emergency services again and said it had been a hoax.' Conrad sure liked to cut in. 'The message went through HEMS and Maya... sorry, The Skylarks, were able to leave the scene.'

Hudson rubbed his hands up his cheeks, let out a long breath, rested his forearms on his thighs.

'Who were the other lads, Beau?'

'Dad...'

'Don't *Dad* me. Who were they?'

'No, no way. I'll take my punishment but I'm not grassing; they'll make my life hell. I've got ages left at that school.'

'But you warned the girl off?' It didn't make sense that he'd expose himself like that if he was worried the others would make his school days hard. And then it dawned on him. 'You like her.' His son had wanted to show his good side; that was why he'd called it in to stop the air ambulance searching for a patient who didn't exist. He'd wanted to impress the girl.

Beau's cheeks took on a telltale crimson shade.

Conrad butted in. 'Ultimately, hoax calls to the emergency services are a police matter.'

'Is he going to be charged?' Hudson asked before looking at Beau. 'You get a criminal record and it'll follow you around. It'll stump your chances of university, finding a job, everything.' Hudson had no idea whether any of these things were true but the look on Beau's face, the utter fear and regret, told him it didn't matter; saying them was making his son see that actions had consequences.

Hudson didn't know whether to yell some more or cry. Had they done this? Him and Lucinda. Had they been such crappy parents, so wrapped up in their marriage problems, that they hadn't seen their son navigating towards other students at the school who thought things like hoax calls were a way to pass the time, fun, a joke?

Conrad told Hudson, 'Whether this is taken further hasn't been decided. There are ways around it, maybe.' But he told Beau matter-of-factly, 'Hoax calls to the emergency services are a criminal offence. You could face up to six months in jail, a five-thousand-pound fine.' Conrad's chest expanded. Both Beau and Hudson were at his mercy now. 'But... I'm human.' He nudged Beau as if they were mates. 'I know we dick around when we're in our teens, boys will be boys and all that, and we make mistakes.'

Hudson wasn't sure whether *dick* was the sort of word a police detective should be using and he hated the way Conrad said *boys will be boys* as if they were all in a club together. He was acting as if he knew Beau personally too, which was odd. Come to think of it, so was Conrad letting anyone off rather than punishing them to the full extent of the law.

'Your mum will be upset about this,' Conrad went on, again to Beau. Hudson wanted to point out that it wasn't his place to be commenting on their family, but he didn't want Conrad to rescind the offer of perhaps sorting this out without it going further.

Conrad addressed Hudson. 'I have a son too. If this were Isaac, I'd want him to have a chance to redeem himself.'

It was a first to have Conrad being understanding. He couldn't wait to tell Maya that one, although then he'd have to tell her what his son had done. Oh hell, everyone would have to know; he couldn't keep this from them.

'How can I do that?' Beau pleaded. 'I'll do anything; I don't want to go to jail.'

'What do you suggest?' Hudson prompted Conrad, putting the police detective firmly in the driving seat on this one. It wasn't like he had much choice.

'Whatever I suggest might not matter if the official body of the air ambulance decide to press charges. That's out of my hands. But we can take steps to maybe prevent that from happening, if we're smart. Like I said, I've got a son too; I'd want him to have the chance.' He patted Beau on the back reassuringly. That definitely wasn't his place but again, Hudson stayed quiet; he didn't want anything to trigger this police detective into making a different decision entirely.

Hudson suspected the only reason Conrad was really doing this was to get in Maya's good graces. Maybe he was so deluded that he thought she'd hear about what he'd done for Beau and she would go back to him eventually. Some men just never took no for an answer.

'I would suggest a very sincere written apology from Beau here,' said Conrad.

'Done.' Hudson would agree to pretty much anything to help Beau out of this mess. And hopefully, he'd learn from his mistake; the fact that he was here with a police detective had to be scary enough to make him think twice about ever pulling something like this again.

'I could have a word with Maya,' said Conrad. 'I'm sure she'd be open to having help cleaning the helicopter; that's a big job.'

'There are plenty of jobs around here that Beau can do,' said Hudson, 'including cleaning the helicopter. Why don't you let me take it from here? I'll ask Maya or Vik; I know how busy you are in your job.' He'd inflate the guy's ego a bit, anything to make sure he wasn't hanging around any more than he needed to.

Beau's dirty trainers scuffed on the floor as he sat up taller. 'Everyone will hate me here for what I did.'

Hudson was inclined to agree. 'Maybe they will. Go wait in the office for me.'

Beau went off without a word while Hudson stood to see Conrad out of the building.

'He'll hate being here under my watch, believe me,' said Hudson. 'But thank you for bringing him in, for making me a part of the decision about his punishment. You didn't have to do that and I appreciate it.' Why had he done it, really?

'Like I said, boys get in trouble; I certainly did at that age.' Conrad looked over Hudson's shoulder. 'Is Maya around?'

'She's out on a job. Do you need me to pass on a message?'

'No worries, I'll send her a text. We're having dinner.'

Hudson didn't respond to that. They had a son together and now Hudson wasn't with Lucinda, he got it; sometimes, you had to be together for the kids, whether you wanted to share your time or not.

He took a deep breath after he showed Conrad out the door and made his way to the office, where he found Beau, feet up on the desk and lolling in a chair. 'Are you serious?'

Beau had the good grace to sit up properly and remove his feet from the desktop. Just when he thought the kid might be having regrets about what he'd done, he showed the arrogance of someone who clearly wasn't all that sorry.

'Go get a cloth from the kitchen, the disinfectant spray, and clean that surface.'

Beau did it without any backchat, without even looking at his dad again.

Hudson waited, stared out of the window. He stayed there the whole time his son was cleaning the desk surface behind him.

'What's next?' Beau asked with more than a hint of the sulks.

'Seeing as I'm your slave for the next God knows how many days.'

'You can lose the attitude right now.' He sat down. 'Do you realise how lucky you are to have a second chance? How lucky you are that this wasn't any worse?'

Beau slumped down in the chair next to Hudson and this time, kept his feet firmly on the floor.

'I mean it, Beau. A criminal record would ruin things for you; I shouldn't have to point that out. Nor should I have to tell you that your stupidity could've cost lives.'

'I know. Conrad went on about it enough on the way here.'

'Where did he overhear the phone call?' Hudson hadn't thought to ask before.

Beau hesitated before he admitted, 'At Mum's place.'

'Mum's place?'

Beau rolled his eyes.

'Oh, don't tell me... your mother is dating Detective Dickhead?'

Beau laughed and before long, Hudson had joined in, releasing the tension that had built up.

'Detective Dickhead.' Beau nodded his approval. 'I like it.'

'Don't repeat it again.' He wagged his forefinger.

'He's actually the best out of the men she's dated since you split up.'

'There have been others?' He held his hand up straight away. 'You know what, I don't need to know. All I know is that he did the right thing by you. Maybe he does have a heart.'

'What do you think will happen when you tell people here, Dad? About what I was involved in.'

'That information won't come from me. It'll be in the form of your written apology, which you will take your time over before I send it to anyone. It's up to The Skylarks whether they agree to you being let off with a punishment that doesn't involve the police in a more official capacity.'

'Do you think they might want me charged?'

Hudson was a little bit glad to see Beau had panic written all over his face.

'Let's just hope they're as forgiving as possible. In the meantime, let's find you something else to do.'

Hudson led the way to the hangar and found a bucket, some sponges and the car shampoo. 'Fill the bucket with hot water, squirt some shampoo in, and you can start by cleaning the rapid response vehicle outside. After that, I want you in the office working on your apology letter.' Hudson intended to have the letter circulated sooner rather than later. Beau could come here and do his homework instead of hanging out with friends after school and only when Hudson was convinced he'd done his time, and if the crew decided they didn't want to take the matter further, would things go back to normal for him.

Beau said nothing, just got on with the task he'd been given as they heard the helicopter on its approach and The Skylarks came in to land.

Although grateful Conrad had chosen to give Beau a chance to redeem himself, Hudson wasn't sure about having the man in Beau's life, but Beau seemed to think he wasn't that bad. His opinion probably had a great deal to do with how Conrad had dealt with this matter and maybe Conrad had been lenient because he wanted to stay in Lucinda's good books by doing right by her son. Who knew what his motives were. And to be honest, as long as Lucinda kept her commitments with her kids, taught them right from wrong and didn't let them down, who she saw in her personal time was up to her now.

He thought about what else he might be able to get Beau to do after the vehicles. The hangar was forever in need of a sweep

– the doors were open often enough that leaves blew in, dirt accumulated. He could get Beau to pull cabinets out from around the edges and clean behind them. He could also put him on tea and coffee duty, make sure nobody else had to do it. And the reception area had a load of glass that attracted fingerprints like nobody's business, especially when kids visited them at the airbase.

He watched his son get to work on the car outside. Perhaps he should've made sure Beau remembered how to wash a vehicle – he'd done it at home but not for years. Once upon a time, it had been a treat to help his dad clean the car.

Hudson quickly went outside and reminded him that if he dropped the sponge, he was to come inside and wash it in the sink to ensure it hadn't picked up any stones that would be rubbed across the paintwork and leave scratches.

He'd only just gone back into the building when Vik came through from the hangar. He shook his head. 'A terrible job. Kate will give you the report but we all need a big mug of coffee after that one.'

'I'm sorry.'

'Yeah, these jobs are the worst.' But he rallied; they had to when some things were out of their control.

With Vik needing to leave early today, Maya arrived at the airbase to take over from him. 'I'm impressed,' she told Hudson as she came through the front door. 'Isn't that your son out there washing the rapid response vehicle?'

'It is.' Beau was facing away from them, stretching up to wash the roof of the car first, tyres last as Hudson had taught him.

'Earning some extra pocket money?'

'Something like that.'

'I hear Conrad came to see you. He texted me when I was on

the job, just called him back quickly. Isaac is coming down for a visit. Have to communicate, unfortunately.'

He knew that feeling well. 'Conrad told you he talked to me?' He hoped Beau's letter would circulate before the team got wind of what he'd been involved in; he wanted his son to have a chance to apologise first if he could.

'Not the details. You know what he's like; he likes to be the one that knows something when nobody else does. Everything okay?'

'Yeah, everything is fine.'

She went off to the locker room and he came face to face with Kate next as he walked along the corridor. He could see the job had been a tough one just as Vik had said.

'Nothing we could do,' she told him as she put the drugs away in their rightful place.

Brad was similarly out of sorts as Hudson went into the hangar and Nadia was the last to step out of the rear of the helicopter.

'Was it horrific?' he asked her as she came up to him.

But she didn't say a thing.

She looked at him, her whole face took on a different expression and she burst into tears.

16

Nadia felt Hudson's arm around her, felt her legs move as she put one foot in front of the other. They came through the internal door from the hangar, bypassed the office, and went through to reception and the privacy of her own office space.

'Wait here, I'll get you a strong cup of coffee,' she heard him say.

And then the door clicked shut.

She closed her eyes. She'd been there plenty of times as a nurse – felt her own hands on a chest performing compressions knowing it was a desperate and final attempt. She'd seen patients die in front of her, heard that there was nothing else that could be done, been the one to declare the fact.

Hudson was soon back with a hot coffee for her. Despite the pleasant temperature of a warm June day, she felt the need to get some more heat by holding her hands around the mug, even though she knew her shivering wasn't from the cold but from the shock.

'Do you want to talk about what happened out there?' he asked after a while.

She looked up at him. 'It was horrible.'

'I know the patient didn't make it.'

'It was worse than that...' Hudson was a good listener. He needed to be in his job. He was a friend too but right now, she needed to think of him in a professional capacity; it was the only way she'd be able to tell him everything. 'When the call came in, I thought the victim was my sister. I thought it was Monica.'

Hudson pulled the chair on the other side of the desk around so that he was sitting next to her. 'That's why you went out on the job.'

'When I saw the woman on the ground, her hair, it was the same colour as mine, the same as our mother's was. I thought...'

'But it wasn't.'

She shook her head. She'd seen the patient lying on the ground, she'd known the team had done everything they could. And for a split second, before she saw the woman's face, she'd really thought it might be Monica.

'I feel terrible, Hudson.'

'It must have been an enormous shock.'

'No, it's not that. It's because... it's because all I felt when I saw that poor woman properly was relief.'

'That's only natural when you thought it might be your sister.'

'It makes me a monster.' She gasped. 'I haven't even told Archie.' She fumbled on her desk for her phone. 'He was here when I went out with the crew and I said I'd let him know. I didn't even think. He'll be going out of his mind...'

She had the phone clutched against her chest. She couldn't make a move to do what she needed to.

'How about I do it?' Hudson offered.

Nadia felt her mouth open but no words came out. She

found Archie's number, pressed the call button and handed it to Hudson.

It was better that she didn't talk to Archie right now. The whole time she was on board Hilda, on their way to the scene, she'd not only been scared stiff that she was going to find out that it was Monica who needed their help; she was terrified that she'd been the one to do this. Her walking away had led to her sister coming to the country to look for her. Her inability to forgive her sister or Archie for everything that had happened had been the reason Monica was out there somewhere and endangering herself and her baby. Nadia had left her family behind and forged a new life without them in it. And for the very first time, she questioned her own actions.

Hudson made the call, succinct and clear, but Nadia gestured for him to pass the phone before he hung up. Archie would want to know some of the extra information and now that he had the basics, Nadia felt capable of that much.

Her voice shook as she told Archie, 'We believe the girl at the scene was Lena's birth mother.' She listened to his exhale of relief. 'The hospital will confirm it for sure.' She'd heard the paramedics; she'd heard her own crew, their assessments and their observations. But not only that; Brad had found identification, the young woman's purse with a photograph of a baby wrapped in the same blanket Nadia had seen once before on the day Lena was left here at the airbase.

She finished the call. 'It's almost 100 per cent certain that it's her, Hudson.' She felt all of her energy drain out of her. 'Poor Lena, she's lost her mother; we'll never get a chance to reunite them and it breaks my heart.'

He put his hands over hers. 'Mine too. What was the woman's name?'

'Marissa. The police say the driver who hit her told them

she'd just walked out in front of the car; there was no chance to stop.'

He clasped her hand. 'Do you know whether she has family?'

'The police will notify her parents.'

'I'll take this case rather than Paige and I'll start going through the details.'

'Thank you.' She appreciated him taking away some of her workload.

'I'll be on standby once I've gone through the crew's notes and pieced together what happened. They'll likely have questions. I expect there'll be a news segment after police talk to the family; the public will be informed that Lena's mother was found.'

Hudson's words washed over her. She remembered the circumstances of the accident. 'The elderly lady who hit her... she'll be devastated. I could've... I should've...'

'I'll get all the details from Brad and Kate and follow it up. Don't worry, she'll be counselled; she'll get the help she needs.'

'What will happen to Lena?'

'The social workers will handle it all.'

'I need to see her. Lena.' She wasn't sure why. She wasn't family, she never had been, and yet Nadia still felt an inexplicable bond. 'I want to tell the social worker, tell Lena.'

'Okay.'

'You don't think I'm crazy?'

'I think you're a kind, sympathetic human being.'

'I don't feel like it, not today. I leapt onto that helicopter for personal reasons.'

'Hey, anyone else would've done the same. How was the elderly lady? Was she hurt at all?'

'They took her away in the road ambulance; she was standing, talking at the scene so only seems to have minor injuries.' She had another thought. 'Do you think Marissa's remaining family might take custody of Lena?'

'I'm not sure.'

'We need to know the bigger story first. The authorities will need to make sure that it's the right thing to do.'

'One thing at a time.' His hand settled on hers again. 'What's happening with Monica? Have you heard anything more?'

'No, not a thing.'

He waited until she'd had a comforting sip of her coffee. 'Would you like to tell me about your sister? About what happened between you?'

'There's so much to say.'

'So start at the beginning.'

It took her a while to get going.

'I spent the latter years of my childhood in Switzerland – my father was originally from there and always wanted to return so took us all back when I was ten years old. You wouldn't know it from my accent – we lived in an area with other expats, I went to an international school with kids from all over the world, and my parents spoke English at home. Even my dad's accent had faded.'

His understanding and patience encouraged her to continue.

'My father passed away a couple of years after we settled in Switzerland but apart from that, I had a relatively normal upbringing. Mum didn't want to disrupt us and leave; she'd grown to love it there. She never married again but the three of us did okay. It was when we were older, when Monica became a teenager, that things really started to unravel.'

She told Hudson about a lot of the good times but she also recalled the punctuation of the moments along the way that set the path for the remaining chapters of their time as a family.

Monica was four years younger than Nadia and looked up to her older sister. When Monica started high school, she began to have real problems. She struggled in class, she was getting behind with her work, and at home, she seemed to get her way no matter how many times she snapped or broke the rules.

Monica got worse as time went on. The way she spoke to their mother made Nadia wince and the disrespect, the condescension and the sheer selfishness of her younger sister really started to affect her. It made Nadia resent her sister's presence, especially when their mother worried so much about her youngest child that she was regularly unwell – there were doctor visits for stress, pills for this and that, and Nadia was worried something serious might happen. Monica meanwhile just continued to take: their mother's time and energy, their mother's money in the form of extra tuition that she often didn't bother to turn up to. She took their mother's focus and left very little for Nadia, who tried to fade into the background until Monica got herself sorted, except that never seemed to really happen. Her little sister was all about take, take, take and didn't care how she did it or who it affected.

'Mum, you have to talk to her; she's a mess,' Nadia told their mother one night as she helped dry up the dishes after dinner. Monica wasn't back yet, late for curfew again: one of the many things she got away with.

'I don't want her to think we're not there for her, Nadia.'

'She knows you're here, Mum, but she needs to take some responsibility.' It was the most polite way of saying that Monica had been getting away with things for ages – no punishment if she broke curfew, no reprimand for not doing her chores, no threat of stopping tutor sessions if she didn't show up and wasted their mother's money again. 'It's the only thing that will teach her how to be a part of the real world.'

But her mum didn't want to hear it. She changed the subject, the way she always did, and when Monica came home stinking of smoke and couldn't even make polite conversation with anyone, she was allowed to eat her dinner and then take a bath.

'I know you think I'm being too easy on her,' said her mum when it was only Nadia and her again. 'She's really struggled at school and I feel terrible; I should've noticed there was something wrong years ago. I didn't, and I'm her mother. I feel like I neglected her when I should have got her more help.'

Nadia gave her mum a hug. 'You're too hard on yourself.'

But the niceness disappeared when she went upstairs.

'When are you going to start putting some effort in?' Nadia demanded when she cornered her sister outside the bathroom.

Monica pushed past without an answer, with no flicker of guilt that she was making things so hard.

Nadia followed her into her bedroom and her eyes were immediately drawn to her sister's bag, which must have fallen off the bed, its contents spilling out all over the carpet.

'What is that?' But she knew even before she paced over to the bag of weed and picked it up. 'You're fourteen years old!'

'All right, Miss Goody Two Shoes.'

She went to snatch it back but Nadia held it out of reach.

'Give... it... back,' she spat.

Nadia tossed it onto the bed. She would've taken it straight down to her mother if she didn't think it would distress her even more. She would rather Monica found her own way out of this, did some growing up without having to upset everyone else in the process.

'You need to sort yourself out, Monica. Mum is tearing her hair out with you.'

'And what are you, her spokesperson?'

'I don't want to see her unhappy.' She softened. 'I don't want to see you unhappy either.'

'Yeah, right.'

'I don't.' She sat on the bed. 'Is school getting better now you've got some extra help?'

'School is great, Nadia. I'm crap in every subject. It's a total ball.'

'No need to get annoyed with me.'

'You're so bloody perfect! You don't struggle with anything and it's not fair. You sailed through school; you're doing the same at university now. You've no idea what it's like for me, getting behind, not able to catch up.'

'It might help if you turned up to the tutor sessions.'

She swore at Nadia then and Nadia saw red.

'You need to stop blaming everyone else apart from yourself, Monica. Take some responsibility for once!'

Their talk ended with Nadia leaving and receiving a slam of the bedroom door behind her.

Her mum didn't even ask about the row she surely must have heard in the quiet of the house. Voices carried after all. But her mum was mending the hem on Monica's school dress when Nadia went downstairs to sit with her and keep her company watching television. She had study to do, but tonight, she'd stay here a while longer even if her mum didn't want to talk. And she'd made it pretty clear she didn't want to do that – when it came to Monica, their mother wasn't just blinkered; she was blindfolded. Monica could do no wrong and whenever Nadia mentioned anything, she had an explanation, an excuse – Monica had problems and Nadia needed to understand, Nadia shouldn't make this into a drama, Nadia should leave her little sister alone. It was hard not to begrudge those things when her mum said them, when she wasn't the one doing anything wrong.

Monica's behaviour didn't change over the months, nor over the next couple of years as she struggled to finish school. Nadia was relieved every time she returned to university, to a world away, a world that was her own as she continued studying for her nursing degree.

Nadia met Archie during her time studying at university in Zurich and it wasn't long before they became firm friends. One winter, in his quest to see Geneva where Nadia's family lived – he lived in Basel although British too – and because his own family were jetting off to America to share the festive season with his brother who had relocated over there, he made the choice to stay in Switzerland and manage his studies and share Christmas with his friend.

Nadia had taken Archie to spend Christmas at her house.

'It's lovely to have you with us,' her mother told him before she wrapped Nadia in a hug that lasted and lasted.

Nadia and Archie had been to several university parties over the last few days and one last night so had driven to the house that morning. It was good to be here. Over the last few months, Nadia and her mother had talked a lot. The distance now Nadia had moved out had brought them closer with even an apology from her mum at how her attentions had been on Monica when they should've been shared between both of her daughters. Nadia had forgiven her, of course, but she didn't find it so easy to move on from Monica's manipulations over the years. And every time she came home, she could see that their mother was still totally blind to Monica's faults.

Monica was by now eighteen, Nadia twenty-two, and Monica still had no plan of what to do with her life. Well, she did: she wanted a year out from education before she did anything else.

'Where is she going?' Nadia asked as her mum covered the turkey with foil and slotted the roasting tin into the oven.

'Going?' She tugged off her oven gloves and set them on the side.

'On her year out.'

'Oh, I don't think she's planned to go anywhere.'

'Nope, no ideas yet,' came Monica's voice from behind her. 'Hey, sis.'

'Hey.' Nadia smiled. She wasn't going to dig any deeper about the year out; she didn't want any unnecessary tension, especially with Archie as a guest: Archie who was in the bathroom and knew a bit about the sibling rivalry but not all of it. She only hoped a guest might help her sister to behave better. Perhaps this year, she wouldn't be rolling joints in her bedroom thinking they had all lost their sense of smell when the aroma drifted down the stairs.

Monica picked up a piece of carrot from the chopping board and crunched into it but stopped when Archie came through to join them.

Archie had had to duck slightly to get beneath the door frame and Nadia didn't miss it: her sister was enthralled by their house guest.

'I heard you were bringing someone home.' Monica beamed in Archie's direction.

'Monica, this is Archie, my friend.'

'Friend?'

'Yes, friend.'

'With benefits?' Monica asked.

'Monica!' Their mother apologised to Archie and reprimanded her youngest daughter. 'Polite, remember.'

'Oh, I'm joking,' she said but one look in Nadia's direction and Nadia knew she had something up her sleeve; she was plotting something either for now or for later.

Nadia hadn't liked the vibe one little bit and she should have taken it as a warning sign.

As Nadia finished recounting that Christmas in Switzerland to Hudson in the office at the airbase, he asked, 'So, were you – just friends?'

'We were at that point. But soon after we returned to university, we started seeing each other romantically. Both of us were twenty-two, neither of us had dated anyone serious; we were exploring things to see where they went, I guess.

'We were seeing each other for a couple of months when I fell pregnant. We were both shocked, but we didn't have much time to get used to it or tell anyone because I was rushed to hospital one night with bleeding and tummy pains. The pregnancy was ectopic. We lost the baby.'

'I'm so sorry.'

She tried to shrug it off, even though it still hurt emotionally almost as much as it had back then. 'We were so young; I think we both felt as though nature had been trying to tell us something.'

'Still, it was a loss.'

'It was, and it happened again when I was married.' She fought the tears. Two chances to have a baby and both of them snatched away just like that.

'You were married?'

'I was. Not for that long, and then when my marriage broke down, I came here to Whistlestop River and started over yet again.' She smiled. 'I warned you there was a lot to say.'

'I'm still listening.'

'The second time I was pregnant was worse – it was ectopic too and I was lucky to survive. I had a ruptured fallopian tube and severe bleeding.'

'Nadia, I—'

She shook her head. 'Both pregnancies were a long time ago.'

'Doesn't mean the pain isn't still there.'

'When it happened with Archie, I needed him; he was my best friend more than anything else. He stayed with me at the hospital, we managed a bit of a joke that it was on-the-job training; he kept my spirits up.'

And then her mind went back to what happened in the weeks after that.

'Archie and I broke up. I think we both realised that we were friends, nothing more. We'd been through a shitty time but it made our friendship even more solid. At least that's what I thought.

'Archie had a clinical placement near Basel; I had one in Geneva. After my placement finished, I went home to surprise Mum for her birthday. Nobody knew I was coming. Not even Monica, who had been swanning around Switzerland, still not working, still without direction. I got home and the rest is so cliché. Mum wasn't there. The house was quiet but I heard giggling coming from Monica's room. It wasn't unusual. She'd get stoned and laugh to herself – still my mother denied she was taking drugs – but I went upstairs to dump my things. And that was when Monica came out of her bedroom wrapped in a sheet. I could tell she was naked underneath; it wasn't hard to work out that she had someone there. I was about to leave the house, give her half an hour to sort herself out with a stern warning that Mum might be home soon and she should get rid of whoever was in her bedroom, when I caught a look on her face. It was a look of triumph, like the one she'd give me when she got away with something and Mum let her off the hook when really she shouldn't have done.

'The next thing I knew, I was walking towards her bedroom.

I looked in and there was Archie in her bed. I didn't want Archie, not in that way any more, but he was my best friend. With everything we'd been through, too, he was a part of my life that Monica hadn't had a say in up until that moment. Both of them had betrayed me and I lost it. I couldn't handle it. I took off and it was Archie, not Monica, who came running down the stairs.

'I told him to stay the hell away from me. I told him to go back upstairs, put on his clothes and get out before he gave our mother a heart attack when she saw her eighteen-year-old in bed with a man four years older than her. I stayed with a girl-friend that night and for a week after; I didn't want anyone to find me. When I returned to university, I refused to speak to Archie. Monica didn't get in touch, I spoke to Mum on the phone as usual, and then I threw myself into my exams.

'Monica took my best friend,' she said. 'Just like that. She took the one thing I never thought she could.'

A knock at the door was followed by Kate poking her head around the frame.

'You okay?' she asked Nadia. She was likely thinking that her distress was the shock of losing the patient at the scene, the fact it was almost definitely Lena's mother.

'Yeah, I'm good.'

'There's a guy in reception for you.'

Nadia didn't have to ask who it was.

And neither did Hudson.

'Want me to deal with Archie?' he asked when Kate went on her way.

'No... I've got this.'

But before she left, Hudson pulled her close, wrapped her in a hug it took her a while to respond to and she felt herself drift back to the night of the dinner dance, what it had felt like to be in his arms.

'You've got me on your side,' he said before he left her to go and greet her visitor.

17

Hudson hadn't had a chance to ask what had happened with Archie yesterday and Nadia had left for the day without another word about it. She'd wanted to get away and he understood. She'd been through a lot both in her earlier life and lately with Archie showing up and now with her sister missing. If it was him, he wasn't sure he'd still be standing after all that. But she was. She was strong, one of the qualities he admired in her. And now he understood her desire to move on. He still wished she'd told him about her family, but he got what it was like to feel the need to keep some things to yourself.

And today, as much as he wanted to talk to Nadia after she'd opened up to him, and especially now the official confirmation had come through that the young woman who'd died was Lena's mother, he had pressing issues of his own to deal with.

Yesterday, he'd called Lucinda to discuss what had happened with Beau. The call hadn't lasted long; she'd had another meeting. She'd told him they'd talk more later.

And now here she was pulling into one of the spaces at the airbase when Hudson was working and Beau, having finished school for the day, was here again as agreed. Beau had worked on his written apology as soon as he arrived and Hudson would go through it later. In the meantime, Beau was vacuuming the inside of the rapid response vehicle.

'You could've just called me,' he said, opening her car door for her. He'd gone outside to bring in the bag of rubbish Beau had cleared from the vehicle and which was in danger of blowing away: a fact his son hadn't noticed.

She sighed. 'We'd only argue.'

'Why would we argue?'

'You know I'm taking Beau and Carys to see a movie this afternoon and then for dinner. And I knew if I called rather than coming here, you'd insist Beau couldn't go, because he was doing this instead.'

'It's important he learns a lesson.'

'I know that; don't you think I realise this was a close call? It's a good job Conrad heard and not another figure of authority.' She paused, presumably waiting for him to say something about her new boyfriend, but he was keeping his mouth firmly shut. He didn't have the energy, especially when he was at work.

'So, can I take Beau to the movies and for dinner?'

It was on the calendar, prearranged, and he hated it when she forgot a schedule, but things had changed. 'What's that teaching him? That he gets rewarded for doing something wrong?'

'He's been going to school when he should, he's working hard in lessons and he has been working hard here, Hudson. Give him a bit of a break.'

He hated to admit that she had a point. Beau had improved a lot compared to how he'd been behaving since their separation.

She leaned on the top of her car door and watched him

retrieve the bag with the rubbish. 'You can't keep him doing this indefinitely.'

'It's better than a hefty fine or a prison sentence.'

She laughed. 'Bit dramatic.'

'So Conrad didn't tell you what the punishment could be for a hoax call to the emergency services?'

'Of course he did; he was very nice about Beau actually. You should be thanking him. Like I said, it was lucky nobody else—'

'Overheard,' he finished for her. 'So you said.' He went over to the big bin outside the airbase and deposited the bag of rubbish in there. 'I don't want to argue with you.'

She crossed her arms in front of her. 'I've arranged time off to do this, Hudson. I didn't think you'd appreciate me changing the schedule even though Beau is being punished.' Her lips formed that hard line that said they were at an impasse.

'Okay, you're right. He has been working hard. Could you please just make sure they're home by Carys's bedtime?'

'Wouldn't dream of doing anything else,' she said but she was already walking over to Beau.

'I'll get his bag from the locker room,' Hudson mumbled.

He hoped he'd get a chance to talk to Nadia tomorrow but tonight, all he had to look forward to was going home to an empty house and a lonely dinner for one.

* * *

The next day, Hudson waited in reception for Nadia to finish up in her early-morning meeting with the fundraising committee. He'd arranged for them to visit the Wallace family – Marissa's parents, Lena's grandparents. The police had already told Mr and Mrs Wallace the basics of what had happened but the family unsurprisingly had questions; they needed to hear about the medical side and it was part of Hudson's job to be that bridge. Hudson and Nadia had all the information they needed. They'd gathered the facts from Kate and Brad's accounts of what happened; Hudson had interviewed the road paramedics who'd been first on the scene.

'Ready?' she asked when she appeared, bag and raincoat in hand in preparation for the dark clouds outside.

'Ready.'

They were soon on their way to the family's home.

'How did it go with Archie?' He'd been desperate to ask her but hadn't wanted to do it until they were alone.

'The police have found Monica.'

He wished he could take his eyes off the road, give her some sort of comfort. 'Why didn't you say anything?'

'I wanted to but I can see you've got a lot to deal with, with Beau, Lucinda.'

'Doesn't mean I can't fit you in too.' He indicated to take the next turning on the right. Something was wrong; she didn't seem overly happy despite the news her sister had been found. 'What aren't you telling me?'

'The police found Monica, but she told them she was fine and she'd take it from there. Archie has heard nothing from her since.'

'She hasn't been in touch?'

'No. And the police wouldn't tell Archie where she is either. They've done their bit, she's an adult, she's okay and still pregnant. They shared that much. Archie told me she went overdue with Giles so maybe this pregnancy has gone the same way. I think Archie is hoping she'll contact him soon. He's terrified of her going into labour when her head is still in a bad place.'

'He must be in pieces.'

'Yes.'

'And you?'

'I'm okay.'

'Do you want to see her?' he asked. 'I know you two have a complicated history, but you were a mess when you thought it was your sister in the accident. That tells me no matter that you turned your back, you'd at least like to face her now.'

'I don't know. Yes. No. Maybe. I'm not sure how I feel. All I know is that I'm scared she'll do something awful.'

'But she'll know you're both looking for her. Surely she won't do anything drastic when she knows people care so much.'

'I've no idea. I don't know her any more. But if she does something awful, it'll all be my fault. She came here for me, she left her husband and child to find me, because I was so stubborn that I cut all ties.'

'You did it with reason. I understand why.'

She didn't say anything else on the drive to the house and soon they pulled in at the kerb.

They sat in the car for a moment. 'This is going to be horrible.' Nadia tipped her head back against the headrest, looked up and out of the sunroof at the vast expanse of sky beyond. 'I can't imagine what these parents are going through. And here we are to make it even more real.'

'They'll be going through hell, but in my experience, they'll want to know more about the medical side of what happened, what help their daughter had, whether she suffered. It's part of the closure they'll need and sometimes, it can be a comfort even when it's unbelievably painful.'

He took the keys from the ignition but Nadia stopped him before he opened up his door.

'Just another minute here. Before we go in.'

They sat side by side, quietly.

'There's more, you know,' she said, looking across at him.

'More what?'

'More to my story, more to what I told you yesterday.' She turned in her seat so she was facing him. Her eyes had lost their dancing sparkle; her face didn't have the usual glow.

'I not only left Switzerland; I made it so that nobody could find me.'

He smiled kindly. 'I worked that out for myself.'

'Part of me wonders whether that's why I got married to Jock so quickly: so I could become Nadia Sutton rather than Nadia Fischer. My mum had gone, it was just me and Monica, but I couldn't bear to be around her. My own sister. I was grieving and we couldn't even comfort each other. She tried to talk to me, so did Archie, but I walked away. I shut them both down.

'Mum didn't have a lot to leave us and the formalities were sorted out via a solicitor. I couldn't bear any contact with Monica because I was so angry, about the way she was when she was growing up, how she demanded all of Mum's care and attention, the way she'd taken my best friend from me.'

Nadia took a deep breath, blew out her cheeks. With all the revelations, it was easy to forget they were working, here to talk to parents about an event so devastating, those people sitting inside the unassuming house on a beautiful tree-lined street, on what was otherwise a very ordinary overcast June day, would never get over it.

'I never told Monica I'd got married, I still had bank accounts in my maiden name having not changed them over, I did all my contact via a solicitor so it was easy enough. I'd walked away once and I knew I was going to do it again and this time, for good.

'Hudson, I walked away from everything. I never looked back. I didn't think she had either but now I know that she did, once before and again now.' She looked up and out of the sunroof as droplets of rain tapped on the glass and bounced right off again.

'How did you leave it with Archie when he came to the airbase yesterday?'

'I told him I didn't know what else I could do. Monica doesn't want to be found. I told him I had a life to live, a job to do.'

'There's a but in there somewhere.'

'But it's not that simple. When I thought the patient at the scene we attended might be Monica, it was as if my past came at me at full throttle – every moment replayed in front of me, every choice that took me in a different direction. I couldn't bear the thought that the victim could very well be my sister and when I realised it wasn't, the relief almost overwhelmed me. And yet, when I saw Archie at the airbase, all the pain they both caused me was all I could think about.'

'It sounds like you need to let him in a bit, talk to him. It might help you and if it doesn't, then you can move forwards in a different way.'

They sat there a couple of minutes more before Hudson put a hand on Nadia's. 'We should go in. Are you ready?'

'Ready as I'll ever be.'

* * *

The Wallaces were welcoming under the circumstances, their grief was hard to judge when they spoke to Hudson and Nadia, who avoided any look of surprise. They'd both had practice at this, with patients and families, where your opinions and your own emotions had to take a back seat.

'We hadn't seen her for almost a year,' said Mrs Wallace, who'd asked them to call her Jane.

'She hung around with a bad crowd.' Bobby, Marissa's father, wasn't good at making eye contact. Whether it was caused by his sorrow or reluctance to talk to outsiders about his only child, Hudson wasn't sure.

Marissa's bag had been found by the police in the hedge at the side of the road; it must have been thrown there on impact. Inside the bag had been the purse with the photograph of Lena wrapped in the blanket Hudson and Nadia had seen the night the baby was left at the airbase.

'We're happy to answer any questions you may have.' Nadia spoke gently and mainly to Jane because Bobby's face and body language was so closed off. He might well still be in shock; sometimes it took a lot longer than hours or days to process something so monumental.

Hudson addressed both parents, a folder of information on his lap even though he didn't want to bombard them with too much detail. Some families wanted all of it; others wanted very little at all. 'We have the full reports from our crew of the emergency pre-hospital care your daughter received, if you'd like us to go through it.'

Jane's fingers traced the edges of the silver crucifix around her neck. 'Did she suffer?'

'From what we know, it was very quick.' Nadia put a hand on the one that wasn't preoccupied with the crucifix and kept it there while Hudson went through the various steps that the road ambulance paramedics and then the critical care paramedics had performed.

'The police say there was a lot of alcohol in her system.' Jane was by now gripping Nadia's hand. 'Was that true?'

Bobby turned away, looked out of the window.

'Yes, that's correct.'

'And that she walked out in front of a car.' Jane gasped, closed her eyes, gathered herself.

'That's right,' said Nadia.

Bobby still had his back to them when he spoke again. 'Marissa was trouble, big trouble, for years. We didn't know what to do with her. In the end, we fought so much about the way she was living her life – the clubbing, the drinking, the drugs on occasion – that one day, she walked out and never came back.'

'We thought she'd have her time away from us and then come home,' said Jane. 'But a few days went by, a week, a month. It was almost a year since she left and we heard from her twice, when she needed money. We paid it into her account; she sounded in a state both times she called. I begged her to come home... I said that we could fix this. And now we'll never get the chance to make things right.'

Nadia wrapped Jane in a hug, rocked her while she cried.

'I'll never forgive myself,' said Bobby. 'If I hadn't been so stubborn, so angry with her...'

'She had a baby without her mum,' Jane wailed, 'a baby, our grandbaby.'

When things calmed a little, Hudson and Nadia talked about Lena, how well she'd been cared for prior to being left at the airbase, they discussed next steps with the social worker, let the couple know that Hudson would liaise with both parties on that.

By the time Hudson and Nadia left the Wallaces, they were spent. The couple had so much grief, so much blame and regret, and none of it was going to change the fact that their daughter was gone.

'What happens next?' Nadia asked as they did up their seat belts ready to leave. 'You probably said when we were in there, but...'

'It wasn't an easy meeting.' He reached across and gave her hand a squeeze. 'I get that.' He started up the car. 'The social worker will be in touch. Grandparents don't always want custody if they feel they're too old, but Jane and Bobby are only in their very early forties so if they're willing, it makes sense that they want to bring Lena up. Did you see the light in their eyes when they talked about their grandchild?'

Nadia smiled and wiped away a tear. 'Actually, I did; it was a little glimmer of hope in a situation that's so...' She didn't finish; there was no word to sum up what this was, not for anyone concerned.

'They'll be able to let Lena know as much as possible about her mother when the time is right; they'll be able to share the happy times and maybe eventually the struggles.'

They were well on their way when Nadia asked, 'Can we go and visit Lena?'

'Sure. Give the social worker a call, check first, but I'll head in that direction.'

Sybil said that of course it was fine to pop over. They didn't stay long but it was enough for Nadia to have a cuddle with Lena, tell her that they'd met her grandparents and that they were kind, they would look after her if that was what was agreed.

As they drove back to the airbase, Hudson barely got another word out of Nadia.

When they parked up outside, he shared with her his own fears. 'If anything happened to one of my kids... well, it would break me. I'm not sure how you move forwards with something like that.'

'It makes me think about Monica.'

'How so?'

She toyed with her handbag on her lap. 'If I'd had my way, my mum would have been harder on my sister, she would have told her to pull herself together, do better. And Monica might have ended up like Marissa, pregnant and alone, thinking she couldn't stay where she was, that she'd been abandoned by those who were supposed to protect her.'

'Nadia, don't beat yourself up about this.'

'But I left Monica; I abandoned her by running away.'

'No, you didn't. She was your sibling, not your child. Your mum made her choices – and I imagine part of you wanting your mum to tell Monica to pull herself together was because you were trying to protect your mum, not because you wanted harm to come to Monica.'

'I would never wish for that.'

'I don't know your sister and I never knew your mother but it sounds as though Monica played a very big part in making things so terrible that her own sibling left. You can't blame yourself for wanting to live your own life away from all the stress and the drama.'

'Mum never once turned her back on her – there were so many times I wanted her to, but she couldn't see my sister's faults; she couldn't see that Monica was taking advantage. Monica got in trouble at school and I lost count of the times Mum went up there to sort things out, the stress she felt and the tears she thought I couldn't hear behind closed doors. Monica would stay out all night sometimes, then she'd waltz in and hug Mum, say a quick "I'm sorry" and it would all be forgotten. But I saw it wearing my mum down. When I said that to Mum, she denied it, said she was parenting; people did it the world over.

'I wondered sometimes whether I was imagining it, whether I was jealous of my younger sister, but then one day, she got picked up by the police for shoplifting and was brought home in a police car. She was let off, the owner of the shop didn't want to press charges, but she was given a stern warning and not just by the police. My mum got angry that day, it was the most furious

I've ever seen her, and she told Monica that something had to change.'

'And did it?' Hudson asked.

'For a while, yes. I thought that finally, we would go back to being a normal family but Monica couldn't help herself; she ran wild, she didn't play by the rules at all but she stayed just on the right side of the law. The potential arrest for the shoplifting had obviously worried her but she went back to blaming all her problems on her struggles at school, her inability to do as well as everyone else.

'I always knew I was loved, I never felt that I wasn't, but any time I spent with Mum was marred with her sadness and her stress over my sister. On my eighteenth, Monica got completely wasted – I've no idea how she even got alcohol when she was so young and she never told my mum either, but my eighteenth, with friends and a posh afternoon tea Mum had organised, along with Pimm's in the garden in the sunshine, was tainted once I saw Monica come in. She almost knocked over the tiered plates full of sandwiches and Mum ushered her away and into the bathroom. She kept her away from me and my friends but the damage was done. It went on for years – different things and yet the same: Monica not caring about other people, only looking out for herself. I had to leave before all the anger and resentment made me into a person I probably wouldn't have liked very much. Monica was never going to stop taking Mum's time, her energy, her focus, and her money, given she didn't pay anything in the way of rent or living costs. Monica stole from me; that's how I saw it. She stole my relationship with Mum because she was always there, always in the background, always causing chaos. I tried to talk to her over the years before I left but...'

'But then Archie was the final straw. Can't say I blame you for that.'

It had Hudson wondering about Beau. Had his son done all these things since Lucinda left to get their attention? Hudson had his kids living with him, which meant he had work, child-care, everything to do around the house, and sometimes the emotional side of parenting was the thing that got cast aside. He barely had enough energy on some days to get through everything else.

'We'd better get inside.' Nadia waved out of her window at one of the Whistlestop River Freewheelers who pulled in alongside them.

Nadia seemed fine as they made their way into the airbase but Hudson knew that deep down, she wasn't. He only hoped she'd be able to resolve things one way or another with her family.

* * *

When Lucinda dropped the kids home that evening, the first thing Hudson did was get Carys organised for bed but then he went into the kitchen and without asking his son, made him a mug of hot cocoa which he took up to his room along with a stack of four chocolate Hobnobs – his favourite.

Beau had said he'd be studying and he was and even managed a thank you rather than a grunt when Hudson went into his room with the drink and snack. For once, he didn't have his headphones fixed in place over his ears.

'I've read through your apology letter,' Hudson told him. 'It reads well. I'll send it in the morning.'

'Then the shit will really hit the fan.'

Instead of reprimanding him for the language, Hudson

smiled at his son, who had done something stupid but was going some way to making up for it with the letter and all the hard work he'd done at the airbase. 'Let's hope The Skylarks are feeling in a forgiving mood tomorrow. You'll stop by after school?'

'Will it be safe?' A Hobnob hovered uncertainly in his fingers.

'Only time will tell.'

He would keep everything crossed that it would be and that perhaps now might be the start of getting Beau back on the right track.

18

Nadia wasn't sure but perhaps Archie had gone back to Switzerland. She hadn't heard from him in a few days, not since he'd told her that the police had been in touch and that Monica had been located, and that as an adult, now that they had found her and were assured that she was okay, it was up to her to get in touch. The fact that she hadn't shown up here since, given she would likely know by now where Nadia worked if the police had spoken with her, had Nadia thinking this was all another one of Monica's stunts: a plea for attention. And that didn't sit well at all. Nadia had been beating herself up about the way she'd been with her sister over the years, how she'd left and made herself untraceable, and now here was Monica causing trouble again. Except this time, Monica was older, she should be wiser and not only was she taking Nadia's time and energy and giving her worries, she was doing it to her husband and her little boy.

And that was even worse than what she'd done before.

Nadia tried to focus on work instead of her sister. No more letting Monica take things from her; she couldn't do it again. If Monica was going to be a drama queen and not put her own family's minds at ease when she knew they'd be beside themselves, then it reaffirmed that Nadia coming here had been the right thing to do all those years ago... At least that was the mantra she'd try to remember to repeat to herself.

The social worker had facilitated a meeting between Lena and her grandparents and let Hudson know. The Wallaces wanted to welcome their granddaughter into their home permanently but it would still be a process to ensure that it was the right decision. Nadia knew she wouldn't get to be updated every step of the way but it was nice that they knew as much as they did. And she felt a certain sense of closure when it came to Lena; that the abandoned baby she'd held in her arms would face a much more stable future very soon.

When her office phone rang, she hesitated before picking it up. She wasn't sure why, Archie didn't have this number, but ever since she knew Monica had been found, she'd been waiting for contact. She supposed over the coming days and weeks that feeling would fade; she'd adjust and return to the way she'd been before.

She smiled when the caller introduced themselves. Frank had already hinted that Marianne might well get in touch, but he'd said the call had to come from her; he wouldn't interfere. Marianne Mayhan hadn't had an easy time over the years but had managed to get things back on track with her life and her relationship with her sons, and getting involved with the community was another step in the right direction.

'Hello, Marianne, what can I do for you?' Nadia wouldn't let it be known that she'd been expecting the call.

'I'm a bit nervous asking this.' She paused. 'You might not want me. I clean. That's my normal job. But...'

'Marianne, I get the feeling you're calling about the voluntary positions we've advertised on our website?'

'I... I am. Like I said, I clean. But I wanted to get involved. I want to be a part of it. A part of the good work you do there.'

'That's great. I'm sure we can work something out. There are plenty of roles.'

Marianne listened to Nadia elaborate and was keen to get involved with the next fundraising event: the car boot sale to be held next month in the supermarket car park.

'Cars will be arriving any time from 6 a.m.,' said Nadia. 'There'll be a lot of movement with vehicles and people, cars will need to be off the road quickly and out of the way, at their allotted spaces, stalls will need setting up.' She went on to give Marianne the date of the meeting to be held by the fundraising committee and ended the call.

Nadia had just emerged from her office when she saw Conrad climb out of his car in one of the parking bays beyond the glass doors.

She went back into her office, turned and leaned against the closed door, her heart thudding.

Was he here about Monica?

No, he couldn't be. The police had already played their part and the rest was up to her sister. He was probably here to see Maya, or maybe Hudson. She'd heard that Hudson's ex was dating the detective, although what she saw in him, Nadia had no idea. If it was between Conrad and Hudson, there really was no choice; they were like chalk and cheese. One was friendly and kind and loyal; the other was arrogant and full of an inflated sense of self.

She heard a call of hello from beyond her office door. He was in reception.

She went out to face whatever was about to come her way.

'Nadia.' Conrad nodded in acknowledgement before checking his watch. 'Is Maya around?'

She felt able to breathe again. 'We've just had a shift changeover. I'll go and let her know you're here.'

'Appreciate it.'

She remembered Maya saying something about another family dinner. She bet Noah would love that, his girlfriend having to go out with her ex-husband yet again, although knowing Maya, she wouldn't be loving it so much either. But she was a good mum; she'd want to make her son Isaac happy.

Nadia found Maya in the locker room, changing into a pair of jeans and chatting to Noah. 'Conrad's here for you.'

'Thanks.'

'If he gives you any trouble, let me know.' But she grinned. 'Not sure what I can do about it if he does.'

'He won't, he knows his place, but I appreciate you looking out for me.'

Noah pulled a pair of trainers from his locker. 'I heard Hudson's ex is seeing him.'

'Apparently so,' said Nadia.

'Does that worry Hudson?'

'Only with regards to the kids.'

'For all his faults,' said Maya, 'I'm sure he won't make their lives bad in any way. He thinks a lot of himself, but if Lucinda is new and he wants to keep her, he'll go out of his way to make things smooth sailing for them.'

'Wow, sticking up for him,' teased Noah. 'Should I be worried?'

Maya grabbed his hand and pulled him in for a kiss. 'Never. Now, how do I look?'

'You look wonderful,' said Nadia with Noah in full agreement.

'I'm a bit nervous. Isaac just called to say he's bringing a date to dinner this time. I want to make a good impression. He's never brought a girl home before.'

And with another kiss for Noah, who hung back so he didn't have to bump into his other half's ex – never a pleasant experience – Maya left the locker room with Nadia.

After Maya went on her way, Hudson came into reception and handed Nadia a form. 'This is the interfacility transfer request for Brian Henshaw.'

She briefly perused it. 'Thanks, all looks good for tomorrow afternoon.' Mr Henshaw would be transferred from one hospital to another via the air ambulance, his health needs too great for the facility he was at now and transportation being time critical enough to require the involvement of the helicopter.

'Was that Conrad's voice I heard earlier?'

She grinned. 'Can't mistake it, can you? Maya has a dinner with him as Isaac is home and has brought a date.'

Hudson groaned. 'This is the problem with splitting up when you've got kids: you're forever linked. I shouldn't moan about it, Lucinda isn't a bad mum, it's just that...'

'You'd rather move forwards than feel like you're in limbo.'

'Exactly. And imagine if one of the kids gets married some day – if Conrad is still with Lucinda, I'll have to play happy families.'

'I think you're getting a little ahead of yourself given one of yours is only a teenager and the other isn't even at school.'

'You've got a point.' He stopped her before she walked back to her office. 'Nadia, I'm about to press send with an email attachment and I'm terrified what this will mean.'

'Ok-ay... not sure where this is going. Should I worry? Oh gosh, you're not resigning, are you?'

'No, of course not. Although once you and the team read the email, you might well want me to.'

When Noah emerged from the locker room, Hudson went over to talk to him about something and Nadia took the form to her office, wondering what it was that Hudson had in an email that could be so terrible, he looked as though sending it was going to have major repercussions.

She'd only just started to scan in the transfer form for Mr Henshaw to all necessary parties when her phone buzzed. It was Archie.

It wasn't anything new – he asked whether she'd heard anything from Monica, whether the police had been in touch. She typed out the beginnings of a reply, deleted it, typed some more, deleted it again.

And before she had a chance to reply, when he'd probably seen three dots appear, disappear, reappear, disappear again, another text came through from him.

> What will you do if she turns up? Because I need to know.

Nadia left her phone in her office and went into the kitchen to make a coffee. How could she reply to the direct question of what she would do when she had absolutely no idea? What *would* she do if her sister were to knock on the front door right now? If Monica were to be standing the other side of the glass looking at her after all these years, would she and could she turn her back?

In the office once again, her fingers hovered uncertainly over the phone keys.

Eventually, she typed:

> I don't honestly know.

And to that, Archie said nothing.

But then Hudson's email landed and her head was in an entirely different space.

Beau had been responsible for the hoax last summer? Or at least partly responsible? She read and re-read the apology letter from him to the entire crew. He hadn't given up any names but was working here voluntarily to learn and hopefully make up for what he'd been a part of.

Nadia went to the kitchen where she found Hudson who'd just finished talking to Brad after he came back to base from a job. They'd clearly been talking about the same thing.

'Well?' Hudson asked as Brad disappeared to the bathrooms.

'I'm shocked, I admit, but he sounds really sorry. And he did call it in to say it was a prank.'

Hudson's shoulders sagged. 'I think he really does regret being involved. I'd be livid if he didn't. What I need to know... and I can't tell you and the rest of the team what to do, but I need to know whether you're going to take this further. Conrad said it was up to you guys, that he didn't have to make it official unless we... or rather you... all wanted to.'

'What did Noah say?' She knew Noah had a history with hoax calls affecting emergencies, one very close to home, so this wouldn't sit well.

'He was the one I was really worried about. But he's spent a bit of time with Beau, he said he could tell he regretted what he'd done, he said he'd go with what everyone else wanted to do, but to him, Beau was learning his lesson. He suggested I get Beau involved even after he's finished his punishment.'

'What do you think to that?'

'If people give him a chance, I think it's a good idea. The air ambulance is vital to the community both nearby and far away and for Beau to really see that for himself can only be a good thing.'

'I'll talk with the team.'

'Thanks for understanding.'

'Of course.' Her brow creased. 'Wait a minute, is this why you're not freaking out about Conrad and Lucinda?'

He let go of some of the tension he'd been holding. 'Yeah, I suppose so. The guy did right by Beau so even though I don't particularly like him, he's gone up a bit in my estimations. Not sure he'll stay there but...'

'Stranger things have happened,' said Nadia.

* * *

Nadia stayed at the airbase long after Hudson had left for the day and she was still there when Maya came in through the front entrance.

'What on earth are you doing back here?'

'I could ask you the same question,' said Maya. 'It's after nine.'

'Admin. Might as well get it done.'

'I left my running trainers in my locker and I really need them to get out tomorrow morning. I'm training for the half marathon fundraiser in a few months and I have to make sure I fit the practice sessions in.'

'How was dinner?' Nadia asked.

On a deep sigh, she admitted, 'Bearable. Conrad was on his best behaviour to impress Sofie, Isaac's girlfriend.'

'Glad to hear it. What's she like?'

'She's adorable. She was more nervous than I was, the poor thing. I like to think I'm not that terrifying.'

'You're not at all; don't be daft.'

Maya came around to Nadia's side of the desk. She seemed

hesitant before she admitted, 'In the car on the way to the restaurant, Conrad told me something. About your sister.'

Nadia's insides dropped. She'd kept the fact she had a sister quiet from all of them for years, and miraculously, the crew hadn't cottoned on to Giles being related to her because they often got kids coming to visit the airbase. Vik must have kept anything he had heard that day quiet and anyone else who'd been around had probably been too busy to think about who Giles might or might not be related to.

'Why didn't you tell anyone you had a sibling?' Maya said softly.

'It's a really, really long story, not one I really like to share.'

'I apologise.'

'No, please don't. It's nice that you care.'

'I get it, though; families can be a nightmare.'

'Something like that.'

'She hasn't been in touch?'

Nadia shook her head. 'It makes me think this is a game to her, that she wanted drama. Without going into the details, it was the way she was for years before I moved over here. I had to get away in the end.'

'It sounds hard.' Maya paused. 'How are you holding up?'

'It's all been a shock. I think I just need to get back to normal.'

'I'm always here if you need to talk. Maybe we'll have a night out, just the two of us, soon.'

'I'd really like that.'

Maya went to fetch her trainers from the locker room and when she returned, talk changed to Beau and the hoax and how the crew felt about it all.

And as Nadia locked up when she left, she felt a sense of

calm. This was her place, right here in Whistlestop River with The Skylarks, and nobody could take that away from her.

19

'You're doing a great job.' Hudson sipped from his mug of tea as he watched Beau finish sweeping down the side of the airbase building.

Beau put the last of the debris into the garden waste bin as Hilda approached, returning from a job, and stirred up the grass surrounds as she came in to land.

It was a lovely dry June day and finally warm enough for short sleeves outside. It felt good to linger in the sunshine for a while, so Hudson didn't rush to get on. They watched the crew disembark, their faces saying their job had gone well.

What took him by surprise was Beau watching the crew so intently.

'Let me take that.' Hudson took the broom and went to put it away. 'Good job, guys,' he said to Kate and Brad as they came inside the hangar and stowed their helmets on the shelf.

They briefly discussed the patient and the mission and by the time Hudson went out to find Beau, his son was talking intently to Vik as the pilot refuelled Hilda, having dragged across the lengthy hose from the bowser.

Hudson wondered whether they'd exchanged any words about the hoax but if they had, Vik had clearly decided the best way past this was to educate, given the information he was throwing in Beau's direction.

'How fast do you fly?' Beau asked once Vik had finished a spiel about fuel consumption.

'We frequently reach speeds of 150 miles per hour.'

'That's fast.'

'Very. We can cover over two miles every minute. It can mean the difference between life and death for a time-critical patient.'

The fuel continued to sloosh into the aircraft.

'I hear today could've been very different if The Skylarks hadn't been there.' Hudson didn't miss Beau's guilt when he said this – what gave it away was the slight dip of his head as he tried to hide behind his fringe again.

'It would've been catastrophic,' said Vik. 'That man would have had no hope without pre-hospital care.' He had Beau hold the nozzle while he replaced the fuel cap and then dragged the hose back to the bowser.

Beside Hilda, Vik put a hand on Beau's shoulder. 'We all appreciate the written apology you sent. It sounds like you won't ever be a part of anything like that again, am I right?'

Beau shook his head vigorously. 'Never. Unless it's to report someone else doing it.'

'Good. And you've been doing a great job around here; nice to have you on board.'

'It's just a bit of tidying and cleaning.'

'It means nobody else has to do it,' Vik told him. 'It means we can focus on other things. It means we don't have to pay someone either, so we can use the funds for life-saving missions.'

'How much does each mission cost?' Beau asked the pilot.

'Around £3,000.'

Beau's eyes widened. Hudson was pretty sure he'd already told his son facts like this over time but he knew the deal: kids listened to others more than their parents, who they assumed didn't know much at all. The thought tickled him sometimes; other times, it was frustrating.

They left Vik to it and headed inside the hangar where Hudson picked up the empty mug he'd put inside when he took the broom in.

'Everyone is being really nice to me,' said Beau. 'I don't deserve it.'

'You made a mistake, you're sorry; that's what they see. And they're a great bunch here. I'm lucky.'

'Yeah.'

In the kitchen, Hudson put the mug in the dishwasher. 'Your apology went a long way; it was much better to admit to the hoax than have it come out at a later date.'

When Brad came into the kitchen for one of the blueberry muffins Nadia had baked and brought in this morning, Beau asked him whether they'd ever had a mid-air emergency on the helicopter. 'I was going to ask Vik but I forgot.'

Brad bit into his muffin. 'No major emergencies, no – we're lucky, Vik and Maya are two of the best pilots around.'

Beau had umpteen questions about Brad's job – when he'd joined The Skylarks, what they'd been tasked with today, what sort of emergencies they might be faced with.

'Honestly, kid, every day is different.' Brad popped the last morsel of muffin into his mouth. 'That's why I love my job: no time to get bored.'

Hudson watched and listened, gauging his son's interest. He'd never seen him focus so intently unless it was when he was talking about his favourite football team, Chelsea. They talked about ventilating a patient at the scene, transfusing blood, emergency surgical procedures on occasion.

'Did you study for ages?' Beau asked.

'Quite a while but it was all worth it.'

'He has to say that,' said Nadia when she joined them in the kitchen. 'He knows he'll be in trouble with the rest of The Skylarks otherwise.'

When Dorothy appeared in the doorway with the fresh supply of bloods, Beau was still eager to know more and Brad didn't seem to mind the line of questioning at all.

'Come with me,' he said, 'let me show you where we keep these blood products and then I'll show you around the inside of the helicopter, all the equipment in the back.'

'He's kind of in his element.' Nadia smiled at Hudson when the other two left.

'Which one?'

She laughed. 'How's Beau doing?'

'In general, pretty good.'

'You still seem worried.'

'I let things slip. I wasn't there enough for him.'

'You can't keep blaming yourself.'

'Who else can I blame? Lucinda and I did this between us. I'm only glad Carys is so young that she had an initial wobble, but more or less settled into our new normal very quickly.' He sat at the table.

Nadia sat down opposite. 'My mum struggled to parent two of us equally, at least from my point of view. But she did try her very best; I never doubted that. She just had no more of herself to give. From what I know about you, Hudson, you seem to have done as much as you could.'

'You have a high opinion of me.'

'I do.' She looked away after the admission, went over to the bench near the sink and brought back the plastic container of muffins. 'These are not a cure-all, but they might help a little.'

'I suppose I could give it a go.' He reached for one and after a few bites, he did feel better, not because of the muffin – although he couldn't deny it was tasty – but rather that Nadia understood where he was coming from. And being in her company always made a situation feel that much lighter.

'Do you think that if your mum had had time for you then you and Monica may have got on better?'

'Not if my sister had behaved the same way; I couldn't stand it. But maybe if Mum had been tougher, who knows, Monica may have made different choices.'

'Hindsight is a wonderful thing.'

'Sure is.' She shook her head when he tried to persuade her she needed a muffin too. 'I've already had two.'

Beau and Brad's chatter and laughter drifted in through the open kitchen window as they emerged from the hangar and strode over to the helipad.

Nadia turned back to face him. 'Beau is a great kid. From what you've told me and from what I've seen, he has nowhere near the issues Monica had, and you're recognising the need to help him now. You made him accountable by having him write the letter of apology and work around the airbase. Mum could've taken my sister back to the shop she stole from, made her do the same. She could've made her accountable for any number of things, but she didn't; she couldn't bear to make things any harder.'

'I didn't enjoy having to punish him,' said Hudson, 'but I know it's way better than the alternative.'

'Who would've thought Conrad might have helped some-one, gone easy on them?'

'Not me, that's for sure.'

'Beau seems to be loving his time here, despite the work you're making him do.'

'He is, and I don't mind telling you that that was unexpected – at first, I thought he'd moan every minute he was here, but slowly I think he started taking it in, and somewhere along the line, he got really interested. For years, I've been telling him about The Skylarks and the airbase and everything that goes on here, but he never really wanted to listen. Until now.'

'Maybe it's a bit like schoolwork – not all kids learn well in the classroom; sometimes taking them outside and having them see things for real can make the difference.'

'He said that he'd like to carry on volunteering. Although he added the caveat that he wouldn't want to be here quite so often and do quite so much scrubbing.'

'There's plenty we can involve him in. Actually, I need someone to hold a collection pot outside the supermarket on Thursday, late afternoon, for an hour to give the volunteer I have down a break. Do you think he'd do it?'

'Would you ask him? It'll sound better coming from you.'

'Of course.' She looked across at him. 'Do you think he'll ever say who the other kids who were part of the hoax were?'

Hudson shook his head. 'He says they'll make his life a misery at school if he does.'

'Poor kid. Taking all the responsibility rather than sharing it by telling us who else was involved. You've raised a good boy there.'

He sat back, let out a long breath. 'Parenting is the toughest job I've ever had. I'm not sure I'm going survive it, if I'm honest.'

'You're doing better than you think.'

He waited a beat. 'Any word from Monica?'

She shook her head. 'I'm trying to return to normal.'

'But you can't. You know that, don't you?'

'I do.'

'Do you think she'll show up here?'

'I'm not sure.' Nadia frowned. 'I don't understand why she didn't come out of hiding when she knew Archie was here looking for her.'

'You think this is all a game?'

'It wouldn't be the first time.'

'Maybe it's like Archie says: her head isn't in a good place.'

'I always thought that was an excuse before, when we were younger, but he says she's changed.'

'You don't believe him?'

'I don't know. I want to.' She put the container of muffins back on the bench. 'I'm confused all the time, Hudson. At first, when Archie showed up, I wanted him to turn back the way he'd come and leave me alone. Even when I saw Giles, my head wouldn't let my heart make the rules. I'd left that world behind, that part of me; I'd made a new life.'

'But you can't ignore it. They're your family.'

'I keep thinking of Monica, pregnant, out there somewhere perhaps not knowing what to do. I hope it's not a game to her, I really do.'

'So do I.'

'I wondered whether she might head back home to Switzerland without trying to contact me, once she knew Archie was looking for her.'

'Tail between her legs, you mean?'

'Something like that.' She made a groan of frustration. 'These are all theories because I don't know her. Not any more. I thought I did, I assumed she was that same person doing the same things she always had, but it's finally dawning on me that with a couple of decades between then and now, I don't know my own sister at all.' She sat back down. 'Do you think I've pushed Archie away so much that he won't let me know when she does get in touch?'

Hudson shook his head. 'From what I've heard, he'll be letting you know and then leave it up to you where to go from there. There's so much history between you all; I think he's a husband, a father, doing what he can and what he thinks is best for his family.'

'You think I should get in touch?'

'It might help you as much as him.'

She took out her phone. 'You know what, I think you might be right.'

'You're going to call him?'

She took a deep breath. 'Yes. If anything, I need the closure, now more than ever before.'

She smiled nervously at Hudson before she left the kitchen and Beau came back in, talking animatedly about the inside of the helicopter.

20

Nadia was a bag of nerves as she waited at the bench overlooking Whistlestop River. She'd got a coffee and there was a playground nearby where Giles would be able to run off some energy while she spoke to Archie. Yesterday when she'd made contact, she'd half expected to have missed her chance. She'd thought perhaps he'd already be back in Switzerland, or at least be on his way, but he was still here in Dorset, which spoke volumes about how much he loved her sister and his family. It also made her realise the hell he'd been going through these past weeks, the emotional turmoil he had to be feeling with Monica still not in contact. She'd focused so much on her own feelings and pushing the past away that she hadn't been able to be a sympathetic ear for anyone. And for that, she was ashamed. At work, she gave it her all, the personal touch, she was a good listener, she advised and counselled. But she couldn't seem to do it with her own family.

'Nadia!' Giles ran over to her at the bench, arms out like he was pretending to be an airplane. Nadia could do nothing else other than embrace him in a hello hug.

'He's been cooped up in our Airbnb all morning given the rain.' Archie was carrying a cardboard tray with three drinks pushed into the sections.

'Can I go?' Giles had already lost interest in the adults with a roundabout, swings, a seesaw and a climbing frame in sight instead.

'Off you go,' said Archie. 'I can watch from here.'

Giles charged over to the climbing frame first.

'I'm glad you called, Nadia.' Archie noted the coffee cup already in her hands. 'However, this was my peace offering, and you've kind of ruined it now.' He was just like the Archie she'd met at university, the Archie she'd hung out with in cosy cafés in Zurich, the Archie she'd studied with and quizzed, him returning the favour, each ensuring that both their brains were packed full of knowledge.

'I've finished this one already.' She slotted her empty cup into the vacant hole on the cardboard tray and he indicated which was hers. She looked at the third cup. 'Giles drinking coffee already?'

'Not quite. The third one is a juice. But he wanted it in a coffee cup like us with the lid with the spout.'

'Ah, I see.' She sipped the fresh coffee. 'That's good. Even better than the first.'

'You always did like your coffee.'

She smiled. 'Have you heard anything from Monica?'

'Nothing. And I don't know what to do. I thought she would've made contact by now. I try and tell myself that she knows we're close by, Giles and me, that we are her family and we love her. But it's eating me up inside that she hasn't reached out. Just a text would do. Anything.'

Nadia watched Giles when he called out from his position at the top of the climbing frame with an, 'I'm the king of the castle!'

She turned back to Archie. 'You must feel helpless. How are you explaining this to Giles?'

'I've explained his mum has a few things she needs to work out, I've turned this into a bit of a holiday, more of a trip to see his auntie. He seems to have accepted it. I don't want to upset him unnecessarily, you know.'

'I think it was the right thing to do. No point having him worry too; you're doing enough of that yourself.'

He nursed his coffee cup in his hands. 'Thank you for getting in touch again. It makes my reasoning with Giles more plausible for a start.'

'Glad I helped. Does he want to go home? Is he missing the familiarity?'

'He's all right at the moment, distraction is working, a new auntie, new surrounds, but I'm going to have to think about it soon. I toyed with the idea of leaving him with a friend back in Switzerland but I thought if Monica was to know he was here too, she might be more likely to come to us. If she gets in touch, I'll get him on the phone; he needs to hear his mother's voice and I think she needs to hear his too.'

'Apart from coming to England when I first left Switzerland, has she ever done anything like this before?'

'Gone off somewhere?' He took a welcome sip of coffee. 'No.'

'What happened that first time?'

'When your mum died, it hit her hard and more so because she knew she'd lost any kind of relationship with you. She became desperate to make amends, she felt totally cut off. I wanted to come to Dorset with her, help her find you, but I couldn't; I'd landed a really good job and I knew her search was a long shot. I also knew I couldn't stop her and so she came over by herself. After a few weeks, when she couldn't find you, she returned home to Switzerland, devastated, her head all over the place. She pushed me away at first; she thought she didn't deserve me because of what she'd done. She knew she'd driven a wedge between me and my friend and that just added to everything else. She knew she'd got away with a lot when she was younger; she told me sometimes, she wished your mum had been harder on her: perhaps it would've helped her grow up a bit. But she never did and so it was left to you to tell her to pull herself together and she never took that well.

'She was so disappointed that she couldn't get in touch with you to invite you to the wedding – she didn't have her sister, she didn't have her mum, she didn't have her dad to walk her down the aisle, and a wedding day without any of her own family was almost too much for her to bear. The day was still wonderful, but it was tinged with a sadness I'm not sure even I could make up for. She told everyone that you were working in England and couldn't get time off, that it was an important step in your career.'

'People must have thought I was terrible. Not coming to my own sister's wedding.'

'Actually, they didn't. Monica made sure people knew you had a great job nursing, that your skills were very much in demand, that taking time off wasn't an option and that you'd celebrate with her when you were next home. I think she even believed what she was saying half the time. She was proud of you.'

'I didn't think—'

'That she cared so much? Of course she did. She idolised you. It might not have seemed that way, but she really did. I'm not a psychologist but from what she's said over the years, that was part of the reason she was always in trouble. She longed to be like you, to be approved of by you, but she knew she wasn't.'

'How did you two even get together? I never asked.'

'Right place, right time, I guess. You might see it as wrong place, wrong time, but I fell in love so quickly with your sister. It was about a month after you and I split up. On a tram in Zurich. She was travelling around and she got on board with the biggest bag of chocolate you've ever seen.' He smiled at the memory. 'We went for coffee, a walk, and we saw each other the day after, then the day after that. At first, I thought she was using me to get one up on you but I soon realised she wasn't. She was different to the girl I'd seen at your house that Christmas, the girl you'd told me about so many times. Away from home, on her own, she seemed to have grown up a lot. She still had all this energy but she put it into things like hiking, bike rides, outdoor swimming.'

'That sounds nothing like Monica.'

His expression said it all: this was the woman he'd fallen in love with, not the woman Nadia remembered.

'She's changed a lot. She had time travelling – she went to every place in Switzerland she could think of, then after your mum passed away and you left, just when I thought she might never pick herself up, she did. She got a job in hospitality working at one of the nicest hotels I've been to, she worked hard, and we were happy. But she never lost the regret for hurting you.'

'When you talk about her, I don't recognise my own sister.'

'That's why I'm telling you all these things. She's a good wife, a wonderful mother. She's a hard worker, she volunteers at a local school helping kids learn to read, and she never gave up hope of seeing you again.'

Nadia tried to absorb everything he was saying. 'Then why hasn't she come forward?'

'I don't know. I wonder if she's scared too: scared you'll tell her to get lost. If only she'd call, I could talk to her, make her realise that you might want to see her as much as she wants to see you?'

It was a question, not a statement.

'I don't know, Archie. It took me time to be happy again. Her taking you from me was the worst – I mean, losing a part of my relationship with Mum because Mum had so much to deal with when it came to Monica was bad enough, but you were the one person I never thought I'd be without. You were something I thought she couldn't take from me.'

'Six months after you caught us together at your mum's place, Monica really broke down over it all. She didn't seem too distraught at first but over time, as I got to know her and her barriers came down with me, I could see how much it had affected her.'

It was a comfort to know that something so major for Nadia hadn't been just a joke to her sister – that was how Nadia had felt and it had given her a pain she couldn't tolerate, an urge to get away that she couldn't ignore.

'I'm glad you found each other, Archie.'

'Really?'

'In an odd way, yes. I didn't see it, not until now, now you're here. Seeing you worry and the fact you're doing everything you can for Monica shows me that it wasn't for nothing. I just hope she does the same for you in return, that this isn't a game for my sister.'

'I swear, if I thought that, I wouldn't even be here.'

They watched Giles for a while until Nadia admitted, 'I'm happy in Whistlestop River, Archie, have been for years, but in the moments I've let myself, I've wondered whether things could've been different.'

'That's human nature. The *what if?* question.'

'Do you ever...'

'Think about us?'

'Well, yes. I mean, there was a baby.'

'I've never forgotten what happened, Nadia. Never.'

'Did you tell Monica?'

'I had to. I wanted to be honest with her from the start and I expected the same in return.'

'Did she care?'

'Of course she cared. But she also knew you wouldn't want her to try talking to you about it.'

'No, I wouldn't have wanted that.' She would've closed the door in her face, physically and metaphorically.

'She did care,' he said. 'I can promise you that. She asked whether I wanted to walk away, said she'd understand if I did because of my friendship and history with you. I'm sorry, Nadia, but I didn't want that. I'd fallen for her by then, I couldn't imagine not having her in my life.'

She looked over at Giles, who leapt off the climbing frame and came barrelling over. Archie handed him his juice without even asking whether he wanted it. He downed it in a few big, thirsty gulps.

'You want some time with your iPad?' Archie asked his son.

But Giles was already running away back to the playground.

Archie smiled. 'I guess that's a no.'

'He's a lovely little boy. And look…'

Another boy about Giles's age had arrived and already he and Giles were racing together around the base of the climbing frame.

'He is, and Monica adores him, which makes this so hard because I'm starting to wonder how she can stay away from him for so long. But if her head is in a similar space as it was when she came back from England last time then perhaps she's not thinking straight at all.'

'Do you think she'd do anything that might put the baby at risk?'

'Apart from travelling over six hundred miles so close to her due date, you mean? No.'

Giles's giggles had them both grinning as they turned to watch him and the other little boy on either end of the seesaw, sending it high enough in the sky that their little bottoms came off the seat each time it was their turn to go up.

'I'm going to have to go back home to Switzerland soon,' said Archie. 'I have work. I just hope she gets in touch with me before that but I can't stay on indefinitely, much as I'd like to.' He turned on the bench to face her. 'I'm sorry about everything, you know. I'm sorry about the way things were in Switzerland and that you felt you had to leave.'

She looked him right in the eye. 'I don't regret it. That might sound harsh but I don't.'

'I understand why you left and Monica does too.'

'You've turned into a wonderful man, Archie. You seem a good husband and father.'

He smiled but before he could reply, his phone rang and when he pulled it from his pocket and answered, his face said it all.

The call was from Monica.

He put it on loudspeaker because he was struggling to hear her.

And hearing Monica's voice after all these years had emotions pinging all over the place for Nadia. It was joyous, painful, hopeful, scary.

'I'm sorry... didn't call earlier.' Her call kept breaking up.

'It's fine. You're calling now,' said Archie. 'Where are you?' He had the phone right close to him, still struggling to hear with the bad connection.

'Outside,' the word came eventually.

'Outside where?'

Nadia looked at Archie; she swore Monica just said, 'Your place.'

Archie must've thought the same. 'You're back in Switzerland?'

It sounded like they'd lost the call, but then came the word, 'Dorset.'

'Where exactly are you?' Archie asked.

The connection seemed to be hanging in there.

'I'm outside the address the police gave me,' said Monica, 'but you and Giles aren't here. Archie...' The unmistakable sound of crying came down the line. 'I shouldn't have come. I want to go home. I've caused so much trouble.'

'You haven't; I'm just glad you called.' Tears welled in his eyes.

'I need you,' Monica sobbed. 'I need Giles. I left you, him, I shouldn't have.'

And now Nadia felt like she was intruding in this conversation by listening in.

'Don't apologise, we just want you to be okay,' said Archie. 'Don't panic. Monica...'

No answer.

'Monica,' Archie said repeatedly until he got a response.

'The baby...' Her voice didn't sound right, it was contorted as if each word was hard to get out.

Nadia waved Giles over but he wasn't budging; he was happy with his new friend. She was about to go over and get him when she heard Monica cry out.

She turned to see Archie's panic and heard her sister wail even louder. 'The baby... I think it's coming!'

21

Hudson admired Nadia for having the guts to call Archie. With everything she'd told him, it couldn't have been easy. But it had helped Hudson do what he needed to do after he picked Beau up from his stint with the collection pot outside the supermarket.

'Is that Mum's car?' Beau asked when they pulled up in the driveway at home.

'It is. She's been waiting with Carys.'

If Nadia could take steps to face up to things, then so could he. And it was about time he and Lucinda represented more of a united front. The snippy remarks, the conflict, it all had to stop, at least in front of the kids. They were both guilty of doing it. He'd called her earlier to ask her to come over so they could talk to Beau together, show that from this moment on, they were still a family, just one that didn't look the same as before. He'd reminded her that it couldn't always be him playing bad cop and her good cop; sometimes, she'd have to lay down the rules too even if it meant an argument with her son and, in years to come, her daughter. When they first split up, he hadn't minded being the disciplinarian, it had made him feel more in control, like he knew what was going on, but for Beau's sake especially, that had to change. He actually hadn't expected to get through to her so easily on the phone call, he'd expected her to say he was being dramatic, but she'd agreed that yes, they did need to do something and that she would come over.

Perhaps pillow talk with Conrad had told her how much trouble Beau could've been in, perhaps her parents had spoken with her because he'd told them about Beau and what had been going on on the phone a couple of nights ago. Whatever had changed, whatever reason she was here now, it was a good thing as far as Hudson was concerned.

He let himself and Beau into the house and he could tell from the sounds that Lucinda and Carys must be in the kitchen. 'You can hit the shower first if you like; I know you didn't get a chance this morning.'

'Thanks, Dad.'

And it would give Hudson a chance to make sure he and Lucinda worked together on this. What Hudson wanted most of all out of today was for Beau to realise that a part of his world might have wobbled but it certainly hadn't ended just because his parents' marriage did.

'Where's Beau?' Lucinda was at the sink rinsing out the yoghurt tub Carys had clearly devoured the contents of – some of it was in her hair.

'Taking a shower.' He gave his daughter a kiss on the top of her head. 'He's had a stint standing outside the supermarket with a collection pot; thought he could use a bit of time before we all talk.'

She dropped the yoghurt pot into the recycling tub in the cupboard below the sink. 'I have told him my thoughts on what he did, you know.'

'I know, but I think hearing it from us both at the same time will help him to see that even though we're not together, we're both very much there for him.' He'd gone over and over in his head the best thing to say so she didn't get annoyed and assume he was picking fault. The last thing any of them needed was a full-scale row to raise the tension around here.

But it seemed he'd been a bit too optimistic.

'You're too strict with him.' Lucinda placed a couple of crackers on the tray of Carys's highchair.

'He could've got a fine, a criminal record.'

'I don't mean with the hoax and his punishments, but you're too strict with the rest of the rules. If we're representing a united front, then I get an opinion. Which brings me to another point – can you please try not to show your frustrations with me so much in front of the kids?'

He was about to argue back but she was right; he did do that. 'Okay, I'll make a concerted effort. I promise.'

'Thank you.'

'What else do you think I'm too strict with?'

'There are rules about homework, seeing his friends, bedtime. He's fifteen; it's no wonder he's rebelling.'

He tried to keep his head; Beau would be down any second. She seemed to be doing her best to cause more upset, despite only just asking him to ease off on any of his criticisms. That would be hard to do if she was going to behave like this.

'He needs rules, Lucinda. He needs boundaries. It'll help shape him into a human being who considers others, who manages his time, who's a pleasure to be around. He already is but rules and ways to behave are there to help him. And you're right, he's fifteen. Fifteen is no age at all. He's still young, still finding his way.'

'He needs to be a teenager.'

'And I'm not stopping him.'

She'd be less combative if she wasn't standing there like she could make a run for it at any moment. 'Would you please sit down?' He gestured to the chair after Carys let him wipe her face, her hair, and her fingers once she'd finished the crackers. He took her out of the highchair and she toddled off along the hallway to pick up her doll, which she merrily brought back to the kitchen to put in the toy highchair. It looked like dolly was going to get some food now.

'For what it's worth, Hudson,' Lucinda said with a sigh after running her hand over Carys's angelic hair, 'I do think, on the whole, you're doing a great job.'

She'd meant it as a compliment but he wasn't sure he could take it as such. 'It's not a job.'

'It's a word. Don't be so paranoid. You're a good dad, whatever phrase gets through to you. I'm not criticising your abilities and I wish you wouldn't criticise mine.'

'We need to treat him the same. We can't have one of us with rules, the other with none at all.' When she opened her mouth to object, she soon closed it again as if finally, he was getting his point across. 'I'm not saying my way is perfect, but otherwise he's going to be all over the place; he won't know what's what.'

She took a seat and it was a while before she said, 'Conrad regrets he hasn't tried harder to get close to Isaac.'

He was surprised at that. From what Maya had said, her ex-husband wouldn't be told when it came to their son; he always thought he was right. 'He still sees him, though?'

'He does but he knows things between them could be better.' Head hung, she surprised him with an admission. 'I want my kids to like me. That's why sometimes I let them do different things; it's why I throw the rules out of the window occasionally.'

'Sometimes, I want to do the same, but it won't help them in the long run.'

It was a while before she asked, 'How's it going with The Skylarks? Are they okay around Beau or are they angry?'

'They've all taken it really well. The written apology was sincere, and I think seeing him helping out around the airbase, without that teenage chip on his shoulder that he sometimes has, showed them all his regret. I was worried someone would want to take it further, but so far, they've all accepted the apology. And you know what, I think Beau has actually been enjoying his time there.'

'He said as much to me.'

'Yeah?' He took a tea cup from Carys, who had given one to Lucinda, one to dolly and now one to him. He pretended to sip from the cup.

Beau's footfall had Lucinda and Hudson look at each other and when their eldest son came into the room, Hudson pulled out a chair for him.

'How was the collection at the supermarket?' Lucinda asked when it seemed their son had nothing to say.

'All right.' Eyes on the table, he slumped in the chair in typical teenage fashion with legs outstretched and face hidden somewhere beneath his fringe.

'Raise much money?' Hudson put in.

'You already asked me that.'

'I haven't,' said Lucinda.

'I don't know, the money goes into the slot, I don't count it.'

'Watch the tone,' Lucinda warned and she looked up, surprised, but Hudson kept a blank expression because he was taken aback by her supportive remark too.

'It seems your apology letter was received well,' Lucinda

began. 'We are really proud of you for taking ownership of the hoax that you were a part of.'

Hudson opened his mouth to ask again who his comrades had been but then he closed it, kept the focus on the reason they were here.

'I like being at the airbase,' Beau confessed. 'They're all really nice, too nice, when they don't need to be.'

'It's part of the job description a lot of the time.' Hudson smiled. 'But you're right, they are.'

'I'm proud of that too,' said Lucinda, 'that you're helping out to make up for what you and the others did.'

Hudson had done most of the hard yards with parenting up until now – the parent evenings, minding the kids when they weren't well, doing the school run every morning and pick-ups from childcare or after-school care. When Carys went through a stage of colouring on the wooden floorboards, it had been Hudson who cleaned it all up and told her off in a firm but gentle way when she was so young. When Beau got into a fight outside school a couple of days after Lucinda walked out, it had been up to Hudson to teach him that no matter what his frustrations, no matter how much someone wound him up, using his fists wasn't the answer. Carys had gone through a biting phase a few months ago and it had been Hudson who went up to meet with the other parent at childcare and apologise. It wasn't that Lucinda didn't care, but Hudson's job, his proximity to his kids made it easier for him to deal with these things. He didn't begrudge her her successful career, but it wasn't up to him to convince the kids of her love for them; it was up to Lucinda to show them both how she felt. And if she didn't, he'd have to be here to catch them from every disappointment, every let-down she was responsible for. He just hoped it wouldn't come to that.

'I didn't realise how much money it cost to send the helicopter on a mission.' Beau started talking unexpectedly, although he still wasn't looking up from beneath that fringe. 'I feel bad about it.'

'Not so bad that you'll tell anyone who the other lads involved were?' Lucinda asked.

'No way, Mum. I told you, I don't want to be a grass.'

'Don't be ridiculous, just tell us who they were,' she went on. 'I've a good mind to go up to that school and ask around – you hang out with Simon and Gareth still; was it them? Beau, tell us.'

'No!'

'Beau, you have to.'

This was spiralling out of control. It had been going so well, but when Lucinda kept asking him, Hudson knew what was going to happen even before Beau pushed out his chair and stomped off with calls from Lucinda of, 'Don't you dare walk away from me,' and, 'Come back here right now!'

She turned her venom towards Hudson. 'That is not okay, you know, to walk away when we're having a family discussion. Are you going to get him back down here? Or am I?'

'Well, at least you're playing bad cop for once,' he said.

'It's what you wanted!'

She had no idea of the difference, did she? That you could be bad cop without blowing the situation up, resolving nothing.

'Maybe we should try this again another time,' he suggested.

'Or maybe we just accept it is what it is, or rather what we are. Divorced. And Beau is going to have to adapt.'

He should've known this wouldn't work and he was tired of arguing about it. He'd done his best.

He waited for Lucinda to hug Carys goodbye and then after she'd picked up her bags and gone out of the front door, he felt the tension dissipate from himself and the house too.

Hudson had intended to give Beau a chance to calm down

before he went up to knock on his door but Beau came down-stairs of his own accord soon after his mum left.

Carys ran over to him and he scooped her up.

'It's past her bedtime,' said Hudson. She was rubbing at her eyes as she leant against her brother's chest and nuzzled into his neck.

Beau sat down, Carys still on his lap. 'Mum left?'

'You know she did or you wouldn't have come down.'

He tried but failed to hide the little turn up at the corners of his mouth.

As Carys leaned against her brother, her eyes almost closed by now, Beau blurted out, 'I was part of the prank because I wanted to get back at you.'

'Get back at me?'

'You were never here. All of a sudden, you'd gone back to working all the time, Mum left, I was angry. Like all the time.'

'I know you were. And I understand why.' And now it felt good that his son was finally being honest and telling him how he really felt. 'I had no choice though, Beau. I upped my hours because I had to. Running a household and raising kids is expensive and it'll only get more so as you two get older. There are always things to pay for – school excursions for you, uniforms, playgroups, childcare. It'll be driving lessons for you soon enough, then university if that's what you decide. And we'll have to do it all over again for Carys. Don't get me wrong, me and your mother want to do those things, but it's hard to do when you live separately and your mum isn't responsible for me. I have to earn my own money for the things that I need, or things that I might want.'

'Mum always loved her job more than us.' Beau, if it were possible, held Carys a little tighter, although Hudson suspected that was only in his imagination. 'It made me feel as if the same would eventually happen with you.'

'What? No way. Never, Beau. I promise. And also, it isn't true to say your mum loves her job more than you. She does love her work, yes, and she's always been career driven. You might not see it but if she really did love the job more than you and your sister then she'd never be here; she would've walked out and not looked back. I'd have let her too.

'You know I felt like the luckiest dad alive when I got to stay home with you guys so much as your mum was happy to work. I'm not blowing my own trumpet here but parenting came more naturally to me than it did to Lucinda. So we agreed, she would work, I would be your primary carer. She does try, though; do you see that?'

Beau nodded. 'I miss the time we used to spend together.'

'You and your mum?'

'Me and you.'

'We spend a lot of time together.'

'I don't mean at home.'

It didn't take long to realise what he meant. 'You're talking about the camping and the fishing trips.'

'Yeah, I miss those.'

'They were fun.' Hudson couldn't believe he hadn't seen it before, that somehow those trips had dwindled away, the memories becoming just that: memories, the past. And over time, he'd got so busy, he hadn't even thought about doing it again.

'I couldn't understand why we didn't go. I knew you had work, but I thought if Mum could take Carys on a weekend, we'd still do it. But we never did.'

Hudson watched his son. 'The divorce didn't just affect your mother and me; I'm realising just how much it affected you and for that, I'm sorry.'

'Someone once told me that an apology could go a long way.' Beau began to smile and Hudson laughed.

'Someone very wise?'

'Old and wise.'

'Cheek.' Hudson had missed the banter between them. But it wasn't too late to see the young boy hidden behind a lot of anger and fear at the world around him changing. 'After your mum and I separated, life kind of spun around for a while and all I could focus on was survival, getting money in the bank and food on the table, making sure you two were all right.'

Beau shrugged. 'It's okay.'

'No, it isn't.' But he did have an idea. 'Your gran and grandad wanted to have you kids over for a barbecue tomorrow straight from school seeing as it's Friday. They're making those burgers you like with the homemade relish.'

'Cool.' Deflated, he added, 'But I can't go as we're supposed to be at the airbase.'

'You're right, we are supposed to be there. But... do me a favour?' He put his arms out to take Carys. 'I'm going to put Carys to bed and while I do that, could you go out to the garage, find the tent, open it up in the back garden and we'll check it. I'm pretty sure it's ready to go but it's always good to be sure.'

Confusion gave way to a smile. 'You mean...'

'Yeah. You can barbecue another time; your grandparents won't mind. They'll get Carys all to themselves, and you and me? We're going camping. I'll call your grandparents, see if they mind taking Carys and we can leave early evening.'

He hadn't seen Beau smile quite so much or move quite so fast since he'd been asking Brad all about the air ambulance.

And the feeling Hudson had right now was priceless.

22

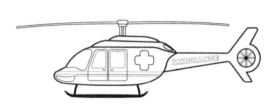

Having not seen her sister for two decades, Nadia always thought that if the time came, she'd be hesitant; it would be a case of forcing herself to put one foot in front of the other to go to see her wherever she was.

She'd never thought she'd rush to her side quite the way she'd done just now.

Monica's wave of pain allowed her to open her eyes momentarily and realise that her sister was here at her side after all this time. 'Nadia?'

'Yes. It's me.' She held back her tears. 'Archie will be here soon.'

'Giles...' Monica didn't get long to speak – contractions were coming thick and fast with no break in between.

'He's safe. With a childminder. And help is on its way; please don't panic.' There was, however, still no sign of the emergency services.

The next-door neighbour had seen Monica outside, doubled over in pain, and come to her rescue and taken her inside her own house while they waited for Archie, Nadia and Giles. The neighbour had called the emergency services and then called Archie's phone and spoken to Nadia. Nadia had had to keep her voice neutral, not give too much away with Giles sitting in the car. The neighbour had offered to go a few doors down to where a registered childminder lived and ask her to look after Giles when the trio arrived and Nadia had agreed, sure that Archie would want the same. And so when they pulled up, Giles had only had to hear that there were a group of kids baking muffins at a house nearby, and that he could join in, to race off happily with his dad.

Archie rushed inside the house, having dropped his son with the childminder, and came straight to his wife's side. The anguish, the emotion, it was all so much to deal with all round.

And Nadia was starting to panic. Crouched down next to her sister, with no sign of an ambulance or extra help, this was down to her. Archie was the emotional support but she now had to make sure that everything was okay medically until they got Monica the proper attention she needed.

She felt her sister's pulse. It was racing, possibly more than it should be. On instinct, or maybe to be cautious, she needed to do an exam. Right now, she had to forget that this was her sister. She had to remember her nursing training. She hadn't trained as a midwife but she'd learned, seen and heard enough to know the basics of what to do.

'Monica, I'm going to try to examine you, okay?'

A groan, a loud one that took away her words.

She was about to palpate Monica's abdomen, assess the position of the baby when the familiar sound of a helicopter's rotor blades had the owner of the house running outside and calling back that an air ambulance had arrived. She'd make sure the paramedics found the house easily. Luckily, the street had tennis courts at the end and Nadia suspected the crew would be landing there. She had imagined a road ambulance would come but sometimes those were in short supply and with the rural location, a helicopter was probably the best bet.

By feeling Monica's abdomen, Nadia was pretty sure the baby was posterior – there seemed to be a lot of movement in the belly, indicating the arms and legs might well be facing out with the baby's spine resting against Monica's. A posterior birth could mean a longer labour, there was a threat of postpartum haemorrhage; it could be a slow and difficult birth as it was harder for the baby to get through the pelvis.

'Is everything all right?' Archie asked.

She nodded. She didn't want either of them to panic, but she briefed the crew at the door. Bess, bless her heart, was surprised to see her but went straight into work mode.

'I suspect the baby is posterior,' Nadia said but not quietly enough.

'What does that mean?' Archie had latched on to the word immediately.

She briefly explained it to him while Bess saw to Monica and gave her an internal examination as well as all the other checks they needed to do. There was no time to waste. She was on the scoop and out of the door almost before Nadia had really had time to reassure Archie that his wife was in good hands.

* * *

Giles had refused to be left at the childminder's when Archie briefly went to the house to ask whether he could stay there a while longer. The little boy understandably wanted his dad and he even left the muffin-making behind.

Archie hadn't argued with his son; there was no time. They

needed to get going on the thirty-minute trip by road to the hospital.

'Where are we going?' Giles asked.

'The hospital.' Archie spoke with a flatness in his voice to mask his panic, his dread, for the sake of his son and to keep this little boy's world stable at least for now. 'We're going to see your mummy.'

Giles sat as upright as he could in his car seat. 'Mummy's here?'

Nadia turned to see his little smile, his hands clapped together. He had no idea of the drama unfolding even when Archie told him that his baby brother or sister was on the way right now.

Nadia did her best to dampen down scenarios that popped into her head – forceps or ventouse delivery, an emergency c-section, an epidural? She wished she knew more about midwifery but perhaps it was best that she didn't.

They pulled into the hospital car park. It was near impossible to find a space but they found the very last one that involved Nadia and Giles getting out of the vehicle first so that Archie could go close to the other car which had parked right on the line.

When Archie climbed out, Nadia told him to run on ahead. 'Me and Giles won't be far behind.'

Giles watched his dad go and as they entered the hospital, Nadia saw the café. 'How about we have a little treat while we're waiting.' The best place for this little boy right now was to not be in the chaos as Archie frantically tried to locate Monica.

'What'll it be?' she asked Giles as they found themselves in front of the cake counter.

He pointed at the apple cinnamon muffins. 'Those are my mummy's favourite. Can I take her one?'

'That's a lovely idea – maybe later on.'

He looked up at her. 'How long does it take for a baby to get here?'

'Sometimes quite a while. It could be hours, days.'

His eyes widened. 'That's a long time.'

But the conversation seemed to placate him enough to study the choices behind the glass counter some more.

'Take your time; you want to choose well,' she joked but really it was to give her enough time to fire off a text to Archie to let him know where they were and to ask for an update if he had one. He might not read the message for a while but it would be there ready for him when he was able.

'Good choice,' she approved as Giles settled on the chocolate chip muffin. 'Make that two please,' she asked the lady behind the counter. 'Plus a coffee and...'

'Apple juice?' Giles requested.

'An apple juice, please.'

Actually coming in here did a lot for Nadia too. It could be hours before they got news, and being here at least instilled some temporary calm.

And it helped her to start processing things.

She'd seen her sister, after all these years; she'd seen her and held her hand. And it was as though with that skin-on-skin contact, she remembered the family that had been together for so long before things began to unravel.

When she caught sight of the framed crochet design of an ambulance on the wall, it sent her mind back to better times. 'Did you know your mummy is fantastically creative?'

Giles seemed more interested in waiting at the end of the counter for service of their order but he did admit, 'She can draw. She drew me, playing with my cars, and then she painted it with paints mixed with water.'

'Watercolours.' Nadia smiled. 'And does she still make things? Like clothes?' That was something else Monica had done before things started to go wrong at school for her and her rebellion seemed to govern her life so much that she stopped doing the things she loved. Nadia hadn't really registered that until now.

He tried to insist he carry the tray with their order but Nadia gave him the job to find them a table instead.

'So does she?' Nadia asked again when she sat down.

He took the little plate with his muffin on. 'She has a machine thing.'

'A sewing machine.'

'Yeah, that's what I said.'

The innocence of childhood, what had happened to that? Why did it all go by so very fast, almost in the blink of an eye?

Monica made Nadia an embroidered handkerchief once with little flowers down one edge in delicate pinks and soft yellows. Nadia wished she'd kept it, been able to remember some of the good. But she'd felt so closed off from her sister even before she left the country and pushing out anything positive became easier for her to handle than letting the better memories change her mind.

They got through their muffins and their drinks, Giles used the toilet and Nadia checked her phone for the umpteenth time but still no news.

They asked at the enquiries desk and found out where Monica had been taken. They got lost no less than three times despite signposting around the hospital and soon enough, they were in a corridor and Giles spotted his dad sitting at the end.

Head in his hands, Archie looked spent and Nadia felt her world twist on its axis.

If something had happened to Monica or the baby, she'd never forgive herself.

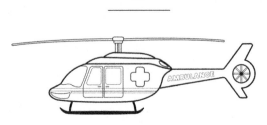

23

It was Saturday morning and Nadia was a bundle of nerves as she and Giles made their way along the corridor in the direction of the maternity ward. It felt more like she was meeting two new people for the very first time, and it was a case of putting one foot in front of the other and hoping this went well.

She would never forget the way she'd felt seeing Archie in the corridor at the hospital last night, his exhaustion evident. It was as though he didn't have an ounce of energy in his body. She'd quickened her pace, she braced for bad news and he looked up with tear-streaked cheeks and said, 'It's a girl.'

He'd hugged Giles when his son had raced over to him, he'd held his son tight and kissed the top of his head. 'You have a little sister.'

Archie did his best to recount the drama in a way that wouldn't be too scary in front of Giles – the baby, posterior, hadn't turned with manual manipulation and it was only after an epidural when the doctors were almost ready to do an emergency c-section that the baby, named Bella, turned of her own accord and an hour later made her entrance into the world.

The family was back together again, the four of them were a complete unit, and Nadia felt almost like an intruder until Archie asked whether there was any way she could look after Giles overnight.

'You'd trust me?'

He looked at her as if that was all that was needed. But he added, 'Yes, Nadia. I trust you.'

'I want to see Mummy,' cried Giles. He hadn't said anything about possibly staying with his auntie who he'd only met recently. Was that a bad sign? Or was he just focused on seeing the mummy who he'd been missing since she left them behind in Switzerland?

Archie still had Giles in his arms, the little boy clearly needing the closeness as much as his dad did. 'Mummy is resting. How about we let her sleep and you see her tomorrow?'

But Giles shook his head vehemently.

'Why don't you go in quickly,' Nadia suggested and as she rubbed Giles's head, told Archie, 'Just let him see her, then I'll bring him back tomorrow morning.'

'Okay. Would you like to come in with us?'

'Not yet. You two go.' She wasn't ready and they needed to be a family of four first before anything else complicated the situation.

Nadia waited and Archie brought Giles back soon enough.

'Mummy is very sleepy,' Giles told her, but he seemed satisfied he'd got to see her and he'd certainly perked up about the idea of staying with his auntie. 'Daddy says I'm going to your house. Where do you live? Do you have an extra bed? Do you have spare covers?'

She couldn't help but smile. 'Yes, of course I have an extra bed. Plenty of bedding too. And my house is in Whistlestop River, not too far from the airbase.'

'What about my pyjamas?'

'I'm staying here tonight,' Archie interrupted, 'so if you like, you can take my key to the Airbnb, get everything you need and head back here tomorrow morning to return it. If that fits in with you.'

'Of course.'

Giles was raring to go after that and so they went to the Airbnb, a cute little place in the countryside on the outskirts of Whistlestop River, picked up a few things and then headed for her place. She was still unsure how this would go – she hoped he wouldn't have a wobble come bedtime.

She found a *Spiderman* movie on demand and after a late fish and chip supper, they settled down to watch it together, Giles's eyes growing heavier and heavier throughout the movie until the credits rolled and he was slumped against Nadia's arm. She woke him to clean his teeth and settled him into the spare bed, leaving the door open just a crack with a little bit of light.

He came downstairs an hour later and this time, they stayed up talking without the television on. He was worried; he might not have shown it during the film, or when they'd been eating, or in the adventure that was staying at someone else's house, but he was showing it now.

'Is my mummy going to be all right?'

'She's going to be just fine.' She lifted up her arm and he came to settle by her side for a hug. 'And you have a sister. That's pretty special.' She gulped at the sound of her own words, the meaning they had for her as well.

She'd ended up making them both a hot cocoa and as soon as he finished his, Giles grew sleepy and he was so comfortable, she settled him on the sofa with pillows and a blanket before she went on up to bed herself.

Now, at the hospital, she had hold of Giles's hand. He had a little backpack with him filled with his things from last night. He'd declared it the best sleepover ever – even though he didn't go on sleepovers yet – probably on account of the fact that he hadn't done much sleeping at all. Instead, he'd got to watch a movie, come downstairs for a chat, a cuddle and two mugs of cocoa when he couldn't settle. And he was up early enough this morning before they were due to visit the hospital that Nadia had made him pancakes.

'Can I stay at yours again?' he asked as they followed the rabbit warren of corridors in the hospital, only going wrong once. 'I could have the bed next time. The sofa was nice though.'

'Glad you think so.'

'Don't tell Mummy I didn't clean my teeth again after the cocoa.'

She grinned. 'I promise I won't say a word.'

'So can I?' he prompted.

'Come stay? If your mummy and daddy agree then of course.'

'What about when we live in Switzerland? That's too far for a sleepover. We won't see you again.'

She stopped before they reached the ward and bobbed down on her haunches. 'I'm sorry I didn't get to meet you before today.'

'You might forget me.'

'Don't worry, no danger of that. I've not stayed up drinking cocoa that late with anyone else; that's your job now.'

'Can we have marshmallows next time too?'

She made a hesitant expression. 'Not sure, I'll think about it.' She reached up to tickle him under his chin. 'You okay?'

He nodded, but he looked suddenly sad. And in true child fashion, he came right out with, 'Daddy says you and Mummy have problems.'

That was one way of putting it.

Kids certainly made you think about what you wanted to say and how to say it. 'We have had a few. But you know, Giles, the thing with problems is that sometimes you can work them out.'

He brightened at that and as Nadia buzzed outside the door to the ward and waited for a nurse to let them in, she started to believe in what she was saying.

And once she saw her sister, spoke to her, she'd know whether there was anything to salvage or whether they were better off carrying on with their separate lives.

As soon as Giles spotted his dad, he charged into his open arms.

Nadia handed Archie the key to the Airbnb and he pushed it into his pocket. She'd texted him a couple of times last night to assure him that everything was fine, Giles was behaving and she was coping, and he'd messaged back to say Monica had already perked up and was feeding the little one.

'Take Giles in first,' said Nadia.

Archie nodded, respecting her need to gather herself. 'We'll have about half an hour – most likely his attention span to sit beside a bed – and then we'll leave you and Monica to talk.'

She wished she'd thought to grab a hot drink to bring up here, give her something to do while she was waiting because the time seem to drag terribly.

But then Giles was running towards her again, boasting about his little sister, laughing at her burps, talking about how she looked like him as a baby.

And Nadia's heart had to catch up a bit with her legs as they took her towards the middle bay in a ward.

They took her to Monica.

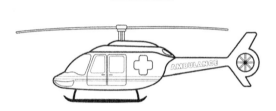

24

Before Nadia left Switzerland for Dorset, she would've described Monica as rebellious, unwilling to bend for anyone else, intent on causing trouble. And yesterday, Nadia had barely registered anything about this woman who was family and who she hadn't seen for twenty years.

Now, when she approached the bed and her sister dragged her gaze from the baby in her arms to the sister who'd left her decades ago, Nadia knew without her saying a word that she was different in more ways than she would ever be able to realise unless they talked properly. Somehow just by watching her sister with a baby showed Nadia that the passage of time had mellowed this woman and turned her into a different person.

And yet she still braced for Monica to let her down, for her sister to open her mouth, speak and for Nadia to realise nothing had changed at all.

That was what she was dreading the most: the fear that any chance she gave Monica would be pointless. And it was hard to talk herself down from that, to make herself open and able to listen.

'Hi.' Monica's voice was small, soft, a buffed version of what it had once been.

'Hi.' She turned her attentions to Bella; it was the easiest thing to do. 'She's beautiful.'

'Thank you. She really is.'

'Is she feeding okay?'

'A little fussy at first but we're getting the hang of it. I'm a bit sore, though.' She winced as if reminded of the pain.

'Did the nurses give you something to apply?'

'They did.'

Nurse-speak was far easier than sister-speak right now.

'Did Giles behave himself with you last night?' Monica asked eventually. Their attentions had been on Bella and her little mannerisms she'd adopted at less than twenty-four hours old.

'He enjoyed himself.'

'Ah, code for very little sleep. I could tell; he was yawning.'

'I'm sorry, I—'

'I'm not complaining, I promise. I'm not having a go at you, I swear.' The words rushed out in defence, little gasps of breaths between the punctuated sentences suggesting Monica was more apprehensive about this than Nadia was herself.

'Sorry, I just expect...'

'Conflict? Yeah, well, we spent so long in that state that I can understand why.'

She sounded grown up. She was, of course. They both were.

'A sleepover would've been such an adventure for him. He's like I was at that age. I still remember my first.'

'At Debbie Mason's house.' Nadia grinned.

'You remember?'

'You fell asleep in our Wendy house the morning after. You were so quiet and out of sight that Mum and I were searching the house for you. She hadn't thought to check in there, at ground level, because usually, you made enough noise that her ears told her where you were at all times.'

Their smiles and laughter settled. 'Well, thank you for taking Giles. It could have been a really stressful day and evening for him following the weeks of hell I've put him and Archie through, so I really do appreciate it. He likes you.'

'And I like him. He's wonderful, Monica.'

She nodded, held back tears.

Nadia wasn't sure whether to ask her question – she didn't want to ignite a fuse that would burn quickly and then explode – that was usually what confrontation did to her sister – but she had to know. 'What made you leave them behind and then not get in touch?'

'It's hard to explain.'

'You could try.' Nadia turned away. 'Maybe you did try over the years and I never understood you.'

'Oh, no, do not take any blame for me. I shoulder all of that and all of the guilt. Have done for years and rightly so.'

'Archie said you struggled with depression for a while. I know you did as a teenager.'

'It's been on and off for me. Mostly off thankfully, but not always. After you left, with Mum gone too, I felt lost, alone, guilty, not good enough. I knew I only had myself to blame for most of it. That was the worst thing. I thought I deserved what I got pretty much all of the time. Even at school, once I'd struggled, it was hard to break out of that mould and be anything other than the kid who got crappy grades, the kid who was slower than others.'

Bella stirred in her arms and when the fussing didn't stop, Monica latched the baby to her breast, wincing at the obvious discomfort at first. 'Whenever you tried to get through to me, I wasn't interested. I pushed you away. It almost made me worse –

I'm not blaming you, but it did – I was so frustrated, so jealous that you were completely together.'

Nadia waited until the baby was feeding. 'I wasn't all that together, you know.'

'Are you kidding me? While I kept making mistakes, you never did.'

'I did well at school but I struggled with friendships sometimes, with things at home. It wasn't always easy worrying about you, worrying about Mum.'

'I was in a bad place. I was selfish; I could only think about myself.' Monica looked down at Bella. 'I can't be that person now; I have to be more. I was doing so well, but then the pregnancy...'

She didn't carry on straight away, her focus stayed on Bella. It must be difficult to talk so candidly after all this time. It certainly was for Nadia.

'You used to ask me about school and how things were going,' said Monica. 'I shut you down every single time. I was embarrassed, I felt helpless. I was so behind with my work and the more behind I got, the more I rebelled, the more I didn't want my big sister having to swoop in and fix everything. It became easier to joke and have a laugh at school than it was to admit I was still struggling. I was a hopeless case; that's what I told myself. And even though Mum went up to school often enough, got me the help I needed with a tutor, I still felt like a failure. I didn't always turn up for those tutor sessions either which was terrible. I apologised to Mum for doing that.' She smiled at Nadia's reaction. 'You seem shocked.'

'I never knew, that's all. But it's nice to know you apologised.'

'Well, I did. And I told her that the way I was wasn't anything for her to feel bad about.'

Nadia couldn't check her sister's claims but something in the way she spoke told Nadia it was the truth even before she said the next thing.

'Mum spent a lot of time trying to sort me out. I'll never truly forgive myself for that, you know. But I didn't see it, Nadia. Not until it was too late.' When she looked up from Bella, her gaze didn't waver. 'I didn't see that I was taking all of Mum's energy, all of her compassion. You were almost her equal, when you should've had time being mothered. And I will always hate myself for that.'

'Hate is a strong word.'

'Well, I do. I wish I'd been able to see it then but I couldn't.'

Nadia wasn't going to say it was okay, because it wasn't. But was there any point getting upset and angry now?

The way Monica was looking at her was completely different from the way her sister had looked at her over the years, as if waiting for a reaction, to gauge how much trouble she'd caused. Now she looked expectant, nervous, when previously, she'd had an air of confidence and hopeful one-upmanship.

Monica shushed the baby as she finished feeding. She looked such a natural at being a mother that it almost tipped Nadia's emotions over; this was the part of her sister that she'd never seen, never had a chance to know.

'I wanted to find you, Nadia, and at least tell you that I was sorry for the way I was back then, for taking all of Mum's time, for not being the sister you deserved.' Her voice broke and she hid the fact behind a cuddle with Bella, gently placing her against her chest to rub her little back. 'And I wanted to apologise for Archie, for the way we got together when you and he... You were friends and more than that, you'd been together. And you two...'

'We lost a baby.' Nadia finished what she thought her sister might be about to say.

The nurse came to check on them and ask Monica about the feeding and how it was going and Nadia excused herself to use the bathroom. She didn't need to go at all, but what she did need was to get a bit of breathing space. She found the bathrooms, then a corridor that looked out onto the car park, an open space beyond the walls. And she stayed there a while, letting what her sister had said sink in. She was apologising, she was sorry, she had regret. But was it enough?

When she went back in, Bella was settled in the little plastic crib beside the bed, bundled up in a pink blanket, her little mouth the perfect 'o' as she slept.

'Was I gone that long?'

'I did wonder if you were ever coming back.' Monica was sitting up; she fussed at the sheets across her, a smile curving her mouth and at odds with the sad tone of her voice.

Nadia perched on the edge of her sister's bed, past the middle, but so that she could reach into the plastic crib and touch the baby's wrapped torso if she wanted. 'I know you tried to find me once before,' said Nadia. And that was another thing convincing her that her sister meant every word she said, every attempt at an apology. 'Archie told me.'

Tears sprang unbidden to Monica's eyes and her voice wobbled so much, she struggled to say anything else and when Nadia offered her a tissue, she covered her eyes rather than wiping them and gave in to her feelings.

Once she was calmer, Monica told Nadia more about the wave of postnatal depression she'd experienced after Giles was born.

'I felt so hopeless, guilty that I wasn't feeling the joy I should be with a new baby. I felt weak, not worthy of Archie or Giles. Eventually, the doctor came out to our home and he was wonderful, really understanding. I think Archie was so lost until that home visit. But I was able to access the right support and over time, I got better.'

'What happened this time? To make you leave your son, your husband, take the risk with your unborn child and come here?'

Monica's head was resting on the pillow and she turned to look up at the ceiling. Nadia waited. She didn't want to rush this; she wanted the truth. They both needed it.

'I don't think... no, I *know* I wasn't prepared to feel the way I did with this pregnancy. Archie and I were wary of what would happen once the baby came; we felt prepared because it happened with Giles. I never expected it to happen *during* my pregnancy. My GP had moved on so I'd lost the continuity of care. I felt good in the early stages but as I got to my third trimester, I started to feel much more anxious. I put it down to being a mother, the pregnancy hormones. I thought that if I got through the nine months, that would be when I'd have to take stock and deal with depression again. Guess the joke was on me; depression found me before I thought it would.'

'And you just packed your bags and left.'

'I was unbelievably sad. And it was a sadness I couldn't claw my way out of; I couldn't see reason. Logic told me I had a gorgeous little boy, a wonderful marriage. But those things were buried by the thought that I had no extended family because I'd driven you, the only one left, away. I became obsessed by every-thing that happened when we were younger; I couldn't let it go. I'd try to talk to Archie but he had work, Giles, and he said we'd concentrate on the baby first then after he or she arrived, we'd think about everything else.

'I felt so alone; I had this overwhelming need to come here, to try to find you. I wasn't intending on staying so long. But when I found no trace of you, I just felt like I'd failed again. So I pushed it, I stayed, thought I had plenty of time. I wasn't thinking clearly at all.'

All those years they'd lost, all the time she'd been a different person to the sister Nadia remembered. The pain Nadia felt knowing that was crushing. 'I can't begin to understand what it was like for you.'

Monica pushed the wobble out of her voice. 'It has been hard. And all I wanted was for us to get to know each other again, to have you back in my life. But I knew I couldn't blame you. I was awful to you; I wasn't much of a sister. I was hard work, stubborn, obstinate – all of those things. On top of that, I was angry at how I struggled over the years. I wanted to be a better person. Even though I could see myself how others did, I still didn't seem able to change.

'My relationship with Archie happened in a whirlwind. I knew I was playing with fire; I often questioned whether that was why I'd done it. You had a wonderful friendship with him even after you two broke up; I'd heard about it from Mum. She was always saying Nadia this, Archie that, and yes, I was jealous. But that wasn't why I fell for Archie, I promise you.'

Nadia couldn't speak; she still remembered the hurt that day finding them together.

'It took time to settle into life with Archie after you left and after I came here but couldn't find you. I felt undeserving, regretful; I felt so many things. We started to get more serious, Archie and me. I eventually found a job in hospitality and when I did, I felt like I'd found a little bit of myself I didn't realise was missing, I was happy. I had so many hobbies, too. I took up hiking, went bike riding, swimming. In my darker days, my interests really only centred around drinking and smoking dope.' She said the last bit in a very quiet voice. 'I haven't done that in almost two decades. The odd glass of wine, but that's it.'

'I'm glad.' And she was. But talking about Archie was still difficult; it was hard to hear all this when she and Archie had once been together. 'Giles tells me you still do some creative things these days.'

Monica smiled, probably glad to talk about something lighter if only for a moment. Perhaps their getting to know each other again would come in waves, with big peaks, and then calmer shores. 'He's my biggest supporter. As well as being so active, I started painting again eventually, and these days I also draw a lot and I sew.'

'I was always useless at those sorts of things.' Nadia laughed.

'I find it therapeutic; it's an escape. It worked well over the years to help me cope. When I couldn't find you, I felt like that silly little girl who couldn't read as well as others in class, who handed in all her assignments late, who was ridiculed when some girl at school got hold of one of my essays and they were falling about laughing at my letter muddling. Archie enrolled me in an evening class to do needlework, I went to appease him, and ended up realising it was exactly what I needed.'

'I wish you'd told me the other kids were mean to you about your struggles.'

She shrugged. 'I developed a thick skin. But also an attitude. Not proud of the second part.' She leaned over and opened the top drawer of her cabinet, pulled out a bag and opened it to retrieve a photograph. She handed it to Nadia.

'It's your wedding day. You look stunning.' She did, she was beautiful, she looked happy and so did Archie.

'My only disappointment that day was not sharing it with my sister. But Archie, well, you know Archie; he's been there for me in ways I never thought a guy could ever be there.'

'He's a good man.'

'I never meant to take him away from you. I promise you that wasn't what I thought at all when I first got talking to him. At first, I saw my sister's friend, then we started hanging out and I forgot that he was your friend and got to know him as his own person. We both knew we had to tell you. I never meant it to come out the weekend you caught us at Mum's.'

'You didn't do that on purpose?'

'No, I had no idea you'd show up when you did.'

'But it was a bonus, right?' Nadia felt nausea rise up. Talking about Archie seemed to chip away at the worst part of their relationship, the utter devastation and sense of betrayal she'd felt back then when she lost her best friend to her sister.

'I admit that yes, it was, at least for a moment. I reverted to that horrible person, not the person I was with Archie. My first reaction was to feel happy that you were hurt by us being together; it felt like payback for all the nagging, the way you saw me as trouble. It didn't matter whether I was being fair or not. I felt like I had one up on you. That lasted all of about five minutes – a high like you get from a drug that is a false reality, then real life crashes down.'

Nadia tried to digest it but it was hard, sitting here going over the past, trying to move on when a lot of it still hurt.

'I'm really sorry, Nadia. About everything. I know an apology can only go so far, but I really want to try.'

But Nadia couldn't say anything else, not yet.

She had to get out of here.

And in tears, she turned and abruptly left the ward.

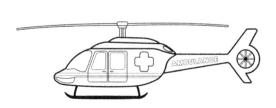

25

Hudson felt the tug on the end of his line and the two young boys to his right on the small boat, neither of whom had caught anything yet, watched in awe as he reeled it in.

They weren't experts in fishing – far from it – and it had been so long since Hudson and Beau had been, but before they left the house to drop Carys at her grandparents' yesterday evening, Hudson had reserved their camping pitch and booked them on a fishing trip today. It was a boat trip for beginners so would be a starting point to getting back into it. Hudson's only regret now was that he'd let this aspect of his relationship with Beau slide. In the business of everyday life, he'd forgotten the simplicity of doing something like this, the joy it gave.

'Dad, it's huge!' Beau got closer to investigate Hudson's catch and abandoned his own attempt for now.

Hudson planted his feet firmly as he reeled in fully and landed his fish. Beau removed the hook gently to avoid wounding the fish or himself.

'What is it?' Beau pulled his phone from his back pocket to take a photograph.

Hudson held the fish up in wet hands. 'I think possibly a bream? All I know is it weighs a lot.'

'It's a bream.' The guy running the fishing trip made the rounds on the boat, helping people get their hooks and bait ready, explaining what to do, and clarifying things like what fish they may have hauled out of the sea like in Hudson's case.

'Are you keeping it?' one of the lads watching asked Hudson.

'We're putting them back,' Beau told the kid.

Hudson had thought before they started that whatever they caught – if they caught anything at all – then they might take it away with them, perhaps do a barbecue. But, before the boat had come to a stop and they'd been allocated their fishing gear, Beau had decided they would use the catch-and-release method. And today was about being together, so Hudson would do it Beau's way without question.

The sea breeze sent goose pimples up his arms despite holding the heavy catch for Beau to take a photograph. The sun had hidden behind a cloud but it was a beautiful day nonetheless. Hudson had forgotten what it felt like to be out at sea, the shore way in the distance, so much peace around them, apart from the occasional excited chatter on board, or a whoop of joy at a catch, but mostly the quiet determination of him, his son and the other family of four.

He leaned over to release the fish, making sure it was well away from the boat so it didn't bash itself, and he watched it swim away to safety.

Over the next couple of hours, Beau helped the two younger boys with their rods. He had a caring side he showed with his younger sister and now with these virtual strangers. It would make him well-suited to a career with an air ambulance if that was really what he wanted to do.

The skipper joked that he should offer Beau a job as he was

so good at helping others out and by the time they returned to shore, everyone on board had caught something – bream, trout, bass and a few crabs, which had been the highlight for the young boys for some reason.

'Well, we don't have any dinner,' Hudson said as they made their way back to the campsite. 'Pub?'

'Can I take a shower first? I feel like I stink of fish.'

'We probably both do, so I should do the same or we'll scare all the other punters away, won't we?'

'Or we could not shower, could work in our favour, scare them off and have our choice of tables.'

Hudson laughed. Nothing could dampen his mood, well, maybe apart from not getting any dinner. All the activity and fresh air had made him unbelievably hungry.

They grabbed washbags from the tent and made their way to the shower block. Hudson hadn't realised how much he'd missed this, what he'd sacrificed when things got difficult with Lucinda and he returned to work full time to pay the bills. It wasn't an expensive trip – camping was cheap, the fishing excursion inexpensive. And the bonding, the time with his son, was priceless.

They headed for the pub dressed in jeans and jumpers – it was June but the sea breeze, the lack of sun and the fact that June really wasn't delivering in the summer stakes this year meant they'd packed more for autumn weather than anything else. Hudson made a quick call to his parents on the way there to check on Carys and was firmly told to stop worrying and they'd see him tomorrow.

'What's it to be?' Hudson had a pint and Beau a Coke and they perused the menu.

'Cod and chips for me, with mushy peas.'

'Think I'll make that two.' Hudson went over to the bar to place the order.

Back with his son, he pointed out, 'You do know that cod is a fish, right?'

'Course I do.'

'You don't see what I'm getting at?'

He shook his head.

'You insisted we catch and release everything today. We could've brought something back to the campsite and cooked it on one of the barbecues.'

'I just didn't want to be the one to do it. It's hypocritical, I know, but I just couldn't.'

When their food arrived, as much as they were hungry, it didn't deter from the fact that these were enormous portions. But they gave it a good go and got through most of it, by the end scraping chips through the ketchup and forcing them in.

'Right, that's it, any more and I'll burst,' said Hudson, willing someone to come and take the plates before he kept going with the chips that tempted him every second no matter how satiated he was.

The other patient and family liaison nurse, Paige, had generously taken on Hudson's workload at the last minute. Hudson had made the call right after he'd put Carys to bed and while Beau was still opening up the two-man tent in the back garden, and he was glad he'd made the quick decision. This was quality time with Beau that both of them really needed. If he'd done this previously, his son might never have done something as irresponsible as taking part in a hoax call to the air ambulance. Then again, maybe Conrad had a point, that they all made mistakes in their youth, and what was important now to Hudson was that Beau seemed to be learning from it.

And as a dad, he couldn't ask for much more than that.

As they waited for their plates to be cleared and let their dinner go down, talk turned to Beau's mum.

'What do you really think of Conrad?' Hudson decided there was no point trying to dress up the question; he may as well be direct.

'He's not so bad.'

'Is that only because he let you off?' Hudson leaned out of the way when one of the bar staff came to take his plate.

'I suppose it's part of it. I think I'm getting used to him. Mum's last boyfriend was awful. It was obvious he didn't expect to have to tolerate kids – whatever age they were.'

'I hope Carys squealed loudly when he was there.'

Beau laughed. 'Actually, she did. I swear that's why he went running for the hills.'

'Does Conrad treat your mum okay?' It wasn't his business who Lucinda dated but he still cared and he'd heard what Conrad was like.

'He does. They seem happy. He works a lot, so does she.'

'Maybe they're a good match in that way.'

'Have you ever thought of dating anyone?'

His beer didn't quite go down smoothly and he coughed. 'Sometimes, but there's too much going on.'

'I don't mind, if you want to.'

'Wouldn't it depend who it was?'

'Well, yeah. They'd have to like kids.' He had more to say. 'You and Nadia seem close.'

'Nadia?'

'Ask her out; I think she'd say yes.'

It felt weird, having this conversation, but he appreciated it. 'Who knows, maybe I will. Now that I have your approval.'

'You'll need Carys's too.'

Hudson laughed loudly. 'As long as she gets a cuddle, Carys

is happy and I don't think her squealing will chase Nadia away either.' He tried to read his son's expression. 'You'd really be okay with it?'

'Sure.'

'Well, thanks.'

'You mean for being okay that my dad actually gets a life.'

'Hey... less making out I'm a sad case.'

'Just do me a favour, Dad.' He set down his second Coke after a generous swig. 'If you date her, or anyone else, don't give me any details.'

He clinked his glass against Beau's. 'Deal.'

The drizzle that had started as they made their way to the pub had turned into a downpour that made them linger inside a while longer. They had a game of darts, which Beau won, three games of pool, which Hudson won, and they made use of the pub's pack of cards.

'The rain has stopped,' said Beau when he came out of the bathroom.

'Shall we make a run for it now in case it starts again?'

They agreed they'd do that; it was only a ten-minute walk and at a fast pace, they made it to their tent, added on a dash to the shower block to clean their teeth and had got beneath the canvas just in time to see the rain start up again. They kept the tent flaps open for a bit. With no other campers in front of them, they had a view of the field stretched out before them, vast open space and freedom.

Bundled into their sleeping bags, they both sat at the mouth of the tent watching as the sky grew dark and the rain comforted them beneath the canvas.

Hudson decided that there couldn't be many moments as perfect as this.

26

Hudson was still smiling about his bonding weekend with Beau when he arrived at the hospital on Monday morning for a meeting.

They'd got back to Whistlestop River yesterday lunchtime and while Hudson played with Carys, who had had the biggest grin for them when they collected her from her grandparents, Beau opened out the tent on the back lawn without even being asked. The rain had gone away and although it still didn't feel like they were almost into the official start of summer, the sun shone and gave it its best effort which was enough for Beau to clean the tent and make sure it was thoroughly dry before it was packed away.

Hudson had texted Nadia yesterday before he started the dinner prep; he told her they'd been camping and that it was the best thing he'd ever done, he asked whether she was okay as she'd been so quiet since she met with Archie. But he got no reply. And eventually, he'd given up holding his phone in his hand like a teenager desperately waiting for a message to come through. Beau had come in after sorting out the tent and as all three of them sat down for dinner, Hudson had indulged in the pride he felt for his kids. He appreciated them for the wonderful human beings that they were, he loved his little family, whatever it looked like.

Hudson attended his meeting with a patient and her family as well as the representative from a brain-injury charity who would provide the ongoing support to the girl who, at only fifteen years old, had had a seizure and fallen down an escalator at a shopping centre.

Following the meeting, he headed for the café and bought a coffee, choosing a table close to the window so he could start work on his report.

His coffee break had only just started when he looked up and saw Nadia emerge from the main hospital building.

He quickly closed down his laptop, put everything into the protective sleeve, and with his laptop under one arm and his coffee in his other hand, took off for the outside.

He'd tried to call her this morning given she hadn't replied to his text but with this case to attend to, he'd ended up leaving a message on his second attempt and just hoped she'd call him back. He already knew from Bess, who'd taken her call yesterday, that she needed the day off today. Bess was also able to share with him the drama of Nadia's sister going into labour on Friday night.

No wonder it had been radio silence. And right now, Nadia didn't look okay at all.

She was sitting on a bench opposite the car park, right near the bus stop and all the smokers.

She looked to the side when he said her name and as soon as she saw him, her face crumpled.

'Come on, let's go around the building,' he said, 'there's

another bench and hopefully nobody smoking or vaping. You don't want to sit here.'

She seemed to register and got up, followed him.

The first bench was occupied, so was the next, but they finally found a seating area and some clean air in a little nook at one side of the hospital.

'What brings you here?' she asked.

'I'm here working on a case.'

'What's the case?'

Was she really doing this? Perhaps talking about something other than what was on her mind helped, so he obliged, gave her an overview.

'That poor family,' she said when he'd finished. 'They'll need a lot of help coming to terms with what has happened.'

'That's what I'm here for.' But then his voice softened and he had to turn the focus to her. 'What about you? I think you need some help coming to terms with everything; at least that's the impression I get. Want to talk about it?'

'I'm fine.'

'You are not *fine*. You haven't seen or been in contact with your sister for decades and now she's here, you're here; I doubt anything about that situation is easy.'

She reached for his coffee. 'May I?'

'Go ahead.'

She finished a big gulp, took another. And then she recapped what had happened since she talked to Archie, from sitting by the river and watching Giles in the playground, to the emergency call, attending the scene with Monica, Monica going to hospital in the air ambulance, the emergency dash to her side.

'I had Giles overnight at my place. I told you that. Sorry, I'm repeating myself.'

'It's fine, keep going.'

'He's a great little boy, and I've missed it. I've missed his growing up. I can't ever get that back.'

'You can't blame yourself.'

'No! Then who exactly do I blame?' She pulled back. 'Sorry, I shouldn't be yelling at you.'

'That wasn't yelling, not even close.'

A small smile curved up the corners of her mouth. The happy Nadia was still in there somewhere. 'I'm here to see Monica again but I got halfway to her ward and turned back.'

'It must be hard after all this time.'

'I was here on Saturday for a while, but yesterday, I couldn't face it. Listening to her talk about what went on years ago, when she got together with Archie, it was all too much. The hurt came back and I haven't seen her since. I wanted to come outside, get some fresh air, then I'll be brave enough.'

'Fresh air? You chose the smoky spot near the bus stop.'

'I know. I wasn't thinking.' She looked back the way they'd come. 'Nobody takes any notice of the no-smoking signs around, do they? I mean, it's supposed to be a place of healing and anyone who comes in and out of the hospital has to walk through all the smoke.'

'Not right, is it?'

'Nice round here, though – kind of hidden.'

'I thought you could use the headspace.' And he knew she was putting off talking about herself again.

They sat in the sunshine; a couple of nurses passed by, exchanged smiles with them both.

'I'll go back inside soon,' said Nadia. 'I just need to get myself together.' She waited a moment before admitting, 'Monica has changed. Archie said she was different and I wanted that to be true but until I was face to face with her on Saturday, I didn't know it for sure. There's a softness; she's lost the hard edges she had all those years growing up. She's apologised and taken the blame, I can't complain at that, and yet...'

'You're finding it hard to forgive?'

'It's not that... I mean I do forgive her, I know she's sorry, but I've buried it all for so many years and now it's coming to the surface. I wish I'd processed my emotions before now. I wish I'd let her get in touch; I wish I hadn't waited so long.'

'But you did. You can't change the past. And wishing that you could or wishing you had will only make all of this more painful in the long run. You need to forgive yourself first and foremost.'

'It's hard to do,' she said. 'Have you forgiven yourself? For Beau. I can tell you think that you're to blame for how he's dealt with the separation and divorce. But it's not all down to you.'

'I'm getting there, feeling less responsible, at least not solely to blame. I'm beginning to realise that maybe I also played a part in him being strong enough and able enough to turn things around. The time he's spent at the airbase has been a big part of that: the interest he's showing.'

'It's really good to see, you raised a great kid.'

'Thank you. That means a lot. I took him fishing, you know.'

'You said in your text. Was it as good as you hoped?'

He smiled at her, his gaze dropping to her lips but only momentarily. 'Better.'

He told her all about the boat trip, the camping, the fact they hadn't taken enough tent pegs and one side of the canvas had almost collapsed by morning.

'Beau took it well, told me it was my fault, I said it was his, and then we just started laughing. It's moments like those that I hadn't realised I missed until now.'

'You'll have to do it again.'

'Definitely. Maybe with the right equipment this time.' He paused. 'We talked a lot over dinner too. Carys and Beau –

although mostly Beau, given he's older – are the reasons I've held back from dating again since their mum and I split up. I thought it would be too much to deal with. But over dinner, Beau came right out with it and told me to basically get a life. Start dating.'

He turned so that he was facing Nadia. 'He seems to think I should ask you out.'

He loved that her cheeks coloured and that she couldn't hold back a smile.

'What do you think?' he ventured when she said nothing at all, just looked away from him, watching passersby in the distance.

'I think I'm an emotional mess right now.' She looked back at him. 'But I'm not saying no,' she added.

'You're not?'

After a beat, she admitted, 'I've wanted a bit more than friendship for a while. With you, I mean.' She covered her face briefly with her hands. 'I'm out of practice with this.' And then her positivity waned. 'After I kept the truth about my family hidden, I thought you'd never be interested. Not after your history with Lucinda and the way she lied to you.'

'I understand why you didn't tell anyone about your family; you had good reasons. You can't compare what you did to the lies Lucinda told. I don't think you're a terrible person for doing it either; I think you have a lot to work through. And I also lied to you, remember. I didn't tell you about the divorce. I wanted to keep that part of my life private and so I did for a while.'

'Are you sure you're ready to start dating?'

'Never been more sure.' He leaned in closer.

'Hudson, I—'

'Don't say anything.' All he wanted to do was kiss her. He

was hyper aware of how close they were now, how much he wanted this.

But the moment broke when a couple of doctors walked past. He hadn't even heard them approaching.

'I should get back inside,' she said.

'You should. Go see your sister again.'

Although he wished they'd found somewhere they wouldn't be interrupted, a moment to themselves so he could show her how strongly he felt about her already.

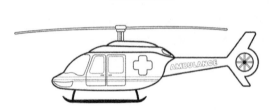

27

When Nadia went inside the hospital, Hudson went with her. He put a hand to her cheek. 'You sure you're okay?'

She put her hand on top of his against her skin. The gesture felt nearly as intimate as the almost-kiss outside. If it hadn't been for those two doctors walking by, it might have happened. But perhaps it was better that it hadn't. Not yet, not here.

'I'm ready as I'll ever be,' she said.

'I'll get back to the airbase before they start wondering where I am.'

He left her to it and then she was on her way to see Monica again, back to see her sister and her niece, apprehensive about where they went from here.

Monica looked up in surprise as Nadia approached her bed. 'I thought you weren't ever coming back.'

'I just needed some time.' She looked at her adorable niece, the baby sleeping so soundly. 'How is she?'

'We had a good night, she's feeding better and I'm less sore.'

'Good.' She took her bag from her shoulder and set it down. 'I'm sorry I stayed away yesterday.'

'I'm sorry I drove you away – that seems to be my strong point.' They shared a smile of understanding. 'Was it me talking about Archie?'

Nadia didn't have to confirm it; her sister knew.

'Archie was devastated that things were never the same with you and him after that day at the house. We got together by chance; I know that's difficult to believe.'

'Archie has talked to me about it already,' said Nadia. 'It's just still a lot to take in.'

Monica reached over and pressed her hand lightly on Bella's blanket as if reminding her baby that she was right there. She was a good mum; Nadia could tell even in the little time she'd spent with her sister.

'After we got together, Archie kept saying we should talk to you, but I kept asking him to wait. I think I was worried that he'd tell you and somehow, you'd persuade him that I was so terrible, he really didn't want to get involved.'

'Maybe I would've done. He was my friend, Monica. We were close, especially after we lost the baby. We weren't a couple any more but he was someone I knew I could turn to, I could rely on. Until...'

'Until I ruined it all.' She paused as if waiting for a torrent of abuse to come her way.

'I missed him so much when he became your boyfriend rather than my friend.'

'I'm sorry.' The words were gentle, heartfelt, and after a while with neither of them talking, she carried on with her story, which Nadia needed to hear no matter how difficult.

'A week after you caught us together, I told him I couldn't do it, I couldn't be with him. I tried to end things between us. But he wouldn't give up. He kept coming back. And although Mum was always there for me, this felt different. He saw me not for the trouble I caused, but for the person I could be deep down. I didn't deserve him. But I'd fallen for him in a big way. I couldn't stay away from him.'

'You seem to have a really good marriage.' Despite the history, Nadia found the words easier to say than she would have expected.

'Apart from me being a little crazy, you mean, and leaving my husband and child, getting on the Eurostar very, very pregnant and having a baby almost on the street if it hadn't been for the kindness of a neighbour. I often wonder what Archie sees in me.'

'He told me how kind you are, how you settled into a job, how much you love Giles and that you are a good mum. He told me how you'd flipped what you thought of as the things that were holding you back and turned them into positives – those were his words. He said you'd refused to let those things ruin your life any more. He even told me about you volunteering at a school helping kids learn to read.'

'He told you all that?'

'We've had some time to get to know each other.' And she'd had some time to accept his side of the story. Perhaps now she needed to delve deep to find the same forgiveness for her sister.

'He hated that he lost his friendship with you.'

'It didn't feel as though we could be friends any more,' said Nadia. 'But also, I never gave him a chance to show me that we could be and for that, I'm sorry.'

Bella started to wake and it wasn't long before she was moving enough that Monica shuffled herself up in bed in readiness to reach over for her. 'She can't possibly be hungry.'

'Maybe it's wind.' Nadia looked at her niece. 'May I?'

'Sure.'

Nadia picked up the baby, nestled her against her chest,

rocked side to side and patted her gently. Her little body relaxed against Nadia's, she quietened, and Nadia thought again about Lena.

'I'll bet you were a good nurse.' Monica smiled as she watched her sister with her daughter. 'I went to a few different hospitals asking after you but never found a trace.'

'I changed names – I'm Sutton now rather than Fischer.'

'That would've made it harder. So, what happened to him, the guy you were married to?'

'Jock.'

'I couldn't even remember his name.'

'I kept him away from family, that was why. I shouldn't have married him really; it was never going to work. We split up but that was a good thing.'

'You're happily single?'

'Something like that.' She hoped she wasn't blushing at the thought of Hudson, the almost-kiss, the way she felt when he touched the side of her face before he left earlier.

'Bella seems happy in her auntie's arms.'

Nadia felt a wave of emotion at the words and holding this precious bundle. 'I was pregnant, you know.'

'I know. And what you went through must've been awful.'

'It was. But I didn't mean that time. I was pregnant again, when I was married to Jock.'

'You have a baby? Archie never said.' Her face lit up but fell at Nadia's expression.

'I lost it. An ectopic pregnancy for a second time; I was lucky to survive.'

'I'm so sorry.'

'There's one thing you do better than me: motherhood.' She regretted the words as soon as they were out. 'I didn't mean that, I swear. Well, I did, but I didn't mean to sound like a bitch.'

'It's fine, honestly.'

Nadia looked at her sister and couldn't help the tears tracking down her cheeks. 'It's still painful; I wanted children, I really did. It just didn't happen for me.' She held Bella, the little girl more than settled again now. 'The Skylarks became my family; the job is more than I ever imagined it to be.'

'What made you leave nursing?'

'It wasn't planned; I saw the job advert for an operational support officer with the air ambulance in Whistlestop River and I was looking to move to a smaller town, somewhere where people knew each other better, and so I applied thinking I'd see what I thought if I got an interview. I did, I loved the airbase and the staff, the town, the sound of the role and what the air ambulance does. It was as though everything fell into place for the first time in years.'

They talked about her job, the teammates she adored, about Monica's work in hotels, which had been on pause since she'd taken early maternity leave with a plan to return once the baby was a year old.

'Archie was going out of his mind with worry about you,' said Nadia. 'I've been so focused on how this has made me feel, the fact that you're okay and your baby is too, that I haven't asked you why you didn't get in touch with him when you knew he'd contacted the police.'

'You wonder how I could've tortured them like that?'

'Kind of, yes.'

'Archie didn't ask me straight away, the birth was too traumatic, he didn't even ask right after. It was only in the early hours of Saturday morning when I opened my eyes and saw him sleeping in the chair near my bed that I woke him and told him why.' She gazed adoringly at her little baby in her sister's arms. 'Did he tell you about the university reunion?'

'No, he didn't mention it.'

'It was for your course: yours and Archie's; I thought you might have got a letter.'

'My course?' She shook her head. 'I never heard a thing. But then I didn't keep my details up to date; I moved here and left Switzerland behind.'

'It was a couple of months ago. Archie went, and when he got home, he said that he'd been asked about you half a dozen times. People talked about how lovely you were; they wondered what you were up to. When he told me, I think he intended to make me think about my sister, but instead, I was thinking about him. He's always put me first and it reminded me of the friendship I took from him. He's never thrown it in my face, he wouldn't, but I knew he missed you. And he wanted our kids to know their family – all of their family. You were the only one who could change that. I had hopes that you were happy, married, with kids. All I wanted to do was find you, for him, for me, for our kids.

'That's another thing that contributed to me suddenly coming here; it added a bit more fuel to my desire, so to speak. I went to all the hospitals in the area, convinced I'd find you or that I'd find something. I showed your photograph at a few places; I must have seemed like a crazy woman. I thought about putting something out on social media but I decided that if you got wind of that, you'd steer clear of me. Face to face was the only way I could ever see me being able to talk to you and tell you how much I regretted everything I did, how much Archie missed you, how much we both wanted you in our lives.'

Nadia's emotions bubbled up; she couldn't have spoken even if she wanted to.

'I've changed a lot, Nadia, but some things are still the same – I'm still that same girl who does things first and then thinks about the consequences afterwards. And this was one of those times. By the time I pulled myself together, realised trying to find you was futile, and so got ready to make my way home, the police showed up at my hotel room to tell me that my husband, my child and my sister were all concerned for my welfare.

'I'd been so stupid. And knowing you were all worried, I sank into the depths of shame for how I'd behaved. That was why I didn't get in touch with Archie. I was devastated at what I'd done. I'm a mother and I'd abandoned my son, left my husband, come to a different country so close to when my baby was going to be born. It was as though I'd stepped onto a set, a stage and was playing a different part and I didn't recognise myself. I'd acted irrationally; I thought I knew what I was doing at the time. For weeks, I'd convinced myself Archie wouldn't disrupt their lives and follow me, but then I saw that he wouldn't have had any choice. Yet again, I'd caused trouble. Just like when I was a teenager.

'I'd only just got my head around it all and went to the address that the police gave me when Bella decided she wanted to amp up the drama. I can't bear to think what might have happened if the police hadn't come, if I hadn't known people were looking for me, if I'd gone into labour when I was travelling to make my way home.'

'Don't think about that now. You're safe, both of you.'

'Thanks to you and Archie.' Her voice caught.

Nadia felt so close to this little baby in her arms, the baby who had made a dramatic entrance into the world.

'I was stunned when you turned up, Nadia. I mean, I knew Archie had located you, the police mentioned you by name, but I never thought you and Archie would be a team and that you would suddenly appear at my side to help me. I almost thought I was hallucinating.'

'I'm glad I was there.' With Bella in her arms, she passed her sister a tissue for her tears.

Monica hesitated. 'Do you think... do you think we can ever go back to being sisters? I think I need to know, I need to process, get my head around it. I'll respect whatever you decide. I know you have a life here, and that that life doesn't include me, us.'

'No... we can't ever go back.' And she knew when she saw how distraught Monica was, the way her face, her shoulders and her whole body sagged, that she really was sorry, that she really did want to repair the damage that had been done over the years.

Nadia put a hand on Monica's as her sister's tears tracked down her cheeks. 'We can't go back. Not ever. But we can go forwards.'

Monica's breath caught. 'You mean that?'

'I think we both owe it to each other to try.'

'It'll take time...'

'And effort.' Their words crossed each other; the tears flowed some more. Both of them wanted, needed, to see what the future held for them.

But they didn't get to do much more talking because Giles barrelled into the ward with a call from his father to walk, not run.

And after Nadia passed Bella to her daddy, she hid her emotions behind a hug with her nephew.

28

Hudson hadn't seen much of Nadia over the last week since that day at the hospital, since their almost-but-not-quite kiss. But he understood. Her family had been absent from her life for such a long while that this, her sister turning up and Archie as well as two kids in the mix, was a lot to get her head around.

When there was a knock at the door that evening, he opened it expecting it to be Beau having forgotten his key again. He did it frequently, had done for years. Beau had improved a lot; he was working hard at school, he'd helped a lot at the airbase. Hudson guessed he couldn't change everything about the kid, and why would he want to?

But it wasn't Beau, it was Nadia, and he didn't mind one bit.

A rumble of thunder came in overhead when he answered the door. 'Come in,' he said.

'I don't want to intrude.'

'You're not intruding. Now come in before the heavens open.'

She looked behind him as if to check who was around. 'Are you sure this is okay?'

'It's absolutely fine.' He took her hand, led her inside. 'Carys is asleep, Beau is out with a friend. How about a cup of tea?'

'That sounds good.'

In the kitchen, he put the kettle on and offered her a biscuit from the tin. 'They're only the packet sort, I'm afraid, nothing like the ones you make.'

'Not for me, thanks, I've just eaten with Monica and her family.'

'*Your* family,' he corrected her and got a smile in return. 'How are they all doing?'

'They're doing well.'

'And is Giles enjoying having a sister?'

'So far, I think he is. He sees himself as her protector by the sounds of it.'

'Just like Beau. I kind of love that about him: that he wants to keep watch for his little sister. God help the boys she goes out with one day – he'll likely have left home by then but knowing him, he'll be keeping a close eye.'

He set the mugs down on the table once the tea was made and she reached for hers. 'Beau is well liked at the airbase.'

He knew she wasn't here to talk about work or about Beau, not directly anyway, but what he'd learned along the way with Nadia was that sometimes, she had to settle into a conversation first before she'd say what was really on her mind.

'He is; it could've gone a very different way. But I'm glad it didn't. And he is very keen on a career with an air ambulance one day; his passion is growing and I'm over the moon about that. I think Brad talking him through some of the stuff he's involved with as a critical care paramedic may well have ignited a flame of enthusiasm. The way he talks about his next years in education is a lot different to the moaning he's done in the past; it's as though he sees the point of it now. It might not last but...'

'I really hope it does.'

'I've told Lucinda too. In the interests of joint parenting and keeping each other in the loop.'

'I'd say that's wise.'

'She hoped he'd go into business, the same way she has, that he'd be in charge of a team and work his way to the top. He might still do that, but I didn't want her to dampen any of his enthusiasm for a possible career doing something else if it came out of the blue.'

'Do you think she'd do that?'

'I don't, not really. But I just need to make sure we're both on the same page when it comes to the kids.'

'You'll always be linked by them.'

'Yep, and that's not easy or pleasant sometimes. But it is what it is.'

Nadia had the fingers of one hand looped through the handle of her mug as she shifted it across the table but didn't lift it up.

'Okay, out with it: there's something on your mind.' He reached for her free hand but she quickly clasped her mug with both hands and his heart sank. 'I thought things with us were good, that it might even be the start of something. Was I wrong to think that?'

'You weren't wrong. But... I'm paranoid about getting in the middle of anything, with your family.'

'In the middle? You mean with me and Lucinda?' When she nodded, he reminded her, 'We're divorced, happily divorced.'

'It's not just Lucinda to consider though, is it? Watching Archie with Giles and Bella today, they're a little family. So were you four at one time and you still need to be in so many ways.'

'Believe me, we're better off apart than we were together. It's upset things, made them unsteady, especially for Beau, but not in the long run. Staying together for them would've been the worst thing we could've done. There's no going back and Beau knows that; it's why he suggested I start dating.'

'But did he really mean it? Is he ready for it? I know you, Hudson; you put your kids first and rightly so. I don't want to be the one to come between you.'

'Is that why you came: because you think you're going to be a problem with the kids?'

'I can't stop thinking about it.'

They were interrupted by another knock at the door. 'This will be Beau, I expect.'

Nadia got up. 'I'll leave you to it; you've got enough on your plate. We can talk another time.'

But Hudson wasn't going to let her make a dash for it. Instead, he took her by the hand before she sensed what he was going to do and went to open the front door, not the easiest with only one hand free.

'Forgot my—'

'Key, yes, I know.'

'Hey, Nadia.' Beau briefly looked at their hands and then closed the door behind him. 'I'm starving.' He headed for the kitchen.

Nadia still didn't seem convinced that this was a good idea.

'Hudson, I—'

He stubbornly kept hold of her hand and led them back into the kitchen.

Beau closed the fridge, having given it a scan, and clocked their hands entwined again. 'Are you two going out somewhere? Want me to look after Carys?'

Hudson let go of Nadia's hand now he didn't think she was about to run off and she sat at the table.

'We're just catching up; no plans to go out tonight. But I

wouldn't mind taking Nadia for dinner at the weekend if you're up for a spot of babysitting?'

'Sure,' Beau replied, his head in the pantry this time.

'You sit down,' Hudson suggested to his son. 'I can make you an omelette.' And then to Nadia, 'He's a teen; all he sees is what he can grab, not ingredients he can put together to make something halfway nutritious.'

Beau rolled his eyes but thanked his dad. 'Do we have mushrooms?'

'We do.'

Hudson didn't miss Beau's attempt to grab a cereal bar from the pantry without him noticing.

'What? This will keep me going. The omelette won't be instant.'

And Hudson didn't miss Beau's cheeky grin towards Nadia either. Maybe Beau, without directly being asked the question, could put a stop to Nadia's fears. Otherwise she might never go out on a date with him and he so wanted a chance with her.

'Can I ask you a question?' Beau said and when Hudson looked round, he realised it hadn't been directed at him.

'Go ahead,' said Nadia.

'I have to arrange work experience next year. I was wondering, would I be able to come in and do it with The Skylarks?'

Hudson beat the eggs with a fork but rather than a stab of resentment that Beau hadn't asked him, he listened to his son talk with Nadia about the side of The Skylarks that Hudson wasn't involved in. He wanted to be out in the field, he said, not just because of the action, but to save lives.

As Hudson prepared an omelette, Nadia answered more questions about the charity. They talked about her nursing degree, her days as a nurse, about the extra qualifications to be a critical care paramedic with the air ambulance, about the experience some of the team had joined up with.

Hudson tilted the pan and let the finished omelette slide onto the plate he'd set in front of his son.

'I'm sure Brad or Bess or any of The Skylarks would talk to you more,' said Nadia, comfortable in his son's company. 'I'll look into getting you a week's work experience. We've never had a student in before, but you've shown how hard working you are on a voluntary basis. I can't see why it wouldn't work.'

As Beau ate, he talked more at the dinner table than he had in a long while and Hudson enjoyed watching the interaction between him and Nadia.

When Beau eventually went off to watch TV, Hudson pulled out a chair. 'Thanks for that.'

'For what?'

'The way you talk to him. It's nice – it's like there's a mutual respect.'

'He's earned it.'

'He has. Now, are you going to tell me why you tried to run off before, just because Beau came home?'

She was far more relaxed. 'I didn't want him to be put out that I was here. I mean it when I say I'm worried. What if he didn't really mean what he said about you dating?'

'I think he meant it. And now you've sat with him, perhaps he's convinced you too?'

'I think he might have done.'

'Well, that's progress.'

'I needed to see it for myself. And a few days ago, I saw Lucinda at the supermarket with Conrad. She seemed happy with him. Seeing her with someone else reminded me that life goes on and even though you will always be linked to her, you deserve the same kind of happiness.'

'Lucinda's romantic relationships are her business now but I'm glad she seemed happy. She isn't exactly likely to tell me. She'll always be the mother of my children; you're right that we'll always be linked. But that really is it, I promise you.'

'I guess I'm worried about making a mess of this... us.'

He got up, looked out of the window. 'No sign of rain yet; how about we take Beau up on his offer and go for a walk?'

He went in to clear it with Beau, who was fine with the arrangement and his main concern was whether there were any choc ices in the freezer.

'Plenty, but just one, okay.'

'I'm not twelve, Dad.'

They left Beau in charge and headed out of the front door, down the garden path and turned left. The moody sky hovered above; another rumble of thunder came. A neighbour called out a hello and urged them to hurry to wherever they were going before they got wet.

'Feel better?' he asked Nadia as he took her hand.

'Better?'

'Being out of my house. Away from my kids so we can have a moment together.'

'I do feel better; this was a good idea.'

'I think so too.' He loved the feel of her hand in his as they walked, turned the corner which would take them all the way down to the river.

'Was that...?' She held out her hand, testing for raindrops.

'I forgot the umbrella.'

And then there was no doubt about it. Nadia's question didn't need an answer because the sprinkling of rain upped its tempo as the clouds gave up on holding it all in.

'There's a bus shelter!' Hudson, with her hand in his, led the way as they began to run. The bus shelter was at the end of the street, with a view overlooking the river and they were a mere fifty or so metres away.

Both of them laughed uncontrollably as they headed for shelter; both of them were absolutely drenched in less than a few minutes.

It took a while to catch their breath once they were under cover.

Nadia squeezed the ends of her blouse, wringing out some of the drips, and did the same with her hair. 'Well, your neighbour did warn us.'

He laughed. 'She'll be looking out of her window later, saying, "I told you so."'

Never had Nadia looked so beautiful. The rain had made her eye make-up start to run, her hair was so wet, it looked shades darker than its natural blonde, but none of it mattered.

Water dripped from his forearms, his upper lip as he reached out and cradled her face with his hands.

And then they were kissing, like they'd both been waiting for this moment forever, like they should've been doing this all along.

He was glad they'd waited, glad he kissed her here, now, in this moment with the beauty of the river in the background, the sound of rain hammering on the bus shelter roof. And they had each other for warmth, huddled together on the bench while the summer storm unleashed and let them all know who was in charge.

When the clouds had passed by, the rain had stopped and the sun had come out once again, they made their way back to Hudson's, hand in hand, no doubt from either of them that this really was the start of something.

29

Archie had dropped Monica at the airbase in time for lunch and she and Nadia made the most of a glorious summer's day. They had Bella with them in the pushchair they'd borrowed from the childminder who had come to the rescue with Giles the day of Monica's labour. They walked from the airbase, followed the road almost to the entrance to the airfield where they cut right and found themselves at a clearing with a bench and view of the surrounding countryside.

As they'd walked, Nadia told Monica a bit about Hudson. It had been a little over three weeks since they went out for dinner and Beau babysat Carys, slightly more than that since their first kiss in the bus shelter which, when Nadia thought about it, still sent tingles all over her body.

'He seems like a lovely man,' Monica told her as they laid out a picnic rug and put the pushchair's wheels on one end in case a breeze picked up on this otherwise sunny, still day.

'He's wonderful.'

Monica had crossed paths with Hudson a handful of times but it was still early days for Monica and Nadia; they hadn't yet reached the stage of being able to confide in each other. Nadia hoped that that was something they could work on.

'Wonderful? That's an understatement; I can tell you're smitten.'

It had taken long enough to admit it to herself but the more she did, the more comfortable she was beginning to feel with the strong feelings she'd begun to develop for the new man in her life.

Over sausage rolls, a cheese and spinach quiche and slices of homemade pizza, they talked about regular things as sisters – the places they wanted to visit someday, home improvements Monica wanted to do to add on a playroom for the kids, plans for Bella's christening, and the relief Monica felt that Giles didn't seem scarred from what had been quite a dramatic summer for him.

'He can't wait to start school,' said Monica, who finished feeding Bella and passed her to her auntie for a cuddle.

Nadia wanted to squeeze in as much auntie time as possible, while she still could.

They talked some more about Giles and when Bella felt so heavy that Nadia realised she was falling asleep, Nadia settled her into the pushchair and with one hand moved it gently back and forth.

'You're a great cook. The quiche is amazing.' Monica lifted up another slice ready to put on a plate. 'Let me take over; you enjoy this.'

'I'm fine; pass it up to me.' She took the slice of quiche with her free hand. 'I'm glad you like my cooking. I thought I'd made too much for us.'

'I'm breastfeeding; it's making me so hungry, I don't think there will be much left.'

'Was it the same with Giles?'

And just like that, they were on to talking about babies, the struggles as well as the triumphs, and Nadia's sadness didn't feel quite so overwhelming. Maybe it was because she had these four people in her life now; there'd been a gap before, and she hadn't realised that there might be more than one way to fill it.

'When are you next seeing Hudson?' Monica asked when they'd had enough and had packed everything away, ready to stow in the shopping basket beneath the pushchair for the walk back.

'I see him all the time.'

'That's at work. When are you seeing him properly?'

'Tonight.' Nadia closed the mini hamper and put it into the basket beneath the pushchair.

'Have you...'

Nadia felt her cheeks redden. 'Not yet.'

'Sorry, that was personal.'

'It was, but strangely, I don't mind.'

A nod of understanding before Monica probed, 'So tonight is the night?'

Nadia laughed. 'Not necessarily!'

'Oh, I bet it is. Didn't you get your legs waxed yesterday?'

'I might have done.'

With a giggle, Monica rolled up the blanket and with that beneath the pushchair too, they were ready to go.

'I want to hear all about it, you know, Nadia. You two are at that exciting early stage where you can't keep your hands off each other so enjoy every second.'

'Oh, I intend to.'

Yesterday in Whistlestop River, Hudson had met Nadia in the main street and clutched her hand before pulling her in for a kiss that took her breath away. The day before, they'd been to the Whistlestop River Inn with work colleagues and Monica and

Archie had collected Nadia afterwards and caught her and Hudson trying to steal a moment with each other down the side of the pub when they thought they had a good five minutes until Nadia's sister showed up.

'I don't care who knows now,' he'd told her when they were sprung. 'I've waited long enough to feel this way about someone again. I thought I could be single until the kids were much older but I'm glad I don't have to be.'

Nadia smiled now as she and her sister started their walk back to the airbase. 'It's early days but I'm falling for him in a big way. I've known him for years. He's always been a friend, someone I've admired.'

'And now he's a whole lot more.'

'Yes, he is.'

'Do you think he'd be up for a bit of European travel? Bella's christening isn't all that far away.'

Nadia felt her cheeks colour. 'I'll have to ask him.'

'It'd be great if you did. We can go out for dinner too, all of us, together.'

'I'd really love that.'

They walked the rest of the way talking about Switzerland, the country Nadia had left and never admitted to missing until now.

Archie's work had been very understanding of his current circumstances. He had been down to take time off following the birth of his second child anyway but instead of spending that month in Switzerland, they'd extended the rental at the Airbnb to spend the time here in Dorset. He'd said it was time for them all to be a family, and that Nadia was a part of that.

Almost at the airbase, they said hello to Bess, who had come off shift and met up with Gio, who had brought their new puppy to meet her by the looks of things.

'Oh, isn't he gorgeous?' Monica wasted no time fussing over the dog which Bess was having no luck making sit. 'Sorry, I'm overexciting him.'

'He has to learn,' said Gio. 'And so do we. Bess here isn't strict enough.'

'I am so!'

Gio shook his head in Nadia's direction. 'She's not. If she had her way, she'd let him on the bed, on the sofas; he'd rule the house.'

Bess grinned smugly as she successfully made the dog sit. 'Good boy, Zeus. See...' She looked at Nadia. 'I'm getting in practice with my disciplining skills.'

'She's pregnant,' said Nadia to her sister. And for the first time, it didn't hurt quite so much.

Monica smiled. 'Congratulations. And might I say, you're brave taking on a puppy and a baby at the same time.'

'It wasn't planned,' said Gio.

'These things never are.'

They let Bess and Gio go on their way and once inside reception, they sat and waited for Archie.

'I expect Giles is missing his little friends quite a lot.' Nadia knew it would soon be time for the family to leave and the thought was hard to get to grips with now that the day had arrived. Small talk seemed the best way to get through it.

'Are you joking?' Monica grinned. 'He seems to make friends just like that – he already has a couple from the local park; I'm sure he'll be talking about more when they come and pick me up.'

Over the last week, the sisters had spent a lot of time together – they'd talked about their childhood, the good, the bad and the ugly parts, they'd cried over the loss of their mother, something they hadn't done together before now. But mostly, they'd got to know each other again.

And the realisation that Monica was leaving had been hovering in the air the whole time.

Archie arrived shortly after they got back to the airbase and he successfully transferred Bella into her car seat with a little kiss on the top of her head and a whispered, 'Goodbye, little one,' from Nadia.

'Well, this is it.' Monica's voice wobbled as they stood next to the car.

Nadia took a deep breath. 'This is it.'

'Are you going to start crying, Mummy?' Giles frowned.

'Of course not,' she said, not convincing anyone given the tremble of her bottom lip.

Nadia hugged her sister tightly and held her for a moment while her own tears came, tears not just about the fact she was leaving but also because she had her sister back in her life.

When they parted, Nadia got down to Giles's level and gave him a tight hug. 'I will see you soon, I promise. You look after your mummy for me, okay?'

'I promise. So you *will* come and see me?'

'My visit is less than a month away.'

'That's a-ges.' He accentuated the start of the word to show just how long he thought he was going to be waiting.

'It'll go really quickly. And then after that, why don't we plan when you're next coming here? Your mummy suggested we do it before Bella starts crawling.'

He rolled his eyes. 'She'll be into *everything*.' That had them all laughing and Nadia fought to hold back tears, happy tears but also tears of sadness that they were leaving.

Monica coaxed Giles into the car and Archie hugged Nadia tightly.

'It's been so good to see you; I mean that,' he said.

'Thank you, Archie, for never giving up on her like—'

But he stopped her mid-sentence. 'You did what you had to do. That's life, and we can't change it. No regrets, eh?'

'No regrets.'

With one more hug from Archie and another from Monica, Nadia finally let the family get on their way. She stayed out front of the airbase building until she could no longer see their car, no longer see three hands waving out of the open windows.

She was about to go inside when she felt a pair of arms slip around her waist. She relaxed into them and closed her eyes against the sunshine.

'You okay?' Hudson murmured in her ear.

'I'm okay.' She turned to face him. 'How do you feel about a trip to Switzerland in a few weeks' time for a christening?'

'I'll have to clear the days off with my boss; she can be a bit scary.'

'Well, that's true... I'll have a word with her, see if she'll be willing to work something out.'

He planted a brief kiss on her lips. They were at the workplace, after all, although when he checked around them and realised nobody was about, he took her face in his hands and gave her a kiss she wasn't likely to forget in a hurry.

A taxi pulled up and they remembered where they were. Hudson straightened his shirt, Nadia adjusted her dress as if the kiss and the clinch had made everything fall into disarray.

A woman emerged from the rear of the taxi. 'Hello, love birds!' It was Maud, their nonagenarian supporter, and she looked full of beans.

'Ah, today is the day.' Hudson beamed at their guest. He hooked his arm for her to slip hers through. 'Come this way, Maud; Hilda and Maya are waiting for you.'

Maud had won the flight on board Hilda at the silent auction of the charity fundraiser after her winning bid – with a remarkably generous sum – had sealed the deal. She'd called yesterday to confirm – for the third time – what the arrangements were and knew that should the helicopter be called out on a job then the trip might need to be postponed, and if they got a call while they were in the air then they'd have to divert.

She wasn't put out at all as Nadia repeated this information when they passed through the doors to the airbase.

'It all adds to the thrill of it, my dear!' Maud was having the time of her life. 'And you know all about thrills with this one.' She nudged Nadia whilst casting a glance in Hudson's direction.

'She's all yours,' Hudson told Maya, who came through to greet their guest of honour. There would be safety talks first, lots of information for Maud to absorb, but Nadia had no doubt she'd love every second of it.

Their jobs carried on around the airbase, Bess and Noah returned from a job they'd attended in the rapid response vehicle and then it was all systems go for Maud.

As the helicopter blades started up, their chopping against the air a sound that Nadia would never grow tired of, Nadia finished up her work for the day and so did Hudson.

And when they left hand in hand from the airbase, Nadia had to pinch herself when she realised that maybe, at last, she had everything she needed in her life.

ACKNOWLEDGEMENTS

My thanks goes to my readers for all the wonderful messages of support and for the reviews of all my books including this latest series. When I created Whistlestop River and The Skylarks, I really wanted the small-town feel but with plenty of action and drama for my characters. I hope that with this story, I have once again been able to deliver those elements.

A huge thank you to Lauren Dyson. Lauren is a critical care paramedic with the Dorset and Somerset Air Ambulance and she has generously given her time to answer my many questions about how things work at an air ambulance base, with the crews, and out on a job. I do a lot of my research online but there's nothing like being able to check your facts with someone who sees what being a part of a crew is like first hand.

Thank you to my wonderful editor Rachel Faulkner-Willcocks for being so invested in my books and helping guide me to write stories that my reader will fall in love with, and a big thank you to the entire team at Boldwood Books for all their tremendous efforts to get my stories to you, the reader, in all formats all around the globe.

And of course as always, a big thank you to my husband and my girls, my biggest support team who never stop believing in me.

Much love,

Helen x

ABOUT THE AUTHOR

Helen Rolfe is the author of many bestselling contemporary women's fiction titles, set in different locations from the Cotswolds to New York. She lives in Hertfordshire with her husband and children.

Sign up to Helen Rolfe's mailing list for news, competitions and updates on future books.

Visit Helen's website: www.helenjrolfe.com

Follow Helen on social media here:

 instagram.com/helen_j_rolfe

ALSO BY HELEN ROLFE

Heritage Cove Series

Coming Home to Heritage Cove

Christmas at the Little Waffle Shack

Winter at Mistletoe Gate Farm

Summer at the Twist and Turn Bakery

Finding Happiness at Heritage View

Christmas Nights at the Star and Lantern

New York Ever After Series

Snowflakes and Mistletoe at the Inglenook Inn

Christmas at the Little Knitting Box

Wedding Bells on Madison Avenue

Christmas Miracles at the Little Log Cabin

Moonlight and Mistletoe at the Christmas Wedding

Christmas Promises at the Garland Street Markets

Family Secrets at the Inglenook Inn

Little Woodville Cottage Series

Christmas at Snowdrop Cottage

Summer at Forget-Me-Not Cottage

The Skylarks Series

Come Fly With Me

Written in the Stars

Something in the Air

Standalones

The Year That Changed Us

Boldw⚭d

Boldwood Books is an award-winning fiction publishing company seeking out the best stories from around the world.

Find out more at www.boldwoodbooks.com

Join our reader community for brilliant books, competitions and offers!

Follow us
@BoldwoodBooks
@TheBoldBookClub

Sign up to our weekly deals newsletter

https://bit.ly/BoldwoodBNewsletter

Printed in Great Britain
by Amazon

57269845R00165